WORKING STIFF

Working Stiff

A Sofie Metropolis Novel

TORI CARRINGTON

A TOM DOHERTY ASSOCIATES BOOK

NEW YORK

WORKING STIFF: A SOFIE METROPOLIS NOVEL

Copyright © 2008 by Lori and Tony Karayianni

All rights reserved.

A Forge Book
Published by Tom Doherty Associates, LLC
175 Fifth Avenue
New York, NY 10010

www.tor-forge.com

Forge® is a registered trademark of Tom Doherty Associates, LLC.

Library of Congress-Cataloging-in-Publication Data

Carrington, Tori.
    Working stiff : a Sofie Metropolis novel / Tori Carrington.—1st hardcover ed.
        p.   cm.
    " A Tom Doherty Associates book."
    ISBN-13: 978-0-7653-1744-5
    ISBN-10: 0-7653-1744-3
    1. Metropolis, Sofie (Fictitious character)—Fiction.   2. Women private inves-
tigators—Fiction.   3. Astoria (New York, N.Y.)—Fiction.   I. Title.

PS3603.A77456 W67   2008
813'.6—dc22
                                                                    2008019507

First Edition: September 2008

Printed in the United States of America

0   9   8   7   6   5   4   3   2   1

As always,
for our remarkable sons, Tony and Tim.
με αγαπη.

ACKNOWLEDGMENTS

"Wonders are many, and none is more wonderful than man." Or woman, as I'm sure Sophocles meant to fall under the "man" umbrella. But let's forget the gender issue for a moment and take a look at the statement itself. While it may be true that there are no new ideas, the human condition enduringly continues to fascinate us all. Why? Well, that's a question we strive to answer in each of our books and through all of our characters. And in Sofie's case we get to have a little fun along the way. If only we could do the same with other of life's many mysteries. . . .

The wonderful men in our lives, our sons, Tony and Tim, still manage to surprise us in ways both big and small. Joyfully so. There are few activities more satisfying than sitting down for four-hour Sunday dinners where no subject is taboo and no answer wrong. Thank you for lovingly challenging us even as we adoringly challenge you.

My (Lori) youngest brother, Stephen Schlachter, is the mirror image of our father, the late Carl J. Schlachter Sr., a blessing he wears with honor even as he forges his own path in life. We wish you and your wife, Lori, and your new daughter, Sophia Grace, love and happiness as your young family grows. My heart bursts with pride. And I know Dad is smiling down on you.

"Dude" Mike Medeiros, for cracking us up when we're least expecting it. You . . . you! You rule, man.

Our exceptional agent, Robert Gottlieb, a true *Yiddisher kop,* who, well, "gets it" on every level. And everyone else who works behind the scenes at Trident Media Group, including Alanna Ramirez and Amy Pyle and Lara Allen: Thank you for covering the business angle of our lives with brilliant aplomb so we may focus on the creative end.

Our remarkable editor, Melissa Ann Singer, who keeps us on track and focused and whose e-mails to catch us up on missed episodes of *Ugly Betty* are more entertaining than watching the show itself.

Additionally, thank you to Linda Quinton, Tom Doherty, Kathleen Fogarty, Elena Stokes, Anna Genoese, Alexis Saarela, Jozelle Dyer, and everyone at Tom Doherty Associates. You're a true dream team!

Fellow writer Robert Knightly and publisher Johnny Temple of Akashic Books: Thank you for including us and Sofie's uncle Spyros in *Queens Noir*. You are princes among men . . . and, of course, with such great names (and that's saying nothing about the noble guys behind them), we're obligated to borrow them along with a bit of each of you for further heroes.

The many booksellers and fellow readers at Borders, B&N, Joseph Beth's, and the countless indies—including but certainly not limited to Books & Co. in Kettering, Ohio, Mystery Lovers Bookshop in Oakmont, Pennsylvania, Black Orchid Mystery Bookstore in Manhattan, New York, Don's Books in Kokomo, Indiana, and the Paperback Outlet in Warren, Michigan. Then there are the libraries and librarians, such as Lynne Welch of Herrick Memorial Library, Heidi McCraw of the Monroe Michigan County Library—Ellis Center, Kym Lucas of the Buckeye Library, Medina County, Ohio, and Wendy Bethel and Laura Hensley and the entire Ohio Library Council. Thank you for your generosity and friendship. (Check out our travel blog at www.toricarrington.net and www.sofiemetro.com for an ongoing list and photos from our adventures.)

Members of the Greek- and Cypriot-American community—including Aphrodite Matsakis, Ph.D., Joyce Anagnos, and Avgi Anagnos (mother and daughter who never fail to include us in Greek goings-on locally), Toledo's own Holy Trinity Orthodox Church, the *National Herald*, *Greek Circle* magazine, AHEPA, to name but a few—for their enriching support and for making us feel we're in the company of family whenever our paths cross. *Zeto E Ellas!*

Finally, we would be remiss if we didn't also acknowledge a place that is far more than "the bedroom of Manhattan"—Astoria, Queens, New York, our Sofie's stomping grounds. Planning a vacation to New York City? Hop the N or W train to Astoria, and once you get to Queens, get off at either Broadway or Ditmars (last stop) and you, too, can walk a memorable mile in Sofie's shoes. Just think of us while you sip a frappé or a glass of ouzo before digging into a great Greek meal. *Opa!*

WORKING STIFF

One

THE DIFFERENCE BETWEEN MEN AND *boys is the size of their toys.*
I slid my Glock 9mm from my shoulder holster and weighed the nearly pound and a half of deadly weapon in my palm along with the old axiom. If the saying was true, what did my carrying around this puppy say about me? And what would be the female equivalent? The difference between women and girls was the sheen of their curls? The height of their espadrilles? The size of their hills?

That was me for you. More than Sofie Metropolis, but Sofie Metropolis, PI. And gender-bending questions like the one I just asked rated among my favorites. Not merely because I am a woman in a typically male-oriented career, but because I am a Greek-American woman of whom nothing more is expected beyond marrying a good Greek guy and providing my parents with grandchildren. Dark-haired, Greek grandchildren that would look cute in their traditional Greek costumes in the annual Greek Independence Day parade down Fifth Avenue every March.

What made the reflection particularly interesting was that seven months ago I came very close to delivering on all of my family's expectations. Good thing I happened across my would-be groom Thomas the Toad's extracurricular activities before the ceremony rather than after (even if I still wished I hadn't found him playing an X-rated version of show-and-tell with my maid of honor five minutes before that same ceremony). Had I found out afterward . . . well, I'd likely still be married to the jerk and probably would be pregnant with our first child, coming to accept my family's promise that Thomas would "grow out" of his need to show Little Thomas to other women. Despite my deep-seated belief that men like Thomas didn't change. They were much like young boys that graduated from Matchbox cars to the real thing as they got older. But in the end, they were still obsessed with cars.

I shuddered as I popped the ammunition magazine and then pulled back the metal slide, emptying the round from the chamber before reaching across the stick shift and putting the gun into the glove box of the old Mustang I affectionately called Lucille. I pushed the single bullet into the magazine and then slid both into my handbag. (Hey, it probably wasn't a good idea to keep the gun locked up in a car that was as easy to get into as an old breadbox, so keeping the ammo separate from the firearm itself made me feel moderately better.) While the reason I was strapped had to do with my visit to a firing range in Woodhaven, I'd been carrying concealed a lot more often lately. Probably because the one time I'd been caught without my gun recently had been the one time I'd needed it most.

Thankfully, my souvenir Mets bat had served as excellent backup against Santos Venezuela, who'd had a long-standing rivalry with his younger brother Reni Venezuela and decided that it was time to prove himself the better ballplayer once and for all by kidnapping Reni and taking his place as relief pitcher for the Mets, albeit not the ambidextrous one fans like me had come to expect.

Lucky for Reni, Santos hadn't gotten rid of him and taken his place permanently before I figured out what was going on. Then I'd guaranteed Santos wouldn't be throwing any balls in the near or faraway future by whacking him in the right arm with a bat he'd autographed, breaking his shoulder.

I stared through the windshield at Broadway. Not the Broadway in Manhattan, but the one in Astoria, Queens, essentially the Greek-American center of the universe, despite how hard the Ditmars Blvd. Greeks were trying to steal the title. The waning light told me that dusk wasn't far off. Which meant I was late. I looked at the clock on my cell to find it was just before six. Actually, I wasn't late. Instead, the shortening autumn days had pushed dusk up further than it had the day before.

A cool, stiff breeze blew leaves across the street and foreboding up my spine.

Of course, my reaction had a lot to do with the fact that I didn't want to be parked in front of my aunt Sotiria's funeral home. Scratch that. I didn't want to attend the viewing of a man I'd never met, but my mother had insisted I come too because, as she put it, "it's our obligation as fellow Greek expatriates."

It didn't help that Nick Papadakis didn't have any family to speak of. Not anymore. After his mother had passed nearly a decade ago, and his father a few years before that, Nick had been left alone, meaning there were no relatives to grieve loudly over his body.

If my reluctance to get out of my car now had anything to do with Halloween looming little more than a week away, I wasn't copping to it.

That went double for the horror movie I'd rented last night that featured flesh-eating zombies.

"Oh, just go in and get it over with," I told myself. "It's not like Nick is going to reach out for you from the casket."

Perish the thought.

I adjusted the rearview mirror, checking that my light brown hair was neat around my shoulders, my mascara evenly applied around my green eyes, and sighed. I grabbed my black trench coat from the passenger seat and then climbed out, closing the door after me. The leaves that had blown across the street swirled in front of my feet and then stilled, as if daring me to cross them in my new pumps. I stepped on them, relishing the sound of them crumpling under my heel.

"It's about time you got here," my mother, Thalia Metropolis, said the instant I entered the east parlor to the left of the entrance.

I repressed an eye roll. My mother. The guilt maven of America. Ever since she stopped working at my father's restaurant a few years ago, it seemed she had an endless amount of time to hound me about what I should or shouldn't be doing. And that extended to every aspect of my existence, including my sorry excuse for a love life as well as my job.

I'd gotten a reminder of that last Sunday when I'd gone to family dinner at my parents' place. I'd forgotten to leave my Glock in the car and had tucked it under my jacket on a chair in the living room. I should have known better, because when I went back to collect it some hours later, I found my coat hanging in the closet and my Glock nowhere to be found.

"What did you do with it?" I'd asked my mother in the kitchen.

She'd pretended she didn't know what I was talking about. "What did I do with what?"

"You know what."

I hadn't been about to announce to everyone in the house that I'd carried a gun inside. Besides, my mother had known exactly what I was talking about.

As did at least one other person, it turned out, as I'd watched Yiayia, my eternally black-clad paternal grandmother, open the garbage can and extract my missing firearm by the grip with her thumb and index finger as if it smelled as bad as the discarded spinach that was draped over the barrel.

My mother had thrown away my gun.

I stared at her now, trying to figure out how her mind worked. And how I might begin to work it to my advantage rather than playing ceaseless victim to it.

"I am not late," I said, taking in the three people milling about the small, nicely appointed room. "You're early."

I didn't see my aunt Sotiria anywhere. Or her vest-wearing, pale son, Byron, who, it was joked, had never really been revived after a boating accident when he was nineteen. Rather, rumor had it that my aunt had somehow found a way to preserve her only child and that he was now officially a member of the walking dead.

I used to laugh at the harmless talk. Until he'd taken much pleasure in repeatedly sneaking up on me during my three-week stint at the funeral home several years ago. That was back when I'd decided I didn't want to wait tables at my father's or grandfather's restaurants anymore (actually, it had more to do with my not wanting to spend more time than I had to around the overbearing

Greek males who, at the time, had likened "daughter" and "grand-daughter" to "brainless slave").

Thalia waved her hand as if it were of no never mind to her. "Anyway, thank God you came. I contacted at least twenty women on the church call tree and I don't see a single one of them here."

I looked toward the focal point of the room decorated with pressed curtains and a single pedestal of white carnations that I knew was included in Burial Package Five.

"Maybe they're running late," I said absently.

Seemed they weren't the only ones late. Where was Nick Papadakis?

No body. No casket. Nothing but an empty spot that had recently been vacuumed, the carpeting bearing sweeper tracks.

I rubbed my arms against the chill I felt. Aunt Sotiria was religious about making sure the body was out on time. No body, no viewing, she'd been fond of saying. Normally the room wasn't open until everything was set up. And the body was obviously of key importance.

My mother seemed more concerned about the few people that had showed up, completely oblivious to there being no body to view.

"Do you have your cell phone?" she asked me.

I stared at her.

She held her hand out.

I didn't fill it.

You see, one of the things for which I'm grateful is that my mother had yet to fully enter the twenty-first century. Twenty-first? My younger sister, Efi, sometimes joked that she would have been right at home in the nineteenth century, an idea supported by my mother's resourcefulness during a ten-day Queens-wide blackout last summer. Thalia not only managed to have a fully cooked meal on the table every day, but somehow had kept the house cool, had hand-washed the clothes we needed, and had even found a way to iron them.

She also viewed my sister's computer as little more than a paperweight to be dusted, and I'd never seen her use a cell phone. Hell, it had taken us five years to talk her into getting a cordless phone at the house.

"What's the matter?" she asked me now. "Give me your phone."

"Who do you want to call?"

"Frosini. She, at least, should be here. I went to her grandson's baptism last year. You remember. The two-year-old boy who ate egg dye and pissed red on Father Ari?"

I didn't want to give my mother my phone. Not because I was afraid she might break it, but because I was afraid that one wrong keystroke and she'd see that half the calls I'd made and received were from one particular Greek that I didn't want her to know I was seeing, and seeing often: Dino Antonopoulos.

I took the phone from my purse and discreetly pushed the button that switched it off. I started to hand it over.

"Oh, look," I said, giving her my best frown. "I forgot to charge it last night and the battery must be dead."

I started to take it back. With lightning speed, she swiped it from my hand in that way known only by mothers used to taking dangerous items from children's hands before they put them into their mouths.

"See," I said after she'd fumbled with it for a couple of moments with no luck.

I reached to take it back.

She found the right button.

Yikes!

Just then the phone vibrated. Thalia jumped as if shocked with a thousand volts of electricity. I caught the phone before she dropped it.

Saved by the vibration.

"Hello?" I answered as I walked toward the area where the body should be on display.

There was no answer. I looked at the display and realized that in the tug-of-war with my mother, the call must have rolled over to voice mail. As soon as the caller was done, Dino's name popped up on the screen. I cleared my throat and pressed the key to banish it.

It was just as well that I hadn't gotten the call in time. I couldn't imagine what I would have revealed had I answered in front of my mother.

Worse, what I would have done had she had the chance to answer it.

Disaster averted.

I switched the cell off again and slid it back into the safety of my purse.

Don't get me wrong. I liked Dino. I mean . . . I *really* liked him. For the past month and a half straight, the two of us had found every conceivable reason to meet. Not for dates. No, I would never consent to anything as official as that. Rather, we met for sex. Hot, sweaty, toe-curling, spine-shuddering sex. His car, my car. His sweets shop, my uncle Spyros' office. His place, my place.

The only condition—aside from the no-date rule—was that no one could know about our secret encounters. Something Dino easily accommodated, finding increasingly inventive ways to "accidentally" run into me.

But if my mother found out, I had little doubt that even as she admired the funeral flower arrangement, she'd mentally be making arrangements for the flowers for Dino's and my wedding.

I experienced a chill of a different sort.

You see, at this point I'm not ready even to think the word *marriage*, much less consider using it anywhere within the vicinity of my name.

I'd reached the viewing area. Nope, I wasn't imagining things. There was no casket there. No body.

I reached across the open area and parted the curtains there.

A cold, pale hand clamped onto my wrist.

I screamed.

The hand yanked me through the split in the curtains.

Two

"I'M SORRY, SOF," MY COUSIN Byron said. "I meant to scare you, but not make you shit yourself."

His laugh belied the meaning of his words.

The curtains fluttered closed, shutting me in the room behind the viewing room . . . away from my mother and the three other mourners who had all probably heard my scream.

"For God's sake, Byron, you really need to upgrade your sense of humor."

He grinned at me. "I really scared you, didn't I?"

If he hadn't then, he would have now.

Truth was, Byron had always given me the creeps. Exaggerated reports of his unfortunate demise aside, he'd always been pale, almost sickly so, the redness around his eyes, nostrils, and mouth only emphasizing it.

And now, in the dimness of the preparation room, with him grinning, he loomed, the Grim Reaper without his scythe.

I looked around. "Never mind that. Where's Nick?"

"Nick?"

I stared at him. "The body that's supposed to be on display for viewing?"

"Oh, him." Byron looked to his right, and I found myself glancing that way as well.

"Don't tell Mom I told you, but he's gone."

I stared at him harder.

Gone.

Gone?

The chill I'd felt earlier returned tenfold.

"What do you mean, gone?"

He motioned toward a casket to his left. "Just as I said. Gone."

"Dead bodies just don't get up and walk out, leaving a note saying they'll be back later." I stepped toward the simple metal casket, immediately recognizing it as one of the cheapest ones this side of a plain pine box. The top was closed.

My throat choked off air as I shakily reached out.

"Boo."

I dropped the lid and jumped away from the coffin, my cousin Byron having moved around to my other side and getting in another scare.

I slugged him in the arm. Something I hadn't done in years, but it felt right.

"Ow. What did you have to go and do that for?"

"*Byronas,* you're one 'boo' away from ending up in that casket yourself."

I went in search of my aunt.

"You're not going to tell my mom, are you?"

I'd opened the casket lid far enough to ascertain that there was nothing in there but satin bedding. "Of course I'm going to tell your mom."

More specifically, I was going to ask her where Nick had gotten off to, when he planned to be back, and when he would be put on view. Because the sooner I paid my respects, the sooner I could leave.

I found my aunt Sotiria in her office, pacing, the telephone plastered to the side of her face. She looked harried. But from experience, I knew that was my aunt's normal modus operandi.

Sotiria was my mother's aunt, my grandfather Kosmos' sister, although there was no family resemblance to speak of. Part of that might have to do with my aunt's frizzy, fire-engine-red hair, which she had dyed that way for at least as long as I'd been alive and had earned her the nickname Bozo the Clown when I was a kid.

Our family and Aunt Sotiria's family didn't socialize much. Aside from the occasional holiday dinner, my father joked that he saw family in Greece more often than he saw my aunt. She said it was because in her line of business there was no such thing as *atheia*—vacation. People didn't take Christmas off from dying.

Of course, her dinner table stories also left a lot to be desired. Another downside of the trade, I guessed.

At any rate, right now she looked even more animated than she normally did. I likened her appearance to that of a dancing, lighted match as she paced back and forth and back again.

"I don't care if there's been a school bus accident on the LIE. I need an officer over here immediately. I've got a missing body."

Well, so much for the viewing being scheduled for any other time today.

I MADE MY WAY BACK to the east parlor the traditional way, wishing that curiosity hadn't gotten the better of me and that I'd stayed put with my mother. I'd not only had the crap scared out of me by my cousin, I'd endured a beg-session from my aunt Sotiria.

"Please, Sofie, I really need you to find the body for me . . . fast! Do you have any idea what would happen to business if word got around that I lost a body?"

No, I didn't, but I was sure it wouldn't be good.

The problem was, I didn't have clue one where to look for a missing body. As my prior experience with just such matters reinforced. The only surefire way I knew of was to wait until the body popped up again somewhere. As they had a habit of doing.

I stepped up next to my mother, who was standing before the empty space where the casket should be. She was reaching out toward the closed curtains, much the same way I had. I caught her hand, afraid that any of Byron's pranks would result in not just a shriek from my mother, but a full-out coronary.

"Sofie!" she said, apparently as unnerved as I was by current events. And she didn't know the half of it. "Where have you been? I heard you scream, and the next minute you were gone."

I waved away her concern. "Byron acting like a five-year-old in a Halloween costume," I explained. "Look, I was hoping I could ask you a few questions about Nick. . . ." I linked my arm with hers and led her away from the curtains and another possible scare.

As we spoke, I noticed that my aunt had taken my advice, and while none of the three attendees watched, the closed, empty casket was being wheeled into the spot where Nick Papadakis' body should have been.

Disaster averted.

Sort of.

"I've already told you everything," Thalia said.

Yes, but then I hadn't really been listening.

I smiled. "Indulge me."

"Oh, all right. Nikos' mother, God bless her soul, and I worked on the festival committee ten years ago. I couldn't say that we were friends, but, well, we did okay. Which was saying a lot because she didn't get on well with the other women. Just the other day, Aliki was saying—"

I cut her off at gossip pass. "Was she his only blood relative?"

Thalia blinked at me as if affronted. "You know it's rude to interrupt, Sofia."

I looked down and grimaced. Would there ever come a time when my mother would fail at making me feel guilty?

"Oh, look," she said. "They've finally wheeled in the casket. It's about time." She made a face. "I wonder why they have it closed. . . ." She started to turn, and I held on fast to her arm.

"Nick's mother . . . ," I reminded her.

"She was Nikos' only blood relative. Which explains why I'm here." She budged the strap of her twenty-year-old purse up her arm. "'Thalia,' she said to me at the end of the festival, clutching on to my arm like she was drowning and I was the closest life preserver, "I want you to promise me something. I want you to promise that if anything happens to me that you'll look out after my Niko.'"

Thalia gave a visible shudder.

"Anyway, two weeks later she was dead. Brain aneurysm."

"And did you?"

She continued to try to make her way toward the closed casket. "Did I what?"

"Did you look after Nick?"

That got her back up. "Of course I did. At least for the first few weeks. I took him food, called him weekly to make sure he was okay, invited him for dinner at the house—though he never came."

I couldn't remember her mentioning Nick. And since my mother mentioned everything, I knew things must have gone south from there. "What happened then?"

"He went off to college in D.C. and I never heard from him again." She made a huffy sound. "Heck of a way to treat the only person who had been looking after him, I say."

"Did he ever get married?"

"No."

"Have any girlfriends that you knew about?"

"No."

"What about friends? He had to have one or two of those?"

Thalia stared at me. "If he did, I'd like to know where they are now. I don't think I've seen a more poorly attended viewing."

I looked around the room, which had even fewer people in it than there'd been five minutes ago. One of the viewers had left before the casket was finally wheeled in.

"I wouldn't be here either except for that promise I made to his mother." She crossed herself three times and mouthed a silent prayer.

I wanted to know why she'd insisted I come but decided not to ask. I already knew far more about the missing deceased dead guy than I wanted to . . . and, interestingly, less than I needed to know.

Without my realizing it, Thalia had led me to stand in front of the empty casket.

"This isn't right," she said, scooting her purse strap farther up her arm and reaching for the lid.

I caught her hands. "I don't think you want to do that."

"Why?" She looked understandably perplexed. "He died of natural causes, they said. Heart attack. No need for a closed casket."

I couldn't tell my mother why she shouldn't open the casket without breaking the promise I'd made to my aunt Sotiria, so I released my grip on Thalia's hands and took a step back.

"Be my guest."

She said something under her breath in Greek about confusing female children and reached out again.

"That's funny. It won't open."

The breath I was holding gushed out. Byron must have found a way to wedge the top shut. I knew they did that in cases where closed caskets were dictated. It would be just like a Greek to open the top and stare down at an accident victim that had lost half his face.

I watched as my mother looked around for something presumably to pry the top open with.

Afraid she might send me out for the crowbar from my car trunk, I took her arm and led her toward a chair.

"Why don't we wait for Byron to come out? I'm sure he'll explain why the casket's closed."

"Oh, look!" my mother said. "Dino came, bless his heart."

Suddenly I wished the casket weren't wedged closed. Not because its empty state would have distracted my mother from the latest addition to the dwindling number of viewers. But so I could jump into it. . . .

Three

THE NEXT MORNING I LAY in bed staring at the ceiling. My eyelids felt glued open, my arms were stiff at my sides. I willed myself to go back to sleep. My mind ignored me.

"I tried calling to warn you," Dino had mouthed yesterday at the funeral home while my mother hugged him as though he were already a member of the family.

Then Thalia had done the reintroduction bit, including details of his owning his own business (a *zaharoplastio* aka yummy sweets shop) and his coming from Eleia, the same area as my father's side of the family (a fact that's mentioned in every introduction, because where a Greek's family came from in the old country was almost as important as the fact that he was Greek).

"You remember Constantinos, don't you, Sofie?" Thalia had asked.

Remember him? His every feature—and I mean *every* feature—was committed to permanent memory.

Now, I finally managed to close my eyes, but only to scrunch them in horror.

While my mother had seemed preoccupied with the fact that the casket was closed, and told everyone within hearing distance, I knew that Thalia missed nothing. And feared that Dino's and my secret connection was flashing like a neon beer sign on my forehead. But rather than spelling out Coors, the tubes formed the word *Whore.*

Still, I'd survived the incident. And determined to make Dino pay for his little transgression.

A small, canine whine drew my attention to my feet. I expected to find Muffy looking at me woefully, figuring that since I was up, I might as well open the window so he could go up the fire escape to the roof to see to his business.

Only the Jack Russell terrier appeared to be fast asleep, the whining caused by something he was apparently dreaming about.

Probably my mother was haunting him, too. Probably he was reliving when she'd chased him out of the kitchen with a broom after he'd liberated half of a roasted chicken from the pan in which it had been cooling, desperately gripping the poultry between his straight little teeth.

I looked at the clock. Just before seven.

Ugh.

At least a half hour before my alarm clock was due to go off.

Okay, so I knew that compared with a lot of New Yorkers, I had it easy when it came to work hours. I had countless friends who got up this early in order to make the half-hour train ride into the city for their jobs and faced an equally long return trip. Me, I lived within walking distance of the agency—even though I usually drove because I used my car a lot tailing targets—and most of my family. Well, at least those that didn't live in Greece.

Still, I felt I was entitled to kvetch a little. Wasn't I? I mean, since I didn't have to get up, I owed it to the others to at least get more sleep.

I peeled off the sheet and comforter and trailed my feet over the side of the bed, shivering as I did. Yes, it was definitely October, with everything the autumn month brought with it, including cooler temps. I had yet to transition my wardrobe from all things summery to all things sweatery, partly because to do so would be to surrender to the changing seasons. Mostly because many of my warmer clothes were still in the closet of my old room at my parents' house a few blocks up the street.

Still, none of that had stopped me from making my first autumn purchase: distressed brown leather Ariat cowboy boots. A comfortable pair of shitkickers that I'd worn nearly every day for the past week and probably would have on for the rest of the season and on into winter. The instant the shoe salesman on Steinway told me they were "roper" boots, I knew I had to have them. I imagined myself an urban cowgirl of sorts who always got her man when I had them on.

Of course, those men usually belonged to other women and were cheating on same, but hey, a girl couldn't be picky.

Unfortunately, the boots were of absolutely no help to me now. If I'd thought the air was cold, I found the hardwood floor even colder as I made a mad dash for the bathroom and the shower beyond. Maybe I could get in a little missing body search time before I went into the office.

THE MOST FRUSTRATING PART OF searching for a body was that you couldn't second-guess the body's mind-set. Namely because it didn't have a mind.

You'd think finding a dead person lying about would be easy. I mean, it wasn't natural even in New York to just walk over where one might lie in the middle of the sidewalk.

Of course, I wasn't exactly searching sidewalks. Instead, last night I'd started with the obvious places, like talking to Aunt Sotiria's hearse driver and two other full-time and five other part-time employees on her books. None of her employees had indicated anything unusual in their daily routine. No, the driver hadn't gone anywhere that night, with or without a body. No, there had been nothing out of the ordinary in prepping the body. No, no one had taken him shopping for a new suit and accidentally left him in a changing room.

The best I could figure it was that Nick must have come up missing right after he'd been transferred to his coffin and before the scheduled viewing. Five hours. That left a hell of a window to try to close.

At least I was reasonably sure that Nick hadn't gotten up and walked out of the place on his own power since he'd already been embalmed. Not that I thought he would have anywhere to go before his veins had been drained and filled with embalming fluid. But, hey, stranger things had been known to happen.

I parked my car up the street from the agency, grabbed my nearly empty frappé travel cup, and got out, a nippy breeze bringing the hair up on the back of my neck.

Oh, stop it. I didn't believe in all things paranormal. I didn't believe in vampires or ghosts, and I most certainly didn't believe that a dead man could walk unless he was taking the infamous final walk down the prison hall toward the gas chamber or lethal injection room. And not even that happened in New

York. Not since the death penalty law had been ruled unconstitutional by the state supreme court a few years back.

I opened the agency's front door and stepped inside. The office assistant, Rosie Rodriguez, was instantly on her feet, reminding me of a Mexican jumping bean even though she was Puerto Rican. She briefly stopped chewing her ever present gum, making her cake-size dimples disappear.

"Sofie, I'd like you to meet Melinda Laughton. You know, the sister of John Warren Laughton?"

I held on to the door, debating the wisdom of ducking back outside.

It wasn't like Rosie to hit me full on with a client the instant I arrived. Usually we both needed at least one cup of coffee (my favorite was Nescafé Frappé, an instant, frothy iced coffee I drank without concern for the time of year) before we could manage to form a coherent sentence to each other, much less to the public at large. But Rosie had been acting a bit out of character lately. There had even been a couple of occasions when she'd forgotten to tell me important details altogether. Like the time we had been hired by both the husband and the wife to prove the other was cheating and the two had crossed paths at the agency.

It hadn't been pretty, resulting in more than the breaking of the front window when the husband had thrown the potted floor plant through it. Neither of them had paid their bill yet, much less repair costs. And I didn't expect that they would.

I considered the pretty young blond woman sitting with her hands folded neatly on her lap. The name John Warren Laughton rang a bell somewhere inside my sluggish brain.

While I hadn't been following the story closely, I knew that

John Warren Laughton was accused of killing his girlfriend last year and that his trial was due to start soon, jury selection scheduled for sometime this week or next. Although the story had dropped from lead to second segment and other news, the progress was being followed to some extent by print media and television, partly because the location of seventeen-year-old Valerie Bryer's body was still a mystery, mostly because her parents were doing a good job of keeping the story circulating, probably in the hopes of a) finding her body; and b) convicting the kid they believed responsible for her death.

Melinda got to her feet from where she'd been sitting in one of the chairs inside the door. She stretched out her hand. "His name is Johnny, not John Warren." She grimaced as I moved my cup from my right to my left hand and shook hers. "I mean, John Warren is his given name, but everyone's always called him Johnny."

Rosie resumed chewing her gum. "Yeah, the police and the media, they like to call people by their given names. Especially when it comes to killers. John Wilkes Booth. Lee Harvey Oswald. Even that Virginia Tech monster was referred to by three names. I think. Only they never used the middle name of that David Berkowitz, Son of Sam guy. That's curious."

I noticed Melinda's shoulders slump lower.

I gave Rosie a look.

"What?"

I looked back to Melinda. "Please, Miss Laughton, have a seat. I'll be right with you." I tilted my head toward the office. "Rosie? Why don't you bring your coffee into the office for a minute."

"What? Oh. Sure. Just a sec. I need a warm-up."

I went into my uncle's office. Well, it was still officially his office, but I figured that since possession was nine-tenths of the law, and Spyros hadn't been in the country for a good six months, much less behind his desk, it was mine. At least for the time being.

Rosie came inside with a fresh cup of coffee. I walked around her and shut the door and then moved to lean against the front of the desk.

"What's up?" she asked, chewing a few times and then sticking her gum to the rim of her cup before taking a sip.

"Nothing. I just wanted a few moments before I jumped headfirst into the day." That wasn't entirely true. I'd been on the clock pretty much for the past hour. But I didn't have to tell Rosie that.

She gave one of her patented eye rolls. "Tell me about it. I mean, who knew something so small could make so much noise?"

I knew she was talking about her one-month-old nephew, Carlos. She'd temporarily moved in with her sister Lupe to help take care of the latest addition to the Rodriguez family tree, and it looked as though she hadn't gotten a lick of sleep since.

"All he seems to do is cry. Sleep? If Lupe or I do manage to get him to close his eyes, they immediately fly back open the instant either of us takes a breath. Poor little Carlito." She shook her head. "Even my mother says she's never seen a baby so fussy. The doctor says it's probably just colic and that it will pass in a month or two." Her dark eyes bulged. "What in the hell are we going to do for two more months?"

My heart went out to her. One of my cousins had had a colicky baby and everyone had tried to help out, but even with the women in the family working in shifts, they all came away looking as if they'd been standing next to an old church bell while it was being rung.

Rosie dropped her voice as if afraid of being overheard. "My mother thinks it's because he knows that no-good, son-of-a-bitch father of his up and abandoned him and his mother before he was even born."

After four weeks of little or no sleep, they were all probably prepared to believe ghosts were sticking pins in the infant's feet. Any explanation would do. Something, anything that didn't support their fear that they were somehow to blame.

"Let me talk to my mother," I said. "Maybe she knows something that will help."

Rosie appeared to relax. "I appreciate it."

For a minute, I wanted to hug her. But the moment passed as quickly as it had come. Which was just as well, because Rosie wasn't the touchy-feely type. Nor, for that matter, was I.

"Is there some specific reason you're running late?" she asked, already looking like the feisty gossip I was used to. "Like a man?"

"Something like that."

Her dark eyes sparkled at me.

"Only not in the way you think, unfortunately." I rounded the desk. "When you're ready, send in Laughton, okay?"

"SO, WHAT CAN I DO for you?" I asked.

Melinda Laughton had seated herself in one of the guest chairs and clutched her purse tightly in her lap as she stared at me unwaveringly. "I want you to find the real killer."

Okay. This was a new one.

I held her gaze for several moments, waiting for her to realize how dumb her request was. Or perhaps even to see if she bought what she was saying. When she didn't look away, I did.

Up until now, my jobs as a private investigator have been limited. Cheating spouse cases, mostly. And missing pets. I did have one missing persons case, but since Uncle Tolly had been voluntarily missing, well, I didn't know if that counted. Then there was the whole Reni Venezuela incident last month, a case I'd initially believed amounted to little more than a cheating spouse with a benefits package (multiple sexual partners by way of groupies, seeing as he was a Mets pitcher), but I'd been proven wrong when I'd discovered Reni's older brother had let jealousy go a little too far and he'd tried to take his brother's place, both in his bed and on the playing field.

But a murder case?

I pushed from the desk and rounded it, sitting in my uncle's expensive leather chair that smelled like heaven revisited.

"I have to admit, I haven't been following your brother's case very closely," I said. "But from what I have seen, all the evidence appears to point to him."

"That's because the cops haven't looked anywhere else."

"Maybe there's nowhere else to look."

Her gaze dropped to where she held her purse, and she appeared to make a concerted effort not to grip the item so fiercely. She closed her eyes tightly instead, as if she couldn't function unless something were clenched.

I could relate to the feeling.

"Look, Melinda, I don't mean to be cruel, but have you considered the possibility that he might be guilty?"

A tear squeezed from under her closed eyelid and slid down her cheek. I grimaced.

She began shaking her head. "No."

I opened my mouth to tell her that maybe she should.

"No, don't. I've heard the 'odds are' speech from every damn PI, detective, attorney, and tarot card reader in Queens, and I'm going to scream if I hear it from you, too."

My mouth snapped shut.

"I know what the evidence says. Better than anybody. But the difference between me and you and the jurors that will be seated is that I know my baby brother could never do anything like this. Ever. He loved Valerie. Heart and soul. He could never have hurt her, much less murdered her."

An image of my own younger brother, Kosmos, entered my mind unbidden.

"Look," she said, opening her purse. "I don't have much money, but, please, take it. One week. That's all I'm asking for. Just look into the case. If you come away thinking Johnny's guilty . . ."

I raised my hands. "It's nothing personal, really it isn't," I said. "But I don't know if I'm the right person for the job."

A kid's life was on the line. If he was innocent, and I couldn't prove it, I didn't want that kind of guilt hanging over my head.

Truth was, while I was growing more confident in my abilities as a PI, I wasn't that confident.

Melinda clasped the fresh one-hundred-dollar bills in her hands on top of her purse. "You're the only person for the job," she whispered. "No one else would take me on."

Well, I suppose that was one way to try to win me over. Knowing that she'd gone to everyone else before me wasn't very flattering. Then again, my name wasn't the one on the door, my uncle's was. And despite my brief appearances in the local news for having shot my own client (self-defense, I swear) and breaking up a dognapping ring (which only served to double requests for the agency to find missing pets), I hadn't made a respectable name for myself in the city. The Venezuela case probably would have helped, but for reasons both obvious (I hadn't wanted to hurt my Mets' chance at the World Series) and not so obvious (I'd grown to like Reni's wife, Gisela, and neither of us had wanted her to know she'd been sleeping with another man), only those immediately involved knew what had gone down.

As things stood in the Laughton case, odds were I wouldn't be able to find anything that the police or the defense attorneys hadn't been able to find.

But there was that slight chance that I might stumble onto something that would exonerate Little Johnny Laughton.

I was not amused that I was already thinking of him as Little Johnny. John Warren sounded more accusable somehow.

But maybe that's exactly what was needed. Maybe a little press on poor Little Johnny Laughton might go a long way toward swaying public opinion to his side. Or at least give him the benefit of the doubt. Hell, even I had tried and convicted him in my own mind based on what I'd seen and read.

If he was innocent . . .

Melinda seemed to sense an opening and stood up, counting out the money on top of the desk. She gave up halfway through and just put it all down. I didn't know if it was because she was too distracted to count or because she didn't have much money and that was all she had in the world.

Either way, the money wasn't the reason I was interested in the case.

"Take it. Take all of it. I don't care. Just get my brother out of that prison cell and bring him home where he belongs."

Four

HOW, EXACTLY, DID ONE GO about investigating a murder?

I sat at my uncle's desk long after Melinda Laughton had left, alternately making notes to myself and scratching my head.

I figured that the word *investigation* was a good place to start. After all, I was a private investigator. Or, according to New York law, a PI-in-training, since I wouldn't be officially licensed for another two and a half or so years while apprenticing under my uncle.

I'm not sure why that is. I mean, medical interns and residents qualified for a temporary permit to practice even while they were still considered students, didn't they? I wondered if New York made it difficult because so many people were interested in being PIs.

Of course, it probably wasn't a good idea to have everyone and his brother flashing a PI ID around town. Or carrying concealed.

At any rate, none of that had to do with the fact that I had an important case to work. And while I had a few ideas on where to start, the mere concept of working it gave me cause for pause. In this day and age, "life or death" scenarios were more fiction than reality. But in this case, Little Johnny's being sent up for life without the possibility for parole was a very real possibility.

Rosie barged through the door like a honey-skinned Tasmanian devil on a mission. All that was missing was a couple of teeth overlapping her upper lip.

"Thank God you're alone," she said, looking behind her to verify that the outer office was empty and then closing the door. "What's this I hear about a missing stiff?"

I leaned back in the chair. How had she found out about the missing corpse? Although the police had been called after the "viewing," they'd seemed preoccupied and had just about outright said that there was nothing they could do, that my aunt shouldn't worry, bodies had a habit of turning up again somewhere.

"Missing stiff?" I asked, trying my best poker face on for size.

Rosie stared at me as if I were a half-teaspoon of Nescafé short of my usual frappé. "Don't give me that. I know you're working that funeral home case. What, the witch who owns the place is a relative of yours, isn't she?"

I suspected that "witch" wasn't being used in place of "bitch," but rather that given my aunt Sotiria's frizzy appearance and her brusque demeanor, some believed she was a practicing witch minus a broomstick.

"She's my aunt."

"Uh-huh. And you told her you'd look for the body?"

"How did you find out about it?" I mentally reviewed the list of Sotiria's employees that I'd questioned.

"My cousin's boyfriend works for one of those independent

ambulance companies as a driver." Rosie's dozen silver bracelets clinked as she waved her hand. "Don't even get me started on that. The guy mostly drives around dead people for a living. What kind of job is that? My aunt almost had a stroke when she found out."

"You mean heart attack."

"No, I mean stroke. Sudden shock to the system that results in an aneurysm."

I gave her my best eye roll. "Yes, I told my aunt that I'd look into it."

"So that's the man responsible for making you late to the office this morning? A dead man?" Rosie gave a dramatic shudder and then crossed her arms under her ample chest, mostly because she was incapable of crossing her arms over her chest because of the aforementioned ampleness. "Uh-uh. You're going to call her back and tell her to let the police look into it."

"Why?"

"Because we ain't looking for no dead body. Not a week before *Día de los Muertos.*"

The Day of the Dead. I was familiar with the Latin day when it was believed that dead relatives returned for an annual visit. It began at midnight on Halloween and stretched throughout the day, if I remembered correctly. When I was young, I'd seen a parade on some Astoria side street in which several of the marchers wore skeleton suits. I'd assumed that the celebration had to do with Halloween, although for us kids, Halloween had ended the night before when house lights went off and we all went home with bellyaches. Besides, the people participating hadn't looked festive. Rather, they'd looked pensive—I've since come to understand it was reflective, the day set aside to think about the past and those they'd lost—and I'd freaked and run home, glad when the next morning came and there was no sign of the walking skeletons.

"Anyway, the neighborhood vampires probably took him, is what I think."

I sighed. "Rosie, there is no such thing as vampires."

"Uh-huh. That's why there's a citywide blood shortage and people have been popping up missing."

"Nick was embalmed before he went missing."

"So? Maybe they got so desperate they're taking even the embalmed."

"I'm not dropping the case."

She tsked at me.

"Anyway, I don't expect the missing body case will be taking up much of my time. Like the police said, missing bodies have a way of popping up somewhere sooner or later."

Rosie made a face, but I continued before she could launch herself dimple-first into her next monologue.

"I just took on the Laughton case," I said.

She dropped her arms to her sides. "Really?"

I nodded and leaned forward to look over the scanty notes I'd taken. "Really."

Rosie inched closer, looking as intrigued as I'd been when I'd finally accepted the case.

"You think he did it?"

"I don't know. But I guess there's one way to find out." I didn't think that's what Melinda Laughton had had in mind when she'd paid me, but I figured it was as good a place to start as any. By looking at what evidence the city had that proved Johnny had done it, I might start spotting errors in their logic and their case.

Rosie met my gaze over the desk. "How can I help?"

I smiled at her. Now that was more like it. . . .

I'D SPENT THE BETTER PART of the morning going over the notes I'd made on the Laughton case, adding to them, making a few phone calls, and finding out that Johnny's lawyer was a public defender (I charged Rosie with making contact with his office to set up an appointment) and that the alleged murderer, Johnny, and by extension his sister, Melinda, had been raised in a public housing building in Long Island City, also in Queens, while the alleged victim ("alleged" was a new word in my vocabulary), Valerie Bryer, was from a wealthy Forest Hills family and that her father was an executive VP of a N.Y. securities firm.

At any rate, my brain was pretty much fried by noon, overwhelmed with everything I'd tried to cram into it in a short amount of time. Since the trial jury was due to be seated any day now, there was a definite urgency to the case. But now I wanted to step away for at least an hour, let everything sink in further as well as provide my body with some much needed sustenance—more specifically, food my mother made.

So I stopped by my apartment to pick up Muffy and drove down the street to my parents' place. As I climbed out of my car, I looked around, hyperaware of the change of seasons around me. It was more than just the nip to the air and the color of the leaves. The very light seemed weaker somehow. Thinner. Eerier. I jerked to look over my shoulder, as if sensing someone there, behind me, even though I knew no one was.

"Muffy?"

Normally when I traveled with him, he stayed at my heel, waiting for me to lead the way. Not that he followed me. Not by any means. Instead, he appeared to think himself equal and fell into step beside me, making for some awkward situations and a few canine yelps when we entered narrow doorways.

Only he wasn't beside me now.

I bent and looked inside the car. Had I closed the door before he got out? Sometimes he was a little reluctant about going to my parents', my paternal grandmother's penchant for sharpening knives while she looked at him a little unnerving even to me.

I heard a low, Muffy growl. I turned to find him crouched low on the sidewalk outside Mrs. K's old place next to my parents', staring at something inside the closed gate.

His interest in the place wasn't so unusual. After all, it had been his home up until a few months ago, when his owner and my mother's best friend, Mrs. Kapoor, had packed her bags and bought a one-way ticket to Hindu heaven. Rather, the way Muffy seemed intently fixed on something inside the gate was what caught my interest.

"What is it, boy?" I said, coming to stand next to him in a bit of role reversal.

His growling intensified.

I squinted at the front yard, trying to spot the reason for his interest. A young Asian family had bought the place a couple of months back and had two young children. I'd hoped that the new occupants would help my mother move on (for weeks after Mrs. K's surprise demise, Thalia had been convinced that her own time must be nigh since the two women had been about the same age), but so far, no good. Since the new family was younger, and they were newish immigrants, they smiled and nodded at Thalia but didn't indulge in her need for conversation, making my mother feel Mrs. K's absence all the more.

"What is it, Muffster?" I asked, reaching down to pet him as he continued to growl at invisible prey.

He snapped at me.

I quickly pulled back my hand, my own mind traveling to times past. Back when Muffy had been Mrs. K's dog. Back when he'd had an insatiable taste for Sofie flesh. And I had the fading scars to prove it.

Huhn.

In the beginning of our forced cohabitation, the dog I had once called the Mutt from Hell and I had carefully steered a wide course around each other. He hadn't liked me, and I hadn't wanted to get bit again. But things had thawed (read: I fed him table scraps and even bought *kalia* for him from time to time), and in due course we'd become friends, if not the best of buddies.

"Sofie! What are you doing over there?"

It was my mother calling from the steps of her house next door, wiping her hands on her ever present apron.

I looked down at Muffy again, only to find that he had finally budged and was running full out for my mother. I opened my mouth to warn her and then closed it again when the little mongrel stopped before her, his tail wagging a million miles a minute as she bent to pat him.

Double huhn.

Then again, Muffy had never bit my mother. In fact, her status as Mrs. K's best friend had automatically qualified her for the same status with Muffy.

"Well, what did I do?" I muttered, and followed in Muffy's wake.

"Hi, Mom," I said, kissing her on both cheeks before I entered the house.

She returned my kiss and then cuffed me in the back of the head as I passed.

"Ow!" I said. What had I done to deserve so much abuse in such a short time span? "What was that for?"

"For not telling me about the missing body last night."

She closed the door and led the way to the kitchen, where I could smell food cooking.

"Now get in here and tell me all about it."

I gave an eye roll, smoothed the back of my hair where it might bear cuff marks, and followed, wondering when I'd ever stop underestimating the power of the Astoria grapevine. . . .

Five

IN THE SCHEME OF THINGS, I supposed I should be grateful that my mother had been distracted by the news of Nick's missing body and not concentrated on something else . . . like, say, the palpable tension between Dino and me last night. But I wasn't. Partly because I'd had to endure endless questions as I ate *fakes*, homemade lentil soup with lots of garlic, to which I generously added Kalamata olives, fresh, crusty bread, and Greek feta cheese. Mostly because I'd had to answer them or risk another cuff to the back of the head.

If I'd been hoping for a little peace to get my thoughts together on the Laughton case, I hadn't found it at my parents'. In fact, so intent had I been on getting out of there, it wasn't until after I'd left that I remembered I'd wanted to pick up the boxes of last year's winter clothes from the closet of my old bedroom.

So I moved on to the next surefire way to bring clarity on a case: work on another one.

———

I SAT IN MY CAR outside the town house where my missing body Nick Papadakis had once lived. I checked my cell phone to find three missed calls: two from my aunt Sotiria wanting to know if I'd found her stiff yet and one from Dino.

I smiled and ran the pad of my thumb over the cell numbers, ready to press the button to call him back. Instead, I put the phone into my purse, looked at where Muffy was snuggled up in the passenger seat considering me through wary eyes, and then climbed out of the car.

For what it's worth, I didn't know what I expected to find here. A living person goes missing, the first place you check is his house. A stiff? I swallowed hard as I took in the neat, two-story brick town house connected to an identical one to the right. Well, while my life would probably be easier if I found the body inside, I wasn't sure what the possible discovery would do to my mental state.

I looked around, finding that the two trees in front of the town houses were almost completely barren of leaves, the branches creaking in the wind.

God, I hated this time of year.

Yet at the same time, I loved it.

Okay, so I'm the type that rents zombie DVDs, screams at the TV while watching them, and then sweats through nightmares, only to go through the whole rigmarole again the next weekend when the latest blood-and-gore flick hits the rental store.

The problem lay in that in reality, I couldn't push the stop button.

Through a little effort, I'd found out that Papadakis had rented his town house and that the owner lived in the connecting one.

Which made things convenient. I consulted my notes and moved to the one where he'd lived. I checked the mailbox—empty—inside the screen door—nothing—and then put my hand to the window so I could peer inside.

"Can I help you?"

I nearly fell back on the cement stairs.

"Um, yes," I said, letting the screen door close as I met the woman who'd addressed me on the sidewalk. "I'm Sofie Metropolis? I spoke to the owner a little while ago about going through the place?"

The woman was either in her mid-forties and in great shape for her age or in her mid-thirties and in bad shape. I couldn't tell which. She had shoulder-length brown hair, held probably twenty extra pounds, and had a thrift shop fashion sense that might work on a grunge band teen but made her look dumpy.

"Oh, hi," she said with a small smile. "I'm Dottie Grear, the owner." She held out her hand and I shook it. "I didn't expect you to be so young."

My chest puffed out. It wasn't all that long ago that I'd have been insulted by someone saying I was young. But after being stamped with a *yerotokori* label—old maid—by my family following my wedding day fiasco . . . well, I found recently that I was flattered by comments like Dottie's.

"Thank you for agreeing to let me in."

"No problem."

She took a set of keys from the pocket of an old cardigan and opened the front door. I followed behind her, holding my breath. I didn't know why until I realized that I expected to be assaulted by the rank scent of decay when we entered the dark place.

"Well, this is it."

I took a tentative sniff. Nothing beyond a hint of dust and stale cologne. Thank God.

Dottie stood near the door and crossed her arms as I switched on the lights. I wasn't surprised to find everything probably much the way it had been before Papadakis had died.

"So how long did he live here?" I asked as I opened coffee table drawers, checked under sofa cushions, and methodically took in my surroundings.

"Two years, two months, and two days."

I quirked a brow.

She smiled. "I figured you'd ask."

"Did you know much about him?"

"No, not really. You know, aside from the obvious. He was quiet, never brought anyone home. Always paid the rent on time."

I leafed through the sheath of mail on a side table. Junk mail, mostly. I frowned. No credit card bills. No utilities.

"What was included in the rent?" I asked.

"Everything. Water, electric, gas."

I nodded and put the generic mail back down.

"I've been collecting the mail and putting it there since . . . well, you know."

I moved into the dining room and then into the kitchen beyond. Dottie followed.

"You know, I was actually hoping you could help me out," she said quietly.

I opened the freezer door. Hungry-Man TV dinners crowded the depths. I closed the door and opened the bottom. Milk, beer, and a loaf of bread. I hadn't answered Dottie, and I had no plans to. One of the things I'd learned on the job, as well as in life, filled as it was with Greeks, is that you never encouraged someone about to ask you for a favor.

"Since Nick didn't have any family to speak of . . . well, I'm not sure what I'm supposed to do with all his stuff."

I closed the refrigerator and moved on to the counter drawers. I didn't know what I was looking for, really. A flashing sign saying BODY HERE might help. But I'd settle for a clue that would lead me further than I'd gotten so far.

"What, like his furniture?"

"Oh, none of the furniture is his. It came with the place."

I looked at her.

She shrugged lightly. "It was my father's house. He was a widower for a decade before he died two years ago. Left me this place along with the one next door where I live."

"So you're talking about clothes and stuff, then?"

Silverware and junk drawers a bust.

"Yeah."

"You married?"

Dottie laughed and then caught herself. "No."

"No husband or brother or someone who maybe might be the same size?"

I hadn't made it to the second floor and his closets yet to see what kind of taste the guy had. Byron had said he'd been found in a new Brooks Brothers suit, though, and that they were going to bury him in it since it was unmarred and clean (well, aside from the pants where he'd dropped into a mud puddle when he fell, but that didn't matter since the open coffin concealed the bottom half of the body—or would, if I ever found the body).

"No. No one."

"So call the Salvation Army or something. Maybe a church. I'm sure they'll be happy to come pick up the stuff."

"Do you think that would be okay?"

I shrugged. "I don't see why not."

I caught myself. The last time I'd given advice of this nature, I'd gotten into trouble. For all I knew, Nick Papadakis had left everything to a dog named Brutus and Brutus' new owner would sue for the return of items Dottie had donated.

"Actually, you might want to consult with your attorney first. See if there was a will or something."

Probably I should do the same. Find out if he'd left a will.

"Oh." Dottie sighed, following after me as I led the way up the stairs. "It's probably better anyway. The place I called yesterday wanted me to pay a pickup fee."

"Really?"

"Really. Forty dollars."

I shook my head as I made a beeline straight for Nick's closet. Given the bit on the Brooks Brothers suit, I'd expected to find a few more suits. Only I hadn't been prepared for the endless line of them, all clean and neatly pressed and bearing designer labels, hanging on wood hangers. There had to be at least two dozen of them, all in dark colors. At first I thought they were all black, but as my eyesight adjusted, I made out shades of blue and green.

"My talents may be a little dubious when it comes to items of this nature, but I'm thinking that place should have given you forty dollars for these." The top of the hangers scraped against the rod as I went through them. "Apiece."

Dottie stepped up next to me. "Apiece?"

"Uh-huh." I jiggled hangers to force out anything that might be in any of the pants pockets. There had to be something that might afford me a clue as to what had happened to the body. Beyond Rosie's vampire hypothesis.

I closed the closet doors and took a few more minutes to go through his drawers and medicine cabinet.

Nothing.

I scratched my head as I stood in the front room again, a contemplative Dottie by my side. This guy had been too neat by far. No man I knew was this neat. But then again, if he had been the mama's boy my mother painted, perhaps it wasn't outside the realm.

I glanced around again, my mind catching on something else.

There was absolutely, positively nothing in the entire place that gave it a personal touch. No photographs. No old love letters. No prescriptions in the bathroom. No "Kiss the Chef" aprons in the kitchen. Aside from his preference for fried chicken TV dinners and his penchant for expensive designer suits, there was nothing to give me a clue as to just who this guy was, Greek or not.

I picked up the remote control and pushed the power button. The sound of a CNN commentator immediately filled the room. I pressed the recall channel button and FOX News popped up. I turned the TV off again.

"Two years, you say?" I asked Dottie.

"Uh-huh."

I fished one of my business cards from my purse and held it out for her. "Well, thanks, Dottie. Should you think of anything, please don't hesitate to call."

"Like what?"

I shrugged. "I don't know . . . anything."

I didn't want to tell her that if she noticed any zombielike beings entering the place with his own key . . .

Speaking of keys . . .

"Thanks again. Oh, and you might want to have someone appraise those suits before you give them away."

"Thanks." She was staring at my card as I left.

What did the coroner do with a stiff's personal items when there was no personal contact around to collect them? Probably my aunt Sotiria had his wallet and his house keys. Did he have a car? I figured there was only one way to find out.

But while I hadn't discovered anything to give me a clue to what had happened to Nick Papadakis' body, I had succeeded in doing what I'd set out to do—namely, get some clues in how to proceed with Little Johnny Laughton's case. Oh, nothing groundbreaking or anything. But I probably needed to start doing what I just had here. Rifling through drawers and peering into closets for anything that might jump out. . . .

Six

I'D HAD MORE THAN MY fair share of run-ins with the Queens Mob lately. Forget that every time I ate pasta, I thought of handsome, wannabe Mafia don Tony DiPiazza . . . and not in a nice way, either. Mostly because whenever I saw the Hell Gate Bridge, I remembered that he'd tried to throw me off it in a brand, spanking new pair of cement overshoes, despite our having gone to high school together and his wanting to share "pasta" with me.

I shivered and pulled my jacket closer as I walked down Ditmars toward an Italian pizza place where Johnny had been last seen with his girlfriend before she'd been reported missing.

As I neared the restaurant—forced to park four blocks up because this part of Ditmars near 31st was always packed this time of day, close to dinner—I started thinking about my Mob encounters and applying my knowledge to the Papadakis' case.

It was well-known that some families liked to keep souvenirs of their kills. You know, tongues from the bodies of snitches, hands from thieves. I hated to think of what happened to those who screwed around with Mob bosses' wives.

But was there ever a time when they claimed full bodies?

Of course, I had no proof that Papadakis had been involved with the Mob. From what I understood, he worked as an insurance underwriter. But even insurance underwriters got in trouble with the Mob from time to time. Gambling debts were particularly newsworthy now.

But why would they take a whole body? And from what I understood, while Papadakis had died young, he'd died of natural causes.

An image of a Mob museum displaying all the various body parts in glass cases sprang to mind, and I pulled my jacket even closer.

My cell rang and I fished it out of my purse.

"Hey," Rosie said.

"Hey, yourself. Did you get through to that PD?"

It was nearly five and she sounded exhausted. "Who? Oh, yeah. Laughton's public defender. No. I've talked to his assistant three times, but she always tells me he's out and unavailable, blah blah. I think she's lying. But I don't know why yet."

"Why do you think she's lying?"

"Because we office managers know how to spot this kind of stuff. Anyway, I'll call again in the morning. I've got to get back to Lupe's. She's one bamboo shoot away from being a full basket case."

"Try holding him up," I said, remembering my mother's suggestion when I'd asked her for advice on handling colicky babies.

"What?"

"She says Carlos probably has gas. So keep him upright. You know, like you do when you burp him, and rub his back and belly to help it pass. Oh, and when you do lay him down, put him so he's resting on his side and shift his position every half hour or so. Only don't put him stomach down." Thalia had also shared a homeopathic remedy involving herbs that probably went back to the old country, but I wasn't sure I should suggest it. My grandmother was still fond of leeches for bad bruises and bloodletting for chest colds and flu.

Which was probably why I didn't much go for anything that didn't involve a doctor's well-informed diagnosis and treatment.

Rosie sounded doubtful. "Thanks. I'll give it a try."

I ended the phone call just as I reached the pizza joint and stepped out of the way of a couple exiting before I entered. I paused, looking at the man and woman who would have been around Johnny's and Valerie's ages. Then I continued on inside.

Minus any hard facts from the PD, Melinda Laughton had filled me in as best she could on times and dates, but I hadn't gotten name information beyond "a waitress at . . ." or "a parking attendant at . . ." Which meant I was on a large-scale fishing expedition.

Probably I should just wait until I met with the kid's attorney before I started blindly seeking out information. But I figured I was in the neighborhood, and I was still hungry since I hadn't eaten much lentil soup in my hurry to get away from my mother, and a slice with pepperoni and anchovies would sure hit the spot right about now.

I stepped to the counter, put in my order, and then leaned forward in a conspiratorial manner toward the girl manning the register where I paid. "Which of the waitresses is the one who served that guy who killed his girlfriend?"

I wasn't surprised when she pointed to someone waiting tables ten or so feet behind me. "Says she still has nightmares about it.

Wished she would have called the cops while they were still here instead of kicking them out."

"Thanks," I said, toasting her with my pizza and Diet Coke.

I headed for the table where the waitress was taking an order from a group of teens. There were no free seats, so I sat at a nearby table where a couple was obviously finished eating but were busy indulging in some heavy PDA.

"I'm sorry, do you mind?" I asked when they didn't even notice me.

The girl pulled away long enough to give me the evil eye. "Hey, find your own table."

"There are no free tables, and besides," I said, pushing their wrappings over to their side and dumping an especially greasy one onto her lap, "it looks like you guys are done anyway."

"Hey, aren't you that girl?" the guy said, earning an arm punch from his girlfriend. "Ow. No, I don't mean in that way. She's that PI that found all those pets last month."

I discreetly watched the waitress as she finished taking the order and skirted around the tables toward the kitchen.

"Sorry. Wrong girl," I said, taking a big, slurping sip of my soda and pulling the other free chair closer with my foot under the table, then purposely pushing it toward them in feigned ignorance before propping my booted feet on top.

"Hey!"

"Oh, I'm sorry," I said, looking under the table. "Did I hit you?"

I made no attempt to move my feet, even though I knew my heel lay against the side of the guy's leg.

"Let's go, Gerald," the girl said in a huff, shooting daggers at me as she got up and pushing her purse handle to her shoulder.

"Table's all yours," Gerald told me.

I gave him a pizza smile.

I watched the couple walk away, Gerald getting another arm hit as they left.

I dropped my boots down and pulled the chair closer to the table with my foot and then followed with the other two in case anyone got the same idea I'd had.

I still had my foot on the last one when it was pulled out again.

"Don't mind if I join you, do you, luv?"

I nearly choked on my pizza.

Jake Porter.

My throat turned to sandpaper, refusing the bite I tried to swallow.

Okay. I wasn't entirely sure what I was supposed to do. Well, beyond spitting the mouthful of food into my napkin. You see, I hadn't seen Jake for over a month. And a lot had happened since then. Specifically, my sex life had taken a huge upswing. Without him.

I winced, recalling that the first time Dino and I had knocked boots, I was afraid I'd given the gorgeous Greek the sex I'd been craving for months with the hot Australian bounty hunter. The same man who had just sat down opposite me at the table. Of course, Jake hadn't wanted the sex. And Dino had. So you didn't have to be a rocket scientist to figure out why Dino was a part of my life and Jake wasn't.

"Holy shit," I said, pretending that his sudden appearance had absolutely no impact on me whatsoever. "Look what the wind blew in."

His grin did funny things to my stomach. Things that it

shouldn't be doing seeing as I was involved with someone else, no matter the secrecy clause.

I squinted at Jake. Or was it a secret?

You see, one of the things that I'd figured out about Jake Porter fairly quickly was that he knew a lot more about my life than I would ever know about his. He used to have a habit of tinkering around with my sheila (my car), even as I'd tried to tempt him into tinkering with something else (me).

Strangely enough, he had a habit of popping up at just the right minute whenever I needed help. Something that didn't sit well with me because I liked to think I could take care of myself.

Actually, that wasn't entirely true. Because I'd gotten into that spot of trouble last month that had required a baseball bat for me to fight my way out of and Jake Porter had been nowhere to be seen.

Hmm . . .

The waitress I was interested in interviewing popped up. "Can I get you anything?" she asked Jake.

"What would you recommend?" he asked me.

I lifted the piece of pizza I still held. "Pepperoni and anchovies."

"Pepperoni and anchovies it is, then. Two slices." He grinned at the waitress. "And bring me a beer. A Foster's if you got it."

"We don't serve liquor."

"Ah. Okay, then. A root beer." He looked at me. "You want anything else, luv?"

Was it me, or was that a challenging look in his eyes? As if he knew exactly who the waitress was and were asking me if I still wanted to question her in his presence.

"No, thank you. I'm fine." I narrowed my gaze, trying to figure out the man across from me.

"Nice boots," he said, distracting me from my thoughts.

I glanced down as if I'd forgotten what I had on. "Thanks. Yours don't suck, either." I put down the pizza slice and wiped my hands on a clean napkin. "To what do I owe the pleasure?"

He leaned back in his chair, making the piece of furniture look pitifully inadequate in light of his wide, six-foot-five frame. He took off his leather cowboy hat and hung it on the chair to his right, not bothering to fluff his light brown hair. I found that incredibly sexy. Most men would never be able to pull off hat head.

"Just out for a bite and saw you here. Thought I'd come over to say hi."

"Right."

"What part don't you believe? That I was out for a bite or that I wanted to say hi?"

He seemed to be looking at me a little too closely.

One of the reasons Jake had given me for not sleeping with me was that he didn't want to be rebound boy and that he believed I still had unresolved issues with my ex-fiancé. It didn't help that he'd been the one to fish my mangled—fake—engagement ring from my garbage disposal or that he'd gotten a gander at the wedding presents still stacked against an entire wall in my bedroom.

But the way he was eyeing me now . . .

There was no possible way in the world that he knew I'd slept with someone else.

Was there?

And if he did? Did that suddenly put me back on the market for him?

The logic made absolutely no sense to me, so I didn't pursue it further.

At least that's what I told myself. But my Jake-deprived brain continued down that nonsensical path all the same without me.

"So how's work treating you?" I asked, taking another bite of pizza. Happily, I discovered I could swallow again.

"Fine."

"Any interesting adventures you'd like to share in the life and times of a bounty hunter?"

His grin widened. "Nope."

"Nope, you don't want to share any stories? Or nope, you're not a bounty hunter?"

"Nope."

I gave him an eye roll and watched the waitress approach with his two slices of pizza and root beer. Root beer. How long had it been since I'd seen someone order a root beer? Not since I'd had a root beer float myself when I was about twelve, I think.

"I got a new case today," I said.

"Did you now?" He sat up so he could eat his own pizza. I watched, mesmerized, as the slice flopped over the side of his large hand.

"No, no," I said, catching the end before all the toppings could fall off onto the questionable tabletop and be lost forever. "You need to fold it in half. Like this."

I maneuvered his long, tapered fingers so that he did as I suggested. In the process, I got cheese on my hand. I began to pull it away when he caught it and lifted my index finger to his mouth. I about died when he sucked on the digit and then released it.

My body's reaction wasn't nearly proportional to the action.

I felt as though he'd just licked a whole different part of my anatomy.

Never, ever, had Jake been so overtly sexual with me. Usually he was dodging my obvious and sometimes asinine advances.

"So what about this case?" he asked.

My mind went blank.

"You said you got a new case today." He took a large bite of pizza, and I stared at the action of his mouth with hyper interest.

"Oh yeah. Little Johnny . . . I mean, John Warren Laughton. His, um, sister came by and hired me to find the real killer. I mean, if her brother didn't do the deed himself."

"That the one where they never found the girl's body?"

I managed a nod and forced myself to focus on finishing my own pizza. "Yeah."

He didn't seem interested in the case. Which meant that he wasn't here because I'd taken it on and he thought I needed protection. Yes!

What was I talking about? No!

"Anything else going on?" he asked.

I slowed my chewing. "There's this missing body thing I'm looking into."

His reaction wasn't that much different from when I'd referenced Laughton's case. But there was the tiniest bit of tightening around his blue eyes.

"Oh, my God!" I said, giving up on the pizza and not finishing a second meal that day. "Is that why you're here? Because Nick Papadakis' body came up missing?"

"Who?"

His response was just a split second too late.

"I can't believe this," I said.

I got up and grabbed my purse.

He grasped my arm to stop me from leaving.

"That's not why I came over to talk to you, Sof."

"Oh? Then tell me what you know about Papadakis."

He shook his head. "Just that you might want to be a little careful. Remember the last pit of snakes you disturbed while working a missing persons case."

Uncle Tolly. The Mob. Cement overshoes.

I shuddered.

"Yes, but this isn't a person, it's a body."

He shrugged.

"Let me go, Porter. Now."

"Not until you tell me whether or not I can call you."

"What do you want to call me?"

His grin made a command performance. "Don't come the raw prawn now, luv."

What did that mean? Don't come the raw prawn? I was guessing it was Aussie speak that I shouldn't play him for a fool. Something I would never make the mistake of doing.

I said, "No, you can't call me. I'm . . . I'm . . ."

Spit it out. Tell him you're dating someone.

"I'm currently unavailable."

He wiped his mouth with a napkin. "So I'll call until you become available."

What did that mean? "What does that mean?"

He released my arm.

"No. Never mind. Don't answer that. In fact, I think I'd better go."

I turned on my heel and hurried toward the door. Although whether it was him I was running from or myself, I wasn't entirely sure.

All I knew was that if nobody let me finish a proper meal today, I was going to scream.

Seven

I NEVER.

Well, okay, maybe I have. But don't tell anybody.

As I sat in my car a full twenty minutes after hearing Jake's latest warning involving slithering snakes, I still couldn't believe that he was back in my life again, period, forget in what capacity. I'd all but finally written him off.

Oh, all right. I hadn't written him off, but I had been so occupied that I hadn't had all that much time to give him any thought. Even if, secretly, he was always somewhere in the back of my mind.

I sighed, watching the sunlight dim as day slid into night. Not one of my most successful days, really. I had an important case that had a lot riding on it that I hadn't really started solid footwork on yet (mostly because a sexily frustrating Aussie had stopped me from talking to that waitress), and there was a missing body that had yet to pop up on its own, as the police had said it would.

The East River was only a couple of blocks down the street,

and I shuddered, remembering the floater they'd fished out a few months back that they'd thought was Uncle Tolly.

It hadn't been. And Uncle Tolly had been fine. Only he wasn't fine anymore because someone had torched his dry cleaner's while he was still inside last month.

Cripes.

I started Lucille and did a U-ie at the next intersection, concluding that the time I was giving myself to recover from my encounter with Jake wasn't helping me recover from anything at all. In fact, it was only making things worse.

My stomach growled, as if understanding where I was heading even before I did.

Okay, so now that I really hadn't had much to eat all day, that meant that I could splurge. And when I said splurge, I meant not just in terms of food. Right now I was in dire need of a one hundred percent Dino fix. I wanted him to look at me as if I were one of his chocolate tortes and he couldn't wait to eat me.

I smiled as I checked my cell phone to find he had called again. I didn't call him back. I didn't need to. I knew his shop would be open for the next half hour. Which meant he would be there. Right where I wanted him.

I found a parking spot and climbed out of the car, rushing toward the brightly lit doorway of Dino's *zaharoplastio*. I pulled open the door and burst inside without thought of who might be there or what he might be doing. In that one moment, I didn't care. I just needed to see him.

And see him I did. Standing far too close to a female someone I couldn't make out because her back was to me. He had his hand raised as if caressing the side of her face, an intimate expression on his too handsome face.

My heart stopped right then and there, as did my feet. I was pretty sure the gasp I heard had come from me.

"Hey, Sofie," Dino said, as casual as you like.

The woman turned, and I found her to be none other than my younger sister, Efi. . . .

"SOFIE, WAIT!"

Efi's words echoed in my ears what seemed like hours later as I paced the length of my apartment and then back again. No matter what I did, no matter how many times I tried to banish it, the image of Dino sharing an intimate moment with my younger sister sent me spiraling back to my wedding day seven months ago when I stumbled across my groom shtupping my maid of honor.

"I had a lash in my eye. Dino was just blowing it out for me," Efi had said even as I'd stalked out of the shop in a state of shock and down the street toward my car.

Oh, yes. The ol' "lash in the eye" trick.

Muffy made a low sound from his Barcalounger, his gaze following my progress back and forth, forth and back.

And just like that, my personal life was thrown back into chaos.

Or maybe it had never really made it out.

I stopped my frenetic movements and leaned against the back of the sofa, crossing my arms over my chest. Okay, so I knew my sister would never do this to me. It was more that she happened to be the only one who really knew what was going on between Dino and me—namely, that we were dating, however covertly. I trusted my sister with my life, much less my guy.

I knew she was in love with a white-bread high school football hero named Jeremy and that odds were Dino really had been helping her remove a lash from her eye. I know that when I got one stuck in one of my eyes, I jumped around and asked for help from anyone and everyone around. And wouldn't hesitate to ask my sister's boyfriend to get it out for me if he was nearby at the time.

Then why did I get the feeling that I'd never be able to erase the inherent intimacy of the action from my mind?

I rubbed my forehead as if I could banish it by force of will.

If only my mother hadn't originally meant Dino for Efi.

I groaned and resumed pacing.

That's right. I'd met the handsome Greek when he'd been invited over for family dinner so he might meet my available sister. Only Efi had ducked out to meet Jeremy, and during the course of the meal, I'd found myself liking the guy. So much so that when I discovered he owned a sweets shop, I hadn't hesitated to pay him a visit, you know, since there was a chance he might end up my brother-in-law, and I could think of worse things to have in the family than a great baker.

"Great" didn't begin to cover it when it came to Dino. In myriad ways I was ill equipped to count just then. Suffice it to say that it was over a chocolate torte that he'd brought me for my name day last month that I'd finally realized I was attracted to him and we'd gotten together. Literally *over* that chocolate torte.

Muffy's low growl gave me cause for pause. I stared at him as I passed him for the hundredth time, only to retrace my steps.

"What?" I asked him. "Am I disturbing you? Well, excuse the hell out of me."

My cell phone vibrated against the coffee table for the third time since I'd come in. I moved closer, bending over to stare at the display. Dino, this time. The first two had been from Efi.

I imagined the two of them still at the bakery, trying to work out how they were going to clear this up. I didn't want to imagine them together in any capacity. Especially not any that had anything to do with me.

I backed away from the table and the phone, prepared to resume my pacing, when a knock at the door made me jump instead.

Muffy didn't even lift his head. That meant it was someone he knew.

Which, by extension, meant that it was someone I knew.

I made a face. If it was Efi or Dino, I wasn't answering.

I peered through the peephole. Nothing. Which meant someone was being sneaky. Or that it was—

"Sofie? . . . Sofie, are you in there?"

Mrs. Nebitz.

I unlocked the door and opened it, smiling down at my vertically challenged neighbor and adoptive Jewish grandmother. "Hi, Mrs. Nebitz. What are you doing up so late?"

"Late? It's not late. It's only eight-thirty."

Was it?

I looked over my shoulder and squinted at the oven clock. She was right. Although it felt as if many hours should have passed since my encounter with Jake and then my happening across my sister and Dino, it had been only a couple.

"What can I do for you, Mrs. Nebitz?"

She reached up to straighten her glasses, holding them in place as she considered me. "Are you all right, sweetheart? You look a little peaked."

Peaked. Now there was a word for you. Did they even use it anymore? Well, obviously they did, or she wouldn't have used it.

"I'm fine. A long day, is all."

She released her glasses and waved her hand at me. "A long day, anyone can handle."

It wasn't rent day, so she couldn't be visiting for that. (When I'd first moved into the building—my biggest wedding gift by far that I hadn't been able to send back—I'd had a little trouble collecting the rent. A problem I no longer had because Mrs. Nebitz now took care of that awkward chore for me. With much more success.)

I narrowed my gaze at where she worried the top button of her blouse.

Mrs. Nebitz worried?

"Maybe I'm the one who should be asking if you're okay," I said.

"Me?" She waved at me again. "Like you, I had a long day."

"Would you like to come in?"

"No, no. This shouldn't take but a minute."

I squeezed the door handle as I wondered if she was going to get to the point soon so I could return to my regularly scheduled pacing.

"Anyway, the reason I stopped by was to tell you that I'm going to be making matzo-ball soup on Thursday. And since my grandson Seth tells me I always make so much, I was wondering if you'd like to come over for dinner and share it with me."

I raised my brows. While Mrs. Nebitz regularly plied me with wonderful Jewish delicacies, we'd never sat down to dinner together. A fact that only now struck me as odd.

"Sure," I said when I realized I hadn't immediately responded and she was staring at me again, her hand on her glasses. "I'd love to share a bowl of matzo-ball soup with you."

"We wouldn't be eating from the same bowl. I mean, my father always wanted to keep kosher, but my mother . . ." She smiled. "Look at me. Babbling on. Of course, you didn't mean that we'd literally share the same bowl. Five o'clock all right with you?"

"Five-thirty would probably be better. If that's okay?"

"Five-thirty would be fine. Good night, Sofie."

"Good night, Mrs. Nebitz."

I waited until she had crossed the hall and disappeared through her open apartment door and closed it before closing my own.

I stood for long moments leaning against the cool wood, considering my large, nicely furnished apartment. I'm not sure exactly when the two-bedroom place had become home to me, but I realized that somewhere along the line, it had. I'd picked out every last thing in it, put them all exactly where I wanted, and cleaned as often or as seldom as I liked.

Cleaning . . .

I passed the vibrating cell phone on the coffee table—Efi, the display read—and made a beeline straight for the kitchen and the cleaning products under the sink. There were few things like scrubbing the place from top to bottom to help a body think.

And it wouldn't wear a hole in my area rugs.

NOT ONLY DID THE APARTMENT smell great when I got up the next morning, since I'd also cooked myself pasta, the scent of garlic drifted on top of that of lemons. Just the way a home should smell.

A small voice tried to tell me that I was avoiding facing the problems currently plaguing my personal life, but hey, I figured I was entitled. It wasn't every day that the man I thought I couldn't have was throwing himself at me (okay, maybe that was taking it a bit too far, but Jake had made his availability very clear) and the man I was dating had suddenly become unavailable to me.

Or, rather, I'd put him off-limits. Temporarily, I guessed, but I couldn't be sure. Right now I wasn't sure about much of anything except that I was damn glad I had work to distract me.

So I got to the agency early, closed myself in my uncle's office, and rather than obsess over the sad state of my personal life, I tried to push aside the niggling fear that perhaps I may have gotten myself in a little too deep with the Laughton case.

It had been two hours since I'd come in, and aside from a morning greeting from Rosie, I'd been going at it nonstop. Making lists, running down possibilities, placing phone calls. One of them had been to Melinda Laughton herself, and she'd stopped by to drop off a few items that I'd asked for, one of them a photo of Johnny and Valerie together.

I'd propped the five-by-seven print against the pencil holder on the desk. It had probably been taken at one of those Christmas drugstore deals, because the young couple was cuddled together inside a red heart and a sprig of mistletoe hung above their heads.

I worried my bottom lip between my teeth as I pondered the fact that one of the kids was gone and the other was currently facing trial for her murder.

A wave of fear washed over me.

I mean, who did I think I was? At best, I was a barely functioning private investigator good at catching cheating spouses. At worst, I was an adequate pet detective who relied as much on luck as on skill in tracking down people's lost pets.

What did I know about murder investigations?

I sat back in the chair and closed my eyes, forcing air past the sudden lump in my throat. Just look at me. I hadn't even officially begun the case aside from some major prep work and I was already psyching myself out. What help was I going to be to Little Johnny Laughton if I couldn't even help myself out of a panic attack?

I had my uncle's computer booted up and was monitoring live news reports from the courthouse where jury selection was about to begin. One of the pieces even spoke on John Warren Laughton's morose, guilt-ridden demeanor as he was transported to the county lockup so he was nearby when the proceedings began.

The door opened and Rosie filled the entryway. Or at least tried to, anyway. Seeing as she was only about five feet two in heels and weighed maybe a buck even, that was quite a feat.

"There's an official citywide blood shortage," she told me, crossing her arms.

I squinted at her, wondering if she'd just said what she had. "What?"

She chewed manically on her gum. "I said that I just heard a report that there's a citywide blood shortage and they're asking everyone to come in and give blood."

I looked at my cell phone for the tenth time. After ten. "I can handle things for a while if you want to go down and donate."

Her mouth gaped open. "Are you serious? Me and needles, we don't get along at all."

I noticed that she looked a little better today. More rested. "How's Carlos doing?"

"Huh? Oh. That thing you told us to try, that your mom suggested? It works sometimes. We all actually got a little sleep last night. Including little Carlito." She waggled her finger. "You're changing the subject, aren't you?"

"I am not." I leaned back in the chair, trying to make sense out of her previous line of conversation. Which should have been my first clue to drop it. "So what are you saying, then? About the blood shortage?"

She gestured with her hands. "I'm saying that maybe you should look into the neighborhood vampire again. I hear he's got visitors."

Her voice had dropped to a whisper at the word *vampire*.

I couldn't believe she was still sold on the idea that there was a vampire in residence in the area. Of course, I was ignoring that lately I was on high alert when it came to all things eerie. But not even I was giving a second thought to the neighborhood vampire.

I shivered as I recalled my run-in with Ivan Romanoff and his tall, dark, and pale nephew, Vladimir, a few months back. Not a memory I revisited often, no matter what time of year it was. But now, with Halloween around the corner, and during a citywide blood shortage . . .

At any rate, last summer the neighborhood had been abuzz with the fact that Ivan hadn't been seen in a good long while. And when I'd unofficially agreed to check into his absence, I'd found his nephew had taken up residence in the old Victorian house that always seemed in shadow, even with the full summer sun beating down on it. And when he'd refused to tell me anything more than that his uncle was ill and being looked after, I'd done a little snooping . . . and ended up trapped in a coffin in the basement.

Okay, so Vlad had told me it was a cello shipping crate, and he had rescued me from it rather than secured the lid so he could save me for some sort of midnight snack. Still, no one had been happier than me when Ivan had returned home, apparently fully recovered.

I hadn't proved one way or another whether the vampire rumors were true. Instead, I'd been content to reinstate my "don't mess with me and I won't mess with you" standoff with the odd family.

Rosie stood staring at me, as if waiting for what I was going to say.

"Oh, for heaven's sake, Rosie, there's no such thing as vampires."

"Uh-huh. Tell me that when you wake up in the morning to find bite marks on your neck and with an incredible thirst for blood. Just don't think you're going to find any with me 'cause I'll be forced to go Buffy the Vampire Slayer on your ass."

She turned to walk out of the office, probably to go count the collection of crucifixes she had in her office drawer and to see if she had any holy water left in her old perfume bottles.

I idly wondered what I'd done with the bottle she'd given me those months ago. Hey, odds were heavily in favor of there being no such thing as vampires. But surely there was nothing wrong with being prepared in case there was.

"Any progress with the PD?" I called after her, referring to the public defender assigned to Laughton's case.

"I'm working on it."

She closed the door.

Eight

A LITTLE WHILE LATER, I did something I normally did without thinking on certain occasions: I crossed myself three times in quick succession while I offered up a prayer of protection to the Virgin. Oh, I crossed myself in church, but mostly because everyone else was doing it and I was usually preoccupied with whatever case I was working on and hoping to duck out before half the patrons asked me for a favor. "I need for you to find my cousin, she ran off with a South Africa exchange student," was one from last week. Or one of my recent favorites: "I think my wife is having an affair." This from a ninety-nine-year-old retired fresh-produce business owner whose wife was a hundred and one and still led a very active social life, mostly through the church.

But I knew exactly why I was crossing myself now, and I put in all the concentration that had been lacking in prior crossings. Because I was standing in a place that I never wanted to be standing in again. At any rate, not on the other side of the steel bars.

County jail.

I sat in the small conference room after having told the officer that I was with the defending attorney's office and gaining access I wouldn't have had otherwise. They didn't have regular visiting hours here. And reporter's credentials—fake or otherwise—wouldn't do it, either.

A clang of metal against metal made me jump, and I turned toward the door. It opened inward, and what looked like little more than a boy in an orange jumpsuit, shackled at the hands and ankles with a chain joining them both in the front, shuffled in, his chin burrowed into his skinny chest where a white T-shirt was visible. The mammoth guard led him to the chair on the other side of a metal table and sat him down in a cacophony of more clanking. Then the guard backed up to stand behind the man I recognized as John Warren Laughton, his own hands behind his back.

"Can't you take those off?" I asked, gesturing toward the hand-cuffs.

"No, ma'am."

I rubbed my neck, wondering how much the shackles weighed. Hell, wondering how much Johnny weighed. Less than me, that was for sure. Probably from having to cart all that metal around all the time.

Jail. The surest fire way to lose weight quick, I thought.

"You're not going to stay here, are you?" I asked.

The guard stared at me.

I cleared my throat, realizing I'd asked the wrong question. "I'd like to be left alone with my client, please."

The guard nodded once and then disappeared through the safety door, the back of his shaven head visible through the small window.

"Thanks," I muttered, wondering if they were listening in. "They" being the jail officials.

Johnny had yet to acknowledge me. His head was still tilted toward his chest, his short, dark, curly hair framing a face that could have belonged to an angel or a devil, depending on what I saw in his eyes. Of course, I actually had to see his eyes to ascertain that fact. And he wasn't looking at me.

I sat at the table opposite him, hoping that my body language wasn't transmitting my uneasiness. "Hi, Johnny."

He finally looked up at me and I realized I'd made the right decision calling him by his nickname. His green eyes were startlingly clear and hopeful, resembling more the boy in the picture with his girlfriend than the perp walk shots I'd seen printed in Queens newspapers.

I released a long breath. I don't know why I was relieved, but I was. I supposed I'd been waiting until that one moment of truth, the instant I made eye contact, to see what my gut would tell me about the kid and his case and whether or not I should proceed. Had I seen hate or apathy, I likely would have walked right back out of that suffocating room and sent Melinda her money back.

I cleared my throat as I extended my hand. "Hi, we haven't officially met yet. My name's Sofie Metropolis."

The cuffs clanked as he lightly shook my hand with just his fingers. His eyes registered recognition. "Aren't you that PI that shot her own client in the knee?"

I smiled. "That would be me." I wasn't sure if he knew the details of Melinda's hiring me. "Your sister came to see me yesterday."

Sadness seeped through his expression. "I asked her to let it alone."

"Why? Why would you do that?"

He broke eye contact again, and his chin disappeared into his chest. "There's nothing that can be done now. Valerie's gone and my fate is sealed."

My heart skipped a beat. Had he just loosely confessed to the crime? I mentally picked apart his words. No, I don't think he had. But then again, it was said that it was up to the listener to interpret the message. And it seemed that no two people got the same thing out of the same material. My grandpa Kosmos had told me that was why there were so many different faiths under the Christian banner. One group believed the Bible said one thing, another saw it differently, and yet another thought it meant something else.

Was I seeing what I wanted to see? Had Melinda managed to turn around whatever prejudice I'd adopted over the past year by calling him Johnny? Was I perhaps seeing a little too much of my own younger brother in him?

"The trial hasn't begun yet," I said.

"It will. And I'll be convicted."

"How can you be so sure?"

He blinked up at me. "Because everyone has already made up their minds. There's no use fighting it."

"So you're tired of fighting?"

From what I understood, John Warren Laughton had never really put up a fight. From the moment of arrest he'd clammed up, refusing to defend himself against the charges lodged against him.

He shrugged again.

I leaned forward. "We're talking about the next fifty years of your life here, Johnny."

He whispered something I couldn't make out.

"What was that?"

"I said what does it matter? Without Valerie, one year, fifty . . . none of it means anything."

There was some commotion outside the room. I looked over my shoulder. Through the window I saw the black guard listening to someone who was apparently shouting. Then the door was thrown open and an obese, balding man that was probably only a decade my senior but looked like he could be my father stood staring at me, out of breath, his round face an unhealthy shade of red.

"Who in the hell are you and what the hell do you want with my client?"

The guard stood behind him, staring at me with the same intensity.

Oops.

In all honesty, I had planned to stop by Johnny's attorney's office before coming to the county lockup. At the very least, I wanted to ferret out why he was avoiding my attempts to contact him. But I'd decided that I had to see for myself first whether the kid was someone I could personally defend. And while the jury was still out on that one, I did feel he deserved a little more digging. And that I could do.

"Hello," I said as casually as possible, as if Gene Shipley and I were meeting in a social environment instead of inside a puke green jail conference room. "It's nice to finally meet you. I'm Sofie Metropolis, and—"

The red faded from his cheeks at his apparent familiarity with my name. Then his eyes narrowed to slits. "I know who you are. Your secretary has been calling my office nonstop since yesterday. Look—"

"You've purposely been avoiding my calls?" I returned his interruptive favor.

"Of course I've been avoiding your calls. The last thing Johnny needs is another snake-oil salesman . . . or in this case, saleswoman, trying to take advantage of a desperate family, sniffing around for money. And, frankly, I could do without another tarot card reader trying to help in my defense of the kid."

Tarot card reader? I recalled Johnny's sister saying something about consulting a seer. Had Melinda sent the woman here?

"I'm not a tarot card reader," I said. "I'm a private investigator."

"And that makes you different how?" he asked.

Okay, so apparently the guy had something against investigators. I might have been in the business for only a short time, but I knew my share of PIs who were interested in securing retainers and then doing little or nothing to earn them out.

Shipley put his briefcase on the table. "Listen, I don't give a flying shit who in the hell you are. You lied to gain access to my client, and I could have your ass thrown into the cell next to John's for doing so."

I raised my brows and looked over his shoulder at the guard, who nodded once.

I swallowed hard.

"My sister hired her," John said quietly.

"Yes, well, your sister also paid for the services of a psychic she found in the phone book, that strange tarot woman she sent to read your and my cards, and has tried repeatedly to make friends with the press only to end up misquoted in tabloid rags."

He looked at the kid, and I glimpsed what I thought was true compassion. Which made me feel at least minimally better for

Johnny. If Shipley was any good as a PD, Johnny would get a fair trial.

Still, that's not what I was hired to find out. And personally, I was a little affronted to be bunched in with a psychic, a tarot card reader, and tabloid journalists.

I puffed out my chest. Which might have made an impression with, say, someone of Rosie's abundant curves, but merely made me look like a wanting chicken. "Hey, listen up, pal. I'm here to help. You can't tell me you couldn't use an extra pair of hands and eyes."

"I have all the hands and eyes I need."

"So you can guarantee, then, that the kid will go free?"

He looked away. Curiously, Johnny didn't seem to be following the conversation. He sat staring at an undefined spot on the wall.

"Come on, Shipley. I've been hired by the family. I'd appreciate any information you could share with me."

"Excuse me if I believe that's not in my client's best interest."

"Well, good thing that's not for you to decide, isn't it?"

The close confines were beginning to make me itch.

"I'll expect a copy of your witness list and evidence log at my office no later than five o'clock today." Ha. My copious researching since yesterday had given me, if not an expert knowledge of criminal proceedings, at least a working understanding. Well, that and years of watching *Law & Order*. I took a business card out of my jeans pocket and slapped it on top of his briefcase. "Fax it, e-mail, courier it, call my office to have it picked up, I don't care. Just get it to me."

I turned toward the door. The guard had his hands behind

his back and he stood ramrod straight, towering over me by a good foot where he blocked my way. I slowly looked up at him, forcing myself to hold his gaze.

Finally, the faintest hint of a smile curved his mouth, and then he moved to the side to let me pass.

"Hey, she impersonated a public official. You're not just going to let her go, are you?" Shipley demanded.

The guard turned to bestow the same stony look on him that he'd given to me. The attorney snapped his mouth shut and moved back a step.

Probably his wife had caught him cheating. Probably it was a PI that had provided the evidence. Probably he was living in a one-room apartment over a fish stall next to the train because his wife had taken him for everything during their divorce.

Whatever the reason he didn't like me, I decided he didn't have to. As long as he did his job and I did mine, maybe between the two of us we could give this kid at least a fighting chance in court.

I leveled one last gaze at Shipley from the door. "By five o'clock."

He made a sound that gave me the impression I wouldn't be hearing from him. If only he knew how determined I could be to get something I wanted.

"Johnny?" I said quietly. He looked up, and I found myself smiling at him, I hoped with reassurance. "I'll see you later."

It was just a general good-bye, not an actual promise to return. If I had it my way, I wouldn't have to come back to the lockup. At least not until enough time had passed for me to get over this visit.

He gave me an absent nod and dropped his gaze. If there remained a niggling doubt as to his innocence in the back of my mind as I exited, I wasn't ready to confront it.

THE THOUGHT OF GOING DIRECTLY to the agency from the county jail didn't appeal to me, so I stopped for lunch up the street from the office. Recently, I'd helped save the owner, Phoebe Hall, from a possible catastrophic "ear found in pea soup" scam. Thankfully, the accusing couple had had a long trail of making just such claims behind them, and I was able to nip their latest swindle in the bud with no harm coming to the owner. (Phoebe hadn't wanted to press charges, but without her knowing, I'd called the law on them anyway. I just couldn't sleep well knowing that they were free to victimize another small-business owner.)

At any rate, I'd finally convinced Phoebe Hall that I didn't need free meals for life since she'd been unable to pay the agency much. So now I could return whenever I wanted without the fear of her trying to force food on me that I wasn't hungry for.

Now I sat with a bowl of homemade tomato soup (I didn't think I'd be able to eat pea soup again, for obvious reasons) and a grilled Swiss cheese sandwich and went over the notes I'd scribbled down after my brief meeting with Johnny, along with a list of leads I could follow up on. Number one was visiting Valerie Bryer's house and trying to talk to her family. Since the public wasn't allowed to view the jury selection process, their time wouldn't be spent in the courthouse . . . yet. I figured it would be a pretty good idea to go around dinnertime.

Of course, I'd also have to come up with a story of who I was and hope they didn't recognize me. Given that they were probably preoccupied with watching the man they believed to be their daughter's killer being brought to justice, I hoped I'd get away with it and perhaps even come away with something useful in the process.

I fished my cell phone out of my purse. My sister had called again since I'd last checked. If my going somewhere she might not easily find me had played a role in my decision to visit the restaurant, I wasn't telling.

I pressed the button for the agency and turned the page of my small spiral notepad to review additional notes.

The line rang and rang.

I checked the time on the clock on the back wall. Half-past twelve. Had Rosie gone to lunch?

That would make sense, except that I knew Rosie rarely left the agency when there wasn't anyone else around to hold down the fort.

I disconnected and tried again.

Rosie picked up on the sixth ring. At least I was pretty sure it was Rosie. Because instead of hearing, "Hello?" I got a shriek.

"Sofie? . . . Sofie! Help! I'm a hostage!"

Nine

SINCE THE RESTAURANT WAS JUST down the street from the agency, I left my car and ran to Rosie's rescue . . . from a black cat.

I stood in the open doorway to the agency, out of breath and scared to within an inch of my life, fearing that an armed robber or a wronged spouse was holding the petite Puerto Rican at knifepoint.

Instead, I found her standing precariously on top of her swivel chair, clutching a nearby filing cabinet to balance herself, a fearless feline with its back arched up, its tail enlarged, on the floor staring up at her, probably more frightened of Rosie than she was of it.

"Oh, for the love of God," I said in exasperation. "I thought you were in mortal danger."

"Sofie! Thank God you're here. I don't know where he came from, I don't want to know where he came from, I just want him out of here. Now!"

"Rosie, it's a cat."

"It's a black cat."

"You're ten times bigger than it is."

"He has questionable intentions."

I laughed and stepped closer. "Here, kitty, kitty, kitty."

The cat hopped so that it was facing me, green eyes huge, growling in a way that would make Muffy proud.

I drew my head back. I'd never had a standoff with a cat before. And I wasn't sure I wanted to be having one now. I mean, dog bites were bad enough. I didn't want to add scratch scars to them.

Was it possible for the feline to pounce on me and do untold damage?

I wasn't sure. But I wasn't ready to find out, either.

I gave a heavy sigh. "Rosie, get down from there."

"Uh-uh. I'm not going anywhere until he's gone."

The phone started ringing. Rosie didn't appear to hear it. I stepped around the cat and snatched up the receiver. "Metropolis, PI."

For a moment, I was afraid it was either Efi or Dino, neither of whom I was prepared to talk to just then. To my relief, it was someone inquiring about fees on a cheating spouse case.

"The office assistant is . . . hung up at the moment. Can you call back in a half hour?"

I replaced the receiver and pressed the button to send all calls to voice mail. With my luck, the next one would be Efi or Dino.

I turned my attention back to the cat.

I hadn't had many missing cat cases yet. I think it was generally accepted that cats liked to go out exploring and eventually would turn up back on the doorstep when they got hungry or cold. And since they usually didn't weigh over fifteen pounds and their teeth weren't registered as lethal weapons, the only problem lay in minor nuisances. You know, like getting into your garbage or spraying your front door or leaving a steaming kitty present in your garden or wherever they could find a warm patch of earth on which to squat. But overall they were viewed as harmless.

Unlike dogs, who not only tended to be dangerous to strangers, but, despite their heightened sense of smell, couldn't find their way home even with the help of a golden cord from Ariadne and a map.

"Do you think it's rabid?" Rosie asked. "I think it may be rabid."

Then there was that. Of course, dogs could also be rabid, but in my six months of pet detecting, I had yet to come across a rabid anything. Mostly the avian flu was more of a concern than rabies.

I stepped closer to the cat, and it hissed. I stepped back.

Then again, there was always a first time.

"Where's that mutt of yours when you need him?" Rosie hissed herself.

I scowled at her. "Muffy's not a mutt."

Technically he wasn't. He was a full-bred Jack Russell terrier. Even though I had occasionally referred to him as a mutt, specifically the Mutt from Hell. But that was before he was *my* mutt. And, as was the case with family, it was permissible for me to call him whatever I wanted but a major infraction when someone else did.

Despite being terrified, Rosie gave me an eye roll. "Whatever. Just get this thing out of here, will you? I don't know how long I can stand like this. I've already broken a nail. I don't want to add my freakin' neck to the list."

I shook my head and walked back toward the entrance, rating another earnest hiss as I went. I opened the door wide and gestured toward the escape route as the cat stared at me.

"Go on . . . scram."

The cat cocked its head slightly—a look I was used to getting from Muffy, who always seemed to think I was one ball short of a full set of worry beads—and then walked right through the doorway as if its visit were over and it was more than happy to leave.

"That's it?" Rosie said incredulously, watching as the cat turned on the sidewalk, twitched its tail, and then continued on down the street. I closed the door. "All you had to do was open the damn door and tell him to scram?"

I shrugged as if I'd known it would work all along, when, of course, I hadn't.

My next step would have been to get the broom from behind the bathroom door.

Rosie let go of the filing cabinet and wobbled on the chair.

"Careful. Or else you'll get a broken bone to match that nail yet."

I helped her down. She stood in front of me, chewing her gum with her mouth closed and giving a visible shiver.

"A black cat. Only a week away from the Day of the Dead." She shook her head. "Do you have any idea what a bad omen that is?"

I looked around at where she'd decorated the place with strings of garlic. "Oh, I don't know. At least as bad as inviting vampires into the place." I walked to my desk to go through my messages now that the emergency was over. Of course, I didn't want to point out that she'd just ruined my third perfectly good meal in two days. "Speaking of which, who invited the cat inside?"

"Hell if I know. One minute Waters came in to turn over money shots, the next that Satan's spawn was about to attack me."

"You could have taken him."

Rosie stared at me, mouth gaping.

"What's this?" I asked, picking up an unmarked package on my desk.

She waved her hand at me, clearly upset. "I don't know. Some creepy, pale guy said he was delivering stuff for your aunt. If he hadn't been out in daylight, I would have thought he was a vampire." She paused. "Maybe he's one of those zombie things that works for 'em. Oh! Don't werewolves keep post during the day? Maybe he was one of those." She frowned as she considered her nail. "No. He was too skinny to turn into anything other than a Chihuahua."

My cousin Byron.

In the past couple of months, I'd learned not to open packages whose point of origin I was unsure about. From dead roses to dead rodents (yes, I received one of those—not a banner day, that one), the cheating spouses in an interesting percentage of my cheating spouse cases felt free to let me know how they felt about my or the agency's involvement in the breakup of their marriages.

Funny how they never blamed themselves and their own skanky behavior.

In this case, however, I knew where the package had come from because I'd asked my aunt to send it.

I shook the shoe box-size carton and then put it down and

opened the top. Inside were Nick Papadakis' personal effects. I fished out his cell phone, discovered the battery was dead, and went through the meager contents of his wallet: an American Express card, his license, about three hundred in cash and change—and a single condom.

I frowned, checked to see if the phone would work on my charger, found it wouldn't, and asked Rosie what kind she had. Turned out she had the same brand I did.

I sighed, put the box on the floor by my feet, and pocketed the phone.

"Where you goin' now?" Rosie asked.

"I'm going to run up the street to the electronics place, and after that I'm going to do a little legwork on the Laughton case. Oh, and I ran into the PD at the county lockup and requested he send the kid's files over. You might want to call his secretary to confirm."

Now that was a polite way of saying what had happened between Shipley and me.

"Fran. And she's a paralegal."

"Pardon?"

Rosie pulled an emery board out of her drawer and went to work on her nail. "The PD's secretary. She's a paralegal. And her name's Fran. Turns out we both dated the same guy three years ago. Or two guys that were cousins. We haven't figured it out yet."

I raised my brows.

"What? When you call a body that many times, you get to know a little about them. She's nice. Her mother's sister lives down the street from my mother."

I had the feeling we'd be talking kindergarten teachers and concert stubs the next time the subject of Fran came up.

"Good. I'm glad you're getting friendly. Use it. Because Shipley is decidedly unfriendly."

She flashed me a dimple. "I'll do what I can do." All expression vanished from her face. "What do I do if . . . he shows up again?"

I stared at her, unclear on which "he" she was referring to. Oh, the cat.

I suppressed an eye roll. "Use the broom in the bathroom and shoo it back out." I opened the door. "Oh, and I need for you to run a background check on everyone I've been able to verify is involved in the Laughton case. The list is on my desk."

I MADE A COUPLE OF stops in addition to the electronics store. One was to pick up Muffy, who was still solidly in whatever funk he was in up to his scrawny little neck. He growled at me when I tried to pet him, made strange whining noises when he drifted off to sleep in the passenger's seat, and had a faraway look on his furry little face whenever I looked at him.

Even his tongue seemed to have disappeared. This from the dog who seemed to be forever panting, his canine breath invading my space.

Now I sat in my car outside a nice, rambling house in Forest Hills. It was the Bryer residence, the home in which Johnny's presumed dead girlfriend had grown up. It was a two-floor Tudor-style place with a big yard full of mature trees and shrubs and fall flowers. I'd been sitting there for twenty minutes watching the front of the house for signs of life—you know, for the father to come home from work, the mother to return from aerobics class, the brother to dribble his basketball down the sidewalk on his way home for dinner.

The only thing that moved was a landscaper busy doing odd jobs around the well-kept lawn.

I sighed and picked up Papadakis' cell phone where I'd plugged it into the lighter charger I'd bought. Finally the screen flickered to life.

"It's about time," I mumbled.

When my cell phone battery went dead, a simple plug-in brought it back. This one had required a waiting period.

I began with the menu buttons, only everything I tried asked me for a PIN.

Great. I went through all that to gain access to a phone I couldn't access.

After trying for a few more minutes, I put the phone back down between the seats, leaving it plugged in just in case I figured out a way to circumvent the PIN.

I settled in more comfortably, watching the landscaper gather a pile of tree branches, tie them off, and then carry them to the bed of his truck. I rubbed the back of my neck, thinking that he never had to worry about keeping up his gym membership. His job guaranteed that he was always in tiptop physical shape.

I looked at my own cell phone for the nth time, sighed, and started the car. My least favorite part of the job was all the waiting. Waiting for a comp case plaintiff to slip up and hoist a refrigerator over one shoulder. Waiting for a cheating spouse to get to the cheating part. Waiting for the person I was tailing to decide on which pair of shoes they wanted in the window.

Waiting.

Lately it didn't seem to be a word associated simply with my career, but was proving to be a metaphor for my life. I was waiting to see what was going to happen with Jake. I was waiting for either Efi or Dino or both to force my hand at the impasse we'd reached.

I was waiting for someone to reassure me that I was making the right decisions in my life.

I pulled away from the curb and determined to come back another time. After all, I wasn't interested in tailing any of Valerie's family members. They weren't suspects.

I frowned as I made a left-hand turn. Or were they. . . .

One thing was very clear. I wasn't going to be able to proceed on this case without more information on the case the prosecution had against Johnny. While Rosie's background check would give me some important information on the key players, it wouldn't detail the witness list. Wouldn't outline the evidence against him. I could only hope the resourceful office manager had made some professional inroads with Fran as well as personal.

I took a corner a little too fast, nearly catapulting Muffy from his resting place in the passenger seat. He got up and dug his claws into the chair leather and then barked at me.

I sighed again. I swear, overnight it seemed that things between us had gone back to how they'd been in the beginning. And damned if I could figure out why.

Of course, even if Gene Shipley provided the information I'd requested, I wasn't entirely sure I'd be able to process everything on my own without a little help. And somehow I got the impression that he wasn't going to be offering it.

I picked up my cell phone and pressed the button for my cousin Antonia Kalamaras. Within three minutes I found out that she was at her tiny office in Long Island City, that she had just won her third case (our grandpa Kosmos had been her unofficial first—unofficial since I had been the one responsible for the "win" because I'd talked my ex into not showing up in court and thus the judge had dismissed the case), and that she was willing to see me.

That's all I needed to know.

Of course, I was still trying to talk myself into a willingness to see her . . .

Ten

MY COUSIN NIA LOOKED LIKE a Greek version of Betty Suarez in *Ugly Betty* or of Toula Portokalos in *My Big Fat Greek Wedding* before her makeover. Oh, she no longer sported the braces she once did, but her refusal to update her hairstyle—correction, settle on a hairstyle, period—and her obvious aversion to makeup and a good skin regimen, and her preference for clothing that looked as if she'd let her grandmother pick out the pieces for her . . . ten years ago, didn't seem to go with her new social status as an attorney.

But who was I to judge? I probably didn't qualify for anyone's idea of what a PI should look like, either.

And if I was going to be completely honest, her appearance was an easy way to dismiss my envy. Although not entirely.

She was an attorney. I barely made it through one course at Queensborough Community College.

Then there was my younger brother, Kosmos, who'd spent the majority of his twenty-five years earning degree after degree and would soon accept the cherry on top, a Ph.D.

But we weren't talking about him, were we?

Oh yeah, Nia.

I found myself making a face even as I knocked on the glass of the outer door to her office on the third floor of an old brick business building and then tried the door handle. It was unlocked, so I opened it.

"Nia?" I called out.

The room was so tiny that the door hit her desk. I closed it, noting books stacked everywhere.

"Nia?" I said again.

Well, for God's sake, where could she possibly hide in this closet of an office?

I heard a scratching sound.

I looked behind me at the door that would be very easy to back out of.

But like that damn cat I'd chased out of the agency earlier, I let curiosity get the better of me.

"Nia?" I said more quietly as I moved slowly around, looking for secret passageways.

A dull *thunk* against the bottom of the desk.

I jumped, then watched Nia pop up from under the desk, her dark hair a tangle, rubbing the top of her head.

I gave an Olympic-size eye roll and took my hand from where it covered my chest.

"Sofie!"

Nia took out her earbuds and then switched off a pink MP3 player in the front pocket of an oversize white shirt that looked as if it might be a man's. (Hey, what a person did in her personal time was her business. But I had the feeling that this shirt wasn't left behind after a roll in the proverbial hay, but was something Nia had bought at the store for herself.)

"Sorry. I didn't hear you come in."

"Obviously."

She got carefully to her feet, holding up a piece of paper. "The wind must have blown this to the floor. It's my law degree. What would I do without my law degree?"

Since there were no windows in the room, I gathered she was talking about the wind caused by the opening and closing of the door.

"So," she said, straightening her shirt and smoothing her hair as she sat down and stared at me through her horn-rimmed glasses. Glasses that were the height of fashion a couple of years ago but that she had worn her entire adult life. "What can I do for you, Sofie?"

I wanted to tell her there wasn't a thing on earth I could think of that I wanted her to do for me, but sense won out over pride and dismissal.

I took books off a narrow chair and sat down. "Do you know a public defender named Shipley?"

"Gene?" she said, perking up. "Yeah, I know him. I interviewed for a job at the Legal Aid Society last month."

And apparently she had liked him.

Nia shrugged. "I decided that I wanted to try to fly solo for a while before I committed to anything else," she offered.

Probably she wasn't offered a job at the Legal Aid Society.

"How well do you know him?"

She smiled widely. "How do you mean?"

"I mean what's your definition of the word *know*? Are you talking a handshake and a five-minute conversation—"

"We went out to dinner."

I drew back, rejecting the image of my cousin on a date with the round public defender.

"Uh, once?"

She nodded. "Yes. It was very nice."

"Will you be going on more . . . dates?"

"Oh, it wasn't a date. It was more of a . . . friendship type of thing. You know, two single people with nothing much to do who would have been eating alone deciding to eat together."

"Ah." I nodded. "Are you two still friends?"

"Of course we are."

"Is he married?"

"Divorced. Pretty nasty, from what I understand."

"Let me guess: His wife hired a PI?"

Nia stared at me. "How did you know?"

I shrugged. "Lucky guess."

I pondered this new information on Nia's ties, however ambiguous, to the public defender. Then I uttered words that I never expected to say in the entirety of my life: "I want to hire you, Nia. . . ."

"SOFIE, WHAT IN THE HELL are you doing? I thought you were better than this. Three days and still no body. What's going on?" my aunt Sotiria demanded over my cell phone as I drove back to the agency from my cousin's office.

I rubbed the area between my eyes. I supposed I should be glad it wasn't my mother calling. But my aunt wasn't all that much better. The difference lay in that I didn't have to face my aunt over Sunday dinner.

Thank God.

"Theia," I said, pretending to be surprised and glad to hear from her; I was neither. "How are you?"

"How am I? How am I? *Sovara milas tora?"* she said in Greek, asking if I was serious. "How do you think I'm doing? I hired my niece, the private detective, to find somebody for me. And not only hasn't she found him, she's telling everyone and his brother that he's missing. What did you do? Take out an ad?"

"Come on, *Theia.* News like that is going to make the rounds no matter how quiet we all try to keep it."

She snorted inelegantly, a Greek trait that left the listener with little doubt as to the snorter's frame of mind. "How much longer is it going to take you?"

Now that was a question.

I wished I could tell her I'd have her stiff in less than twenty-four hours. Unfortunately, there wasn't any kind of missing body handbook I could refer to to help me out on this. The police had already signed off on the case. There was no family to complain. Short of an eyewitness who saw someone dragging the body out of the back of the funeral home, I didn't see how I was going to solve this one.

It looked as though I were going to have to talk to some of her staff again. Someone had to have seen something. Something they didn't want to report to me or the police.

I pulled up into a nice empty parking spot right in front of the agency, immediately recognizing the car in front of me as well as the person leaning against it.

Speaking of police . . .

"Look, *Theia*, I'll call you as soon as I have something, okay?"

"Is that the best you can do?"

"Yes." I hung up on her in midsentence and considered the man in a freshly pressed navy blue policeman's uniform. Pino Karras.

I grimaced. That was all I needed right now.

I cut the engine and climbed from the car, shutting Muffy in when he tried to get out with me. Probably he would try to bite Pino. Probably Pino would ticket me for not having him on a leash.

Probably I would want to bite Pino, too, if I were a dog.

I wasn't and I still wanted to bite him.

The reason it had been easy to find a spot was that it was after seven and most of the businesses on this block had closed for the night. I looked over my shoulder at where the sun was quickly setting into a nest of orange clouds, robbing the air of the warmth that had built up during the day.

I shivered and contemplated ignoring Pino altogether and going straight into the agency.

"Sofie," he said, pushing from the car.

"Pino."

Sometimes I had to try really hard not to add "Pimply" to his name. Not because he had acne now, but because I'd called him Pimply Pino more times than I'd called him Pino in the past months since I'd become a PI and he'd taken it upon himself to wreak revenge for sins stretching back to when we both went to school at St. D's, showing up where I least wanted to see him.

What was I talking about? I didn't want to see him anywhere.

He hiked up his pants in that way that made even me cringe and drew nearer. "I hear you're working that missing body case."

Rosie had locked up for the night, so I took out my keys and unlocked the agency door. "That would be me. A regular working stiff." I pushed the door inward. "You want some coffee or something?"

Pino looked shocked at the offer. Of course, I never thought he'd accept. "Sure. One sugar, a little milk if you got it. Thanks."

Damn. I should have known better.

I made a face as I switched on the overhead lights and went about making two cups of instant Nes (shorthand for hot Nescafé). I craved a frappé but figured since I was making him hot, I might as well drink a cup myself.

"Why'd you take the case, Sof? I thought degenerate cheating spouses were more your forte."

"Forte. Ha. Funny."

As the plain water percolated through the ancient coffee machine, I leaned against Rosie's desk and crossed my arms.

"I took the case because the police refused to do anything about it." I cocked my head to the side. "Why is that, Pino?"

He tucked his thumbs inside the front waist of his slacks. "I'm working it during my spare time."

"Have a lot of that? Spare time, that is?"

I measured the coffee into two mugs along with the sugar, added a few drops of water, and began quickly stirring the mixture with a spoon, hitting it against the sides of the cup.

"Not much, but I don't like the thought of there being a dead body out there floating around."

Tell me about it.

Pino sniffed. "So . . . I thought we might compare notes."

I stared at him. *"Sovara milas?"* I used the same Greek my aunt Sotiria had used minutes earlier.

"I couldn't be more serious."

I squinted at him. Pino had never been a very good liar. And I don't think that was a talent you could ever truly learn. He had something that I didn't. I could tell.

The key lay in getting him to tell me what it was. And in order to do that, I had to play like I knew something that he'd want to know.

I added water and then finished off the two cups of coffee with a dollop of milk and handed him his while taking a sip of my own.

I wasn't sure how I felt about playing "I'll show you mine if you show me yours" with Pino. We'd been on opposite sides of the fence for so long, I didn't know if I had what it took to cross to his side. Or tempt him over to mine.

"You go first," I said with a smile.

"I thought you might."

"I have his cell phone."

He sipped his coffee. I was reminded of a scene from one of my favorite westerns, *The Good, the Bad and the Ugly*. I imagined myself a combination of the good and the bad, while Pino was definitely the ugly.

Then again, maybe I was fooling myself. No matter how hard I tried being bad, I always ended up doing good.

"Do you have the PIN?" he asked.

I raised my brows. So he'd already had a look at the phone. Probably at my aunt's. Huhn.

"I might."

"That means you don't."

"That means I might." I tried on my brightest smile for size.

He narrowed his eyes.

"What do you got?" I asked.

He shrugged. "I might have some info on who his employer was."

"He was an insurance underwriter."

He gave me his brightest smile.

Then I remembered Jake, his warning me away from the case, and a light bulb went off. Papadakis hadn't worked as an insurance underwriter. Not if he was able to afford the expensive suits in his closet. Which meant he worked elsewhere. But where? And in what capacity?

"And?" I prompted Pino, playing it cool.

"That's all I'm going to say unless you can unlock that cell phone."

I took his coffee cup.

"If you don't give me more, then you won't ever know whether or not I unlocked his cell phone."

He chuckled at that.

Fine.

He turned toward the door.

"You know," I said, putting both coffee cups on top of the low filing cabinet, "having all this happen now . . . well, it's a little weird, don't you think?"

"How so?"

I shrugged. "With Halloween around the corner and everything."

"The Greeks don't believe in Halloween."

"The Greeks don't believe in a lot of things, but that doesn't necessarily stop them from wearing the evil eye to church."

He looked outside and then back at me. "Good point."

He left me wondering just what in the hell that meant.

Eleven

I STOPPED BY MY FAVORITE souvlaki stand on Broadway and 32nd before heading back to my place, all the way thinking that even for a Wednesday night, things seemed a little too . . . quiet. Eerie. I hadn't had to dodge traffic when I crossed the street to get my food. Paper blew across the pavement along with fallen leaves, and the wind itself seemed nippier still, reminding me I had yet to get my winter clothes from my parents' house.

Winter. Was it really almost here already? Since I'd been working steadily for my uncle since March, I hadn't really had time to stop and consider the changing seasons. First summer, now autumn. And I'd been grateful. The less time I had to think, the better for me.

I opened my apartment door and let Muffy go in before me. Oddly enough, he didn't run circles around my ankles, begging for bits from my souvlaki. Instead he went straight for his chair, not even bothering with his usual ritual of finding exactly the right spot there, either.

I shook my head, bolted the door, and then shrugged out of my brown barn coat that went so well with my new cowboy boots as I switched the bag I held from hand to hand. I'd left the kitchen stove light on along with a lamp, so the apartment looked cozy even if it wasn't as physically warm as I would have preferred. I put the bag on the coffee table, switched on the TV with the remote, and then freed one of the souvlaki.

"Mmm," I said, keeping Muffy in my line of sight as I peeled back the foil wrapping. "Been a long time since I had souvlaki."

His eyes regarded me even as he gave a long-suffering sigh and turned his attention to avoid having anything to do with me.

"I don't know if I'm going to be able to eat all this by myself." I refused to give up as I rounded the sofa and walked toward the chair as if going to my bedroom. "Shame I don't have anyone to help me with it."

I took a big bite, making sure I made all the appropriate sounds of appreciation that normally went along with eating my favorite food. The grilled pork topped with fresh tomatoes and onions and parsley along with a healthy dollop of *tzatziki* was exactly what I needed. I swallowed the bite and then freed a piece of pork, happily sucking the garlicky cucumber yogurt sauce from it before holding it out to Muffy.

"Are you sure you don't want any? It's very good. They've really outdone themselves this time."

He didn't even sniff it, merely growled at me and then got up so he could turn the other way.

Hookay.

I didn't know if I liked this new Muffy. I'd put up with being bitten by him, suffered through a nonstop series of noxious clouds, and thought we'd finally advanced to a comfortable cease-fire that included moments of affection (merely remembering him duct-taped to the commode, his delicate little snout missing tufts of hair from where I gently removed the adhesive, his grateful licks to my chin, was enough to make my eyes water even now).

Now we were back to hellhound status.

I twisted my lips and took another bite of my souvlaki, ignoring where my cell phone vibrated on the coffee table next to the bag.

Ah, yes. The Efi and Dino dilemma.

I'd made a point of not thinking about what had happened yesterday. I'd purposely kept myself busy, focusing on the two urgent cases I had rather than my personal dramas.

But now that I was at home, alone, the quiet pressed in on me, allowing my mind to fill with unanswered questions.

Would Efi betray me in that way, knowing what had happened with Thomas the Toad?

No, I truly didn't believe she would. Some people might be built that way (my ex–best friend, Kati Dimos, sprang to mind), but not Efi. She did what she said and said what she did. There wasn't a devious bone in her beautiful, slim body.

Dino . . .

Well, I didn't know if he and I had been acquainted long enough for me to judge his moral fortitude or possible lack thereof.

My chewing slowed as I reached the doorway to my bedroom. I leaned against the doorjamb, staring at the towering piles of still wrapped wedding gifts that had been sitting there for the past seven months.

Seven months.

The other day, I'd actually had to dust them.

I peeled open the souvlaki further and took another bite, although I'd stopped tasting my favorite food about five minutes ago.

A couple of months back, Jake had told me he wouldn't get involved with me because he didn't think I was free of the past yet. An image of myself on the day of my wedding—still wearing my dress, tossing my engagement ring into the garbage disposal, and then sitting on the roof in the late March chill, watching family members come and go, no one the wiser to my whereabouts as my long train blew in the wind—grew large in mind.

Sometimes that day felt like yesterday.

Okay, maybe it was more than sometimes. Maybe it was like most of the time.

I covered the unfinished souvlaki and dropped it to my side.

Had Jake been right? Were my feet still mired in a past that I couldn't change no matter how hard I tried?

Not that I would alter events. I shuddered. I couldn't even fathom being married to Thomas.

But where did that leave me now? I was standing there staring at the gifts I had no intention of returning to the groom's family (no matter how much my mother begged me otherwise), reflecting on another ostensible incident of infidelity in my love life. This time involving my sister.

I sighed and turned from the door, grabbing the bag from the coffee table, dropping the uneaten souvlaki inside with the other, and then putting the bag in the refrigerator, where it would stay until I threw it out (there were few things worse than cold souvlaki; each ingredient was separate but equal).

I plopped down on the sofa, braced my boots against the table, and stared at the television, although I really wasn't interested in what was playing. My thoughts had turned inward. I watched my cell phone vibrate next to my feet and used the toe of my boot to turn it so I could crane my neck to make out the display.

Efi.

I sighed, tucked my hands under my behind, and concentrated on watching the flickering images without connecting with them.

A knock at the door.

Muffy's closed eyelids stayed closed. Mrs. Nebitz again? Probably. Our dinner wasn't until tomorrow night, but maybe she wanted to know what kind of bread I liked with my matzo-ball soup.

I forced myself up from the couch, crossed to the door, and opened it.

Efi.

Figured. The first time I don't look through the peephole and she's the one knocking.

I moved to close the door again.

Efi put her own combat-booted foot between the jamb and the door to stop me.

"Nice try," she said, pushing the door the rest of the way open and stepping inside.

Don't get me wrong. I didn't try to close the door on my sister because I was mad at her. I just wasn't ready for this confrontation. And judging by her serious expression, I knew this was going to be one of those sisterly confrontational conversations.

"You're not answering your cell," she said.

"No, I'm not."

I turned and walked back to the sofa, where I plopped back down into my previsitor position.

Efi picked up the remote and pressed the mute button. I continued staring at the screen as she shrugged out of her short leather biker jacket and laid it on the back of an armchair before sitting down.

My little sister. Really, there was nothing so little about her anymore. Aside from her being a few years younger than me. Oh, it wasn't her size. She was as thin as ever and had inherited the only breast genes that seemed to run in the family. But more than that, it was her out-and-out coolness factor that ceaselessly fascinated me. It was more than the borderline goth, rocker clothes she wore. Confidence and irreverence seemed to ooze from her every flawless pore. She'd kept her hair cropped short for years but changed the color depending on her mood. Now it was jet black and shiny, hanging in a soft, dark curtain around her pretty face.

It killed me that I hadn't been able to talk to her about my fears. Scratch that. "Talk" wasn't the word I was looking for. Rather, I missed being able to lean against her and know she was there for me.

The problem lay in that she played the starring role in my current personal nightmare, however unwittingly.

"Sofie, we need to talk."

I glanced at her and then stared at the TV again. "No, we don't."

She picked up the remote and flicked the television completely off and then tucked the remote between the cushion and arm of her chair where I couldn't reach it.

"I like what you've done to your hair," I said.

"Fuck my hair."

I raised my brows. "I know that you usually spike it up, but even *that* would be difficult to do, don't you think?"

"Fuck you."

"Oooh. Two f-words in a row. The narrowing of your vocabulary says this must be really serious."

Efi sat forward, clasping her hands between her jeans-clad knees. Her nails were short and painted black. Her jersey T-shirt bore a picture of Nixon holding up his fingers in two peace signs and underneath read, "I'm Not a Crook." I could make out the tail end of one of her many tattoos peeking out from under her right sleeve.

"Let me make this very clear, Sofie. There is absolutely nothing—I mean, *nothing*—going on between Dino and me."

I pretended nonchalance. "Who said there was?"

The color in her pale cheeks rose. "You, by refusing to take my calls, with every look you throw in my direction, with every goddamn breath you take—"

She bit down on her bottom lip to put a stop to her spiraling agitation.

I considered the buttons on my own jeans. "I know nothing happened."

Efi blinked at me. "Then why are you acting like you caught us going at it full coital on his display case?"

I made a face. "Now there's an image for you."

"Sofie, stop with the cracks already. This is serious."

"Is it? Because I don't think it is."

Efi sat back. "This is about Thomas, isn't it."

The mention of my ex-fiancé catapulted me from the couch. "Do you want a beer?"

To my dismay, Efi followed me into the kitchen. "Answer my question."

I popped the cap off the second bottle of Amstel Light and put it down on the counter a little harder than I intended. Some of the beer splashed out. "Damn it, Efi, I'm not ready for this."

"Ready for what? Finally dealing with the truth?"

I shoved the beer in her direction, and she accepted it. After taking a long hit off of mine, I said, "Whose truth? Your truth? I'm having enough trouble dealing with my own without considering yours."

I leaned against the counter, and she did the same on the connecting counter. "Tell me what's going on in that head of yours, Sofie."

"Honestly? Nothing."

"Bullshit."

"No, it's the truth. I haven't thought about it much since it happened." Liar. But I had avoided coming to any conclusions about it.

"Then why are you refusing my and Dino's calls?"

My throat nearly closed on another sip of beer. "You and Dino are talking about this? About him . . . me? What's going on?"

"Only because you're not talking."

"Oh, that's big of you."

I wasn't sure I liked what was happening inside of me. Jealousy raged like an out-of-control dragon, snaking through my veins with a vengeance. I pushed from the counter and walked back into the living room.

"You're not going to solve anything by running from it, Sofie."

"No, but I can put it off until I'm ready to deal with it."

She stood behind the chair while I stood behind the couch, both of us seeming to stay at acute angles to each other. "And when might that be, exactly?"

"I don't know," I said, enunciating each word for emphasis. "What I do know is that it's not now."

She began to open her mouth again, and I quickly raised my hand to fend her off.

"No, don't. Stop right there, Efi. I don't want to hear another word." I put my beer down on the console table behind the sofa. "I love you to death. I love your spirit, your honesty, your integrity. But I'm not you, okay? I . . . I don't run headlong into problems, determined to solve them come hell or high water. I need . . . time." I realized I was gesturing fervently but didn't stop myself. "Time to wrap my brain around things. Time for the heat of the moment to pass. Time to allow my thoughts to catch up with my emotions."

"On the battlefield, wounds need to be tended to immediately."

"Is that how you view life? As a battlefield?"

"In a manner of speaking." She rounded the chair and sat in it, staring at her hands between her knees. "Look, Sofie, if you don't tend to the wounds you're suffering from—both real and imagined—then they're just going to fester and become infected and they're never going to go away."

Fester, fester, fester. "I'm all right with amputation." I tried for a joke.

"Including amputating your sister?"

I looked down, hating that I'd stepped right into that one.

"And what about the rest of the family? Are you going to cut them off, too?"

Her words caught me up short. I slowly slid my gaze in her direction. "What do you mean, the rest of the family? No one but you knows about Dino and me."

The exasperated look on Efi's face shot dread straight through me.

"They know?" I asked, skirting the sofa so I could move closer to her. "You told them?"

"I didn't tell them anything," Efi said, getting up to face me. "They already knew. In fact, they knew before even you and Dino knew."

I felt suddenly nauseated. I sank into the sofa, my heart beating a million miles a minute.

I remembered the circumstances surrounding Dino's and my first meeting. How I'd gone home for dinner and Dino had been there, a potential groom specifically handpicked by my mother. But Efi had had other plans and ducked out to meet Jeremy for pizza instead, leaving Dino with the family for dinner.

Leaving Dino with me . . .

"That's right. Dino was never intended for me, Sofie. All along he's been intended for you. . . ."

Twelve

MUCH LATER THAT NIGHT, I lay in bed unable to close my eyes. Because every time I did, I experienced a falling type of sensation, as if I'd gotten on a bad carnival ride where the floor dropped out and I was stuck against the wall; there was no exit, no escape, only the knowledge that I'd have to wait for the floor to raise back up.

Events and conversations and brief snapshots swirled in my mind, from that day at my parents' when Dino first smiled his sexy, one-dimpled smile at me to the other night when my mother had seemed to completely miss the unspoken words that had passed between Dino and me.

It was like a jump into the icy waters of the East River to discover that she hadn't missed anything. She'd known exactly what was going on. Had probably inherited Mrs. K's binoculars so she could watch Dino's comings and goings from my apartment building. Likely had marks on the calendar indicating all the times he and I had met, seemingly on the sly, when in reality our movements were being secretly documented.

I wasn't sure what bothered me more about the entire sce-
nario: that I had been deceived or that they had deceived me.

The day before, I'd asked Rosie to have a freestanding whiteboard delivered ASAP, and it had been placed in my uncle's
office. On one side I was using different-colored dry-erase
markers to list items on the Laughton case I needed to do. On
the other was a corkboard on which I'd tacked photos and reports and notes I'd made.

At around four A.M., I gave up on trying to sleep, slipped out
of my empty bed (Muffy remained on his chair), and came into
the office, where I did computer research until Rosie got in and
brightened my day by telling me I looked like shit.

"Damn, Sof, what happened to you last night? You look like
something that black cat dragged in here from the Dumpster out
back," were her exact words. Then she waggled one of her purple
talons at me. "You know, you should do like I do and get in twelve
hours of sleep at least two nights a week and start a daily beauty
regimen. Well, before little Carlito blessed our lives, anyway. But
I still try to stick to it. Especially since I have a man in my life—
not my wailing nephew—that I'd like to keep."

Hell, I'd settle for two hours of sleep and an exfoliating soap.

"We ain't getting any younger, girlfriend. We single women
need to do what we can to keep up with the competition. And
those girls keep getting younger and younger every year."

I cringed at that one.

Apparently, my parents thought I was too old. Specifically,
too old for them to wait for me to find a man on my own.

Or maybe they thought I wasn't old enough. Or, rather,
mature enough. So they'd set me up with a man they thought
would be a good match for me.

I was currently ignoring that what had happened between Dino and me had nothing to do with my parents—and everything to do with wild passion. Hey, we've already established that I'm not a headlong, straight-into-it kind of person. I needed at least a week to sort through the complicated emotions before I could settle on the most important one.

At any rate, I'd asked Efi to leave shortly after dropping her bombshell, and she had. But not without first giving me a hard hug.

"Call me, Sofie. Please. I can help you with this if you'll let me."

That had made me cry and threatened to do so again just thinking about the concerned, loving expression on her pretty face. I hadn't realized how much I'd missed her.

I gave a loud sniff and pushed my hair back from my face, considering the green, blue, and red words on the whiteboard in front of me, trying to concentrate.

Sometime around nine-thirty, Rosie came in with a file box. "Ta-da."

"What is that?" I asked.

"The files from the PD's office."

I plucked off the lid, as excited as a kid on Christmas. "You're kidding me?"

"Nope." She crossed her arms and popped her gum. "Told you I had my ways."

"Yes, well, I think both you and your new friend Fran deserve at least a lunch out on the agency for this one."

I couldn't believe she'd pulled it off. Not only did I have the PD's witness list, I had the NYPD's evidence list, reams of paper including pretrial hearings, witness interviews, and background material not only on Johnny, but on Valerie, and a sheath of photos of the evidence due to be used in the trial.

Some hours later I faced the whiteboard, considering what I'd done with some of the information.

Under the "Miscellaneous" column, I'd jotted down "tooth tat."

I ran my tongue along my own teeth. I'd discovered that body ink was no longer limited to flesh alone. There were actually people out there that would tattoo your teeth. Valerie's back left molar bore the initials *JL* in flowery script in honor of her boyfriend of the past three years, Johnny Laughton. My Internet research had shown that the process originally had been meant as a means of identification for Alzheimer's patients and for children. It had since evolved into an extended form of body art.

I thought of Eugene Water's gold tooth and grimaced as I moved on to another column on the whiteboard.

"Nine out of ten female murder victims are killed by someone they know."

I'd written out the fact I'd unearthed online because it had been shocking to me. Underneath, I'd noted a simple "62/bf," indicating that in sixty-two percent of the cases the intimate partner had been the offender (John Warren being the bf, or boyfriend).

Those were some pretty staggering stats. And they definitely didn't work in the defendant's favor. Did the prosecutor plan to introduce like material to the jury? I certainly would.

Of course, the fact that I was once again referring to Johnny as John Warren wasn't a good sign.

"Rosie?" I said through the open door, where she'd just hung up with a client asking for a status report. "Have you made any progress on the background checks?"

She got up, fingered through papers on her desk, and then came into the office holding a few files. "I've got information on nearly everyone. I'm still waiting for one report to come through, though."

I accepted the papers and browsed through them.

"By the way," she said, "I saw that black cat again when I came in. He was lurking outside. He was standing in front of the fish store, but it's like I just knew he was waiting there for me."

I immediately realized she'd run more reports than I'd asked for. "How do you know?"

"Because he was looking at me with those glowing eyes, that's how." She gave an affected shiver that seemed to shake every inch of her petite body.

I ignored her and waved the papers. "What's this?"

"What's what?" She turned back from where she'd been exiting the office.

"I didn't ask you to run a check on everyone."

"Uh-huh, yes, you did. You said everyone on the list." She pulled the slip of paper from inside the sheath.

I realized she'd used the paper on which I'd written down every name associated with the case, up to and including Valerie Bryer's parents and even John Warren Laughton's attorney, Gene Shipley.

Cripes.

"Something wrong?" Rosie asked.

I caught a whiff of something that made me wrinkle my nose. "What's that smell?"

"What smell?"

I leaned in closer to her and then pulled back. "What is that? Garlic?"

She straightened her shoulders. "Sure is. I couldn't believe my luck when I actually found garlic oil in the vitamin aisle of the supermarket. Saved me from having to make some myself."

"You're wearing garlic oil as perfume?"

"No, silly."

I relaxed. Probably she had spilled it on her clothes or something while cooking or taking her supplements. Hell, for all I knew, it could be part of her aforementioned "beauty regimen."

"I'm wearing it to scare off vampires."

I dropped my hands to my sides and stared at her.

"What? You want some? Hold on, I bought two bottles. I'll give you one."

I gave her retreating back an eye roll and then tossed the background reports onto the desk. I picked up the red pen and wrote under possible alternate murder suspects, "Vampires."

Rosie watched me finish as she came back in. She gasped and slapped her hand over her chest. "Do you think maybe that's what happened to the Bryer girl?"

She held out the bottle of garlic oil, and I took it and put it on the desk on top of the reports. "Not a chance in hell."

She glared at me. "Then why did you write it down for?"

"To show you how ridiculous you're being?"

She *tsk*ed and showed me her palm in the universal expression of "talk to the hand."

It wasn't until that moment that I understood that the expression quite possibly had originated with the Greeks. The Greeks, dating back centuries, had used the hand to show distaste. And how many fingers you held up while doing it indicated the severity of disgust. Five fingers was the maximum. Two or three was the usual.

Rosie was now giving me *pente*, or five.

"I don't care what you say. You haven't heard the flapping around of little vampire bat wings because you're not listening. And then there's that blood shortage going on. I was talking to my sister the other day and we think there must be a vampire convention or something going on here in Queens, you know, in honor of Halloween, and that's why there's no blood."

"There was a bus accident and the demand for blood affected supplies."

She made a face. "Whatever. But those schoolkids aren't turning into bats at night and flying around outside my bedroom window."

"Have you ever thought that it might be actual bats?"

"I know from bats. And those ain't no normal bats. They're hungry for blood."

"Whatever," I said back to her.

"There are even stars that are vampires."

"Stars?"

"Yes, you know, celebrities. Take John Travolta, for one. He can't even go out in sunlight without wearing sunblock five thousand. You've heard it, I know you have. How he stays up all night and sleeps all day. Even his family does it. His kids are home-schooled and everything so no one has to find out."

"Whatever," I said again.

She began to huff away and then stopped and made her way back to me. She picked up the bottle of oil from the desk and put it into my hand, wrapping my fingers around it. "Please, Sofie. Just do me a favor and wear the garlic oil, okay? If something happened to you . . ."

If something happened to me, what? She'd still work for my uncle, and life would go on as it always had without me.

Now that was a reassuring thought.

"Well, you know," she finished.

I didn't, but I wasn't going to tell her that. Sometimes following Rosie's logic took every last brain cell I had, and then it was only to find out that what she'd said wasn't worth understanding to begin with.

My gaze caught on the file box. What was even stranger was that in some instances she was one of the most brilliantly efficient people I knew.

"What's going on?"

I looked at the open door to find my cousin Pete standing there. The way Rosie was staring up at me, still holding my hand around the garlic oil bottle, I could only imagine what his young, oversexed mind was making out of the display. Something that had less to do with the truth and more to do with those *Girls Gone Wild* videos they advertised on late night TV was my guess.

Rosie gave an eye roll. "Nothing." She released my hand and sauntered from the room.

I instantly put her from my mind and concentrated on my cousin, even though I was afraid he was more concentrated on what he thought had been going on.

I ACCOMPLISHED MORE IN ONE morning working on the Laughton case than I had in the past three days. Namely, I'd finally spoken to the pizza place waitress, who'd had an uncanny recollection of events that night if only because the victim had accused her boyfriend and alleged killer of flirting with the woman.

Gwen Stefani—yes, I said Gwen Stefani, no relation to the No Doubt, Harajuku Girls one of the same name—had red-rimmed eyes after having spent a sleepless night tossing and turning, thrown back in time as the case was coming closer to trial. I'd wanted to tell her I could so relate but hadn't. I didn't want to distract her from whatever she was about to tell me.

"I get it all the time, you know?" she'd said where we stood outside the pizza joint on the sidewalk. She'd lit a cigarette and exhaled a long line of smoke into the air. "Guys coming on to me. Don't get me wrong. I don't think I'm all that." She'd grimaced. "But I've come to learn that so long as your ass fits into a single-digit size, and you're female, most men will sniff after it."

I had nodded, having come to much the same unfortunate conclusion myself.

"What about that night, Gwen?" I'd encouraged her. "Do you remember clearly what happened?"

She'd gotten a faraway look on her face as she'd stared down 31st. The W train was pulling into the final station, the brakes squealing against the rails. "Are you kidding me? Sometimes it's all I can think about. Especially with the trial coming up." She'd looked at me. "I've been called to testify, you know? Relive the whole night all over again. And the DA says that the defense attorney will probably rake me over the coals, try to find something to incriminate my memory of events." She'd squinted at me. "Who did you say you were with again?"

"Just an interested party," I'd said. "So the couple came into the place at around six?"

She'd nodded. "Yeah. They were laughing and holding hands, you know, like lots of other couples that come in. . . ." She'd stopped as if remembering the night blow by blow but deciding which parts to share with me. "I'd served their pizza and everything appeared fine, and I'd made my normal rounds to see if they needed anything else, you know, like a soft drink refill, etc., and everything had changed."

"Changed how?"

She'd looked at me point-blank. "Where they'd been loving before, now they were fighting." She'd sighed and briefly closed her eyes. "Sorry. The DA's office has tried to help me describe everything, but I keep forgetting."

The sun had ducked behind the clouds just then, and a brisk wind had stolen away my breath. It didn't surprise me that the district attorney was coaching his witnesses. What did surprise me was my own realization about how easy it would be to spin events one way or another, depending on your point of view.

Not that unlike my viewing the presumably innocent exchange between my sister and Dino as something tawdry because of the tainting of my own experience.

"She, Valerie, was visibly upset. Her face was red and she was talking to the defendant in a quick, staccato way. I didn't hear much. Snippets, really. Stuff about how she was tired of having to deal with his heavy-handedness, and that maybe they should break up. Stuff like that. Then he grabbed her arm to keep her from leaving by herself. She slapped him across the face. . . ."

Gwen had bit her lip then. "I see it all the time. Lovers' quarrels, spats. I didn't make too much of it at the time. Not until . . ."

Not until the following morning, when Valerie went missing. And two weeks later, when John was arrested. And three months later, when Valerie was declared presumed dead and the story had dominated the front page of every Queens newspaper and led local television news broadcasts.

"It's hard to believe it's been a year ago already," Gwen had said.

I'd nodded, agreeing with her.

It had taken a frappé at my grandpa Kosmos' Cosmopolitan Café on Broadway—where I was thankfully left alone to go over my thoughts and notes while he entertained his friends in the back—before I was capable of moving on from the conversation and the images of an arguing John and Valerie that Gwen had stamped into my brain.

Thirteen

"SOFIE, CALL ME."

I checked my voice mail in the early afternoon to find five such messages from my aunt Sotiria. I knew that calls from my mother wouldn't be far away.

Or would they?

Considering what had happened when my parents tried to reunite me with Thomas the Toad a few months back, I'd fathom a guess that my mother had found out about Efi's and my conversation last night, and she might not have the *mouri*, the face, to confront me just then.

What was I talking about? Thalia Kalamaras Metropolis didn't possess any such propriety. She did what she did, and either you accepted it or you didn't. She never apologized. Never backed down from an argument. Even if later she figured out she was wrong, she'd just magically switch positions (once she'd done it as a result of a "dream" she'd had starring the Virgin Mary, who had told her that I was having problems and that she should step in before I really did something stupid) with no further mention of the previous stance.

There was something strangely reassuring about her predictability.

There was something ultimately frustrating about her stubbornness.

As I stood in front of the whiteboard, marker in hand, I wondered what she had been thinking when she'd concocted her latest scheme to match up Dino and me.

Of course, I was choosing to ignore that I'd found myself drawn to him seemingly without my mother's manipulations.

I uncapped the blue marker and caught myself taking a quick whiff. Okay, so I was beginning to feel the effects of little sleep and little food. Probably I should go to my parents', ignore my mother, and fix myself a plate of food, then go home for a siesta. Maybe that would help clear my mind.

"Anything other than cheating spouses going on?" Pete asked, appearing in the doorway.

I hadn't heard the bell on the front door ring, but that meant little because I was used to tuning out Rosie's nonstop chatter as she talked on the phone to her mysterious boyfriend or sister or a client or carried on a conversation with her new computer in her Puerto Rican Queens *r*-less accent. "There's nothing the matter" became "They's nuttin' tha matta."

I glanced at my cousin. "I don't know. I think a couple of missing pet cases came in yesterday."

He looked ready to spit. I didn't blame him. Merely speaking the sentence aloud made me grimace.

Strangely enough, Eugene Waters, one of my more recent hires that took pride in resembling a seventies pimp, complete with platform shoes, large Afro, and printed polyester shirts, enjoyed taking up missing pet cases between cheating spouse cases and delivering papers. He said it mixed things up, kept things interesting.

I suspected he enjoyed creeping around in people's backyards and having the police called on him, only to be vindicated when they called the agency to verify his identity.

I picked up the bottle of garlic oil that Rosie had given me and then put it back down before leaning against the edge of the desk, taking in my cousin.

I have to admit, in the past month since I'd begun sending him out on cheating spouse cases, he'd impressed me. Where before my uncle Spyros' eldest son had come around only to fish money out of his father's office (I actually caught him trying to drill a hole in the combination dial of the safe in the corner), and lifting a few dollars out of my purse, he'd morphed into a guy who was all business.

Take now, for example. He wore nice slacks, a crisp white shirt, and a tie.

I smiled. "What's the occasion? Court date?"

"Funny, Sofie. Funny." He jabbed a thumb over his shoulder in Rosie's direction. "Just delivering the latest money shots." He made a low sound. "Got 'em last night at the Quality on Queens Boulevard. Guy spotted me and gave chase. Almost caught me, too."

"How close did you get?"

Pete grinned. "I picked the lock on the motel room door and caught them going at it full-out, like a shot from a triple-X porno film."

"You're kidding?"

"The gap in the curtains wasn't big enough and they went in separately." He shrugged. "I figured if I didn't want to tail the guy another night, I'd have to get inventive."

"Inventive is acting like a pizza deliveryman. Stupid is breaking into a motel room with the flash blazing."

"Hey, I got the pics."

"Yeah, well, just don't do anything like that again."

He looked around, catching sight of my gun holster where I'd hung it on the back of the chair. "I've been meaning to ask you how I go about getting one of those."

"Are you serious? After the story you just told me?"

"I'd think it would be because of the story I just told you."

"Think again." I crossed my arms and sighed, realizing I was acting more like Thalia than a boss. It hadn't been all that long ago that my uncle had only cracked a grin and given me a step-by-step on not only how to obtain a gun, but how to get certified to carry concealed, which was essentially his vouching for my position at the agency.

"Do you really want one?" I asked, dropping my arms to my sides.

Pete was quiet for a moment, staring at my Glock. "I don't know. I'm thinking about it. After what went down last night . . . well, I don't want to get caught with my guard down again."

"Your guard should have been way up to begin with."

"Yeah, well, who knew the guy was going to chase me buck naked, for crissakes?"

"He was naked?"

"Uh-huh. As the day he was born. As a jaybird. In full birth-day suit—"

I held up a hand. "I get the picture. Perhaps a little too vividly."

I'd never been chased by a cheating spouse. Mostly because I chose to use my brother's Olympia complete with zoom lens, which meant I never had to be within fifty feet of the offenders.

Unlike Pete, I didn't feel the need to go a-knocking. Mostly taking pictures of the perp's car in the lot, him or her entering the motel room and who they were meeting going inside the same room, all photos time-stamped, and my expert testimony stating the time the couple was in the room was enough for any client I ever had.

"What's this?" he asked, catching sight of the whiteboard.

"A case I'm working on."

"You're working the Laughton murder?"

I switched my attention from the board to him. "You're familiar with it?"

"Hell, yeah, I'm familiar with it. I've been working different conspiracy theories since that girl went missing a year ago."

Like every other female in the triborough area, I'd watched news reports and read newspaper pieces with interest around the time Valerie Bryer had gone missing. But I hadn't thought up any conspiracy theories. I only wanted the person responsible to be put behind bars so I wouldn't have to worry about going out late at night by myself.

Over the years, I'd come to learn that there were two types of people in the world: the kind that like to pass the time figuring out who really shot JFK, and those—like me—who thought it was enough to know that whoever it was, they weren't around anymore.

A secret part of me had always envied the former, because usually their talents didn't end there. They could do crossword puzzles without looking at the answer key every sixth word, a

Rubik's Cube was child's play to them, and they always got the high score at the video game at my grandfather's café.

Okay, I didn't so much envy them. I hated them.

But having one working at the agency could turn out to be a definite asset.

And who knew it would be my once lazy, good-for-nothing cousin Pete?

"I'm hungry," I said. "Let's go get a bite together so you can share some of these theories of yours. . . ."

THE PERSON YOU LEAST SUSPECT is usually the one who done it.

The sentence played in my mind like an MP3 file on repeat as I sat at my uncle's desk that afternoon. I propped my head up with my hand and yawned, going through the background checks Rosie had run up for me on basically everyone associated with the Laughton case. Up to and including the assistant DA, who was twice divorced and was arrested ten years ago for propositioning a prostitute for sex. That's not what made the entry interesting, however. The fact that the assistant DA was white and the prostitute had been an underage black male transsexual dressed in women's clothes was.

We paid a monthly fee for access to myriad databases, but I wondered at the paper cost as I fanned the two-inch-thick sheath with my thumb.

I'd finally had a halfway decent meal. I'd treated Pete to lunch at Opa! Tony's Souvlaki on 31st near Newtown and passed on my usual souvlaki and ordered a plate of *marides*/pan-fried smelt and shared a Greek salad with my cousin, who'd ordered the *brizoles*/grilled pork chops. I'd been hoping that the up-swing in my day would continue and that what Pete would offer would inspire the second ta-da moment of the day. One that would get Little Johnny Laughton off the hook.

What I hadn't factored into the equation was that Pete was so happy to have someone listening to his conspiracy theories that he shared every last one with me, filling my brain to over-flowing and making me want to knock over his chair to get him to shut up.

"No, think about it, Sofie. This could have been an alien ab-duction, you know, like you hear on *Coast to Coast AM* all the time." He'd counted off the possibilities on his fingers. "One, no body was ever recovered. B, there were no witnesses."

I'd have corrected his one-to-B move, but after the word *alien*, I'd essentially tuned him out.

Tucked somewhere within the ridiculous UFO theories, how-ever, had been a couple of interesting possibilities that might warrant a little follow-up.

I stretched my arms out above my head, longing for a nap so I might sleep off all the fish I'd eaten, but instead began sorting the reports into separate piles. The first was those of the attor-neys involved in the case. The second belonged to Johnny and his family. The third was about the victim's family. The fourth was witnesses.

I came across one report on a Floyd Sackett that merely stated his profession was landscaper and that he had a sealed juvenile record.

I squinted at that one, remembering the guy that had been working in the garden at the Bryer house. Same guy? I haz-arded a yes.

I put the report into the witness pile and then pulled the victim's family pile forward.

"What if the family was having financial difficulty?" Pete had said, olive oil running down the side of his handsome chin. I'd gestured for him to wipe it off.

"Johnny's family?"

"No, no, the victim's family. . . ."

Successful. Well-heeled. Father a VP and board member of a prominent N.Y. securities firm. Mother an NYU American lit professor. I couldn't imagine either one of them needing money and being willing to sacrifice the life of one of their two children in order to obtain it. But, hey, I watched *Dateline NBC* and *Primetime* and *20/20* and Court TV all the time and knew that strange things happened. Just look at the JonBenét Ramsey case. Or O. J. Simpson.

I made a face at the fact that I'd chosen one case that had never been solved and another where the murderer had never been criminally convicted.

I went through the report, finding nothing that indicated that the family either needed money or had any other motivation to collect on the reported one hundred thousand in life insurance they'd had on their daughter's life and, from what I understood, every cent of which had gone into the memorial service they'd held for the girl whose body was never found (I'd called up Internet newspaper shots of large white tents and fields of flowers and a mammoth marble headstone).

Melinda had also told me that the Bryer family was largely to blame—or credit, depending on your point of view—for the case against Johnny proceeding at full steam. Dad had his connections, after all, and Mom was not without a few of her own.

It was those same connections, apparently, that kept the story circulating in the news, when the fickle N.Y. media would have likely preferred to move on.

But I couldn't really draw a line, either directly or indirectly, from Pete's theory to either of the Bryer parents. Which didn't mean anything, really, but didn't exactly motivate me to look further in that direction.

I turned the page and found Valerie Ann Bryer's name at the top of the next report.

I suddenly couldn't swallow. Rosie had run a check on the dead girl?

But that wasn't the most interesting. What was, was what she'd found. Namely that Valerie's paternal uncle had been convicted of molesting a "ten-year-old" niece—purportedly Valerie, whose name was never used—and had served four years in prison and moved to the Midwest upon his release.

I wondered if he ever returned to the New York area—say, to visit family. And if any of those dates were around the time that Valerie had gone missing. . . .

Fourteen

A WHILE LATER, I WAS still pondering the possibilities of the information I'd uncovered. If a simple background search had pulled up the conviction for me, then surely the prosecution had obtained it.

Then again, the prosecution might not have run a background check on the victim, as Rosie had.

I stood on the sidewalk in front of the agency. Rosie had gone home for the day and I'd already locked everything down, waiting for Waters to stop by as he'd promised to. Of course, he'd said five minutes and it had already been twenty.

I sighed, looked at my cell phone for the time—at this rate I'd be late for my dinner with Mrs. Nebitz—and was just about to give up when I heard a car horn.

Since most of the businesses up and down Steinway had already closed for the night, the exception restaurants and cafés, parking was relatively easy to come by. A twenty-year-old gold Cadillac pulled to the curb in front of me, the bass from the seventies funk Eugene was fond of vibrating the windows. He switched off the car and got out, looking like the old-time pimp he was trying to emulate. The only thing he was missing were the ho's.

I shook my head and tried to hide my smile as he joined me on the sidewalk.

"You like?" he asked, grasping the lapels of his full-length leather coat and doing a Prince-like move as he turned around.

"Is it real leather?" I touched the shoulder. His platform shoes put him at almost the same height as me.

He shrugged me off, appearing insulted. "Of course it's real."

"Well, then, I think we must be paying you too much." I squinted at the car. "How can you afford all this and rent, too?"

"Who says I pay rent?"

I remembered the first time Eugene and I had crossed paths. I'd been trying to deliver landlord dispute papers to him, and he'd been staying at his girlfriend Dolores' (I had yet to ascertain if they were married or not—and honestly I wasn't sure if I wanted to).

I fished around in my purse for Nick Papadakis' cell phone. "You sure you can crack this code?"

"Am I sure? Sure as the day is long, mama."

He took the phone and stared at it. "Yep. Locked up tighter than a thirteen-year-old Catholic girl's va-jay-jay."

I nearly choked. "Her what?"

He grinned, and his gold tooth glinted at me. "You need me to give you an anatomy lesson?" He slid his thumb into the waist of his lime green polyester pants and lifted them a bit, openly sucking his teeth with his tongue as he gave me a once-over. "Because I'd be happy to oblige. Won't even charge you nothing, neither."

"No thanks. I'll pass." I gestured to the cell. "How long do you think it'll take you?"

He shrugged and tried a couple of combinations before sliding the phone into his pocket. "Oh, I'd say I could have something for you in an hour or so."

"Good. Drop it by my place when you're done."

He grinned again. "You going to make me dinner?"

"No, I'm already having dinner with somebody."

He shrugged. "You don't know what you're missing."

Oh, I had a pretty good idea. And I'd be thanking God for years to come.

I walked toward my car. "Thanks, Eugene."

"Don't mention it, baby. Don't mention it. You know how I like to take care of my ladies."

"SIT, SIT, DEAR. I CAN take care of it."

Which, translated into Greek, meant that Mrs. Nebitz needed help.

I got up from the old large, round kitchen table that made it nearly impossible to navigate around the cramped interior of her kitchen and stood next to her while she got out drinking glasses. She handed two to me and then pointed toward a top shelf. "There's a tray up there. Be a dear and get it for me, won't you?"

I put the glasses on the table and turned to do as she asked.

"No, no, not that one. The smaller one."

I showed her the next one.

"Smaller than that."

I took out something a little larger than a plate with a simple blue-and-gold-edged design.

"Yes, that's it." She accepted it. "Thank you, Sofie."

"You're welcome. Tell me what else I can do."

Mrs. Nebitz had turned her attention to the platter. She wore a faraway look on her wrinkled face as she ran a towel over the old ceramic.

"This brings back memories, it does." She leaned closer to me and turned it over. "See there. It was made in Israel."

"Oh, yes. Yes."

I didn't see more than a couple of faded markings, but I did make out a small blue Star of David.

"Me and my Noah were married in Israel, you know. One of the first couples back in 1948."

I raised my brows. "Really?" I mentally did the math. You see, I didn't know Mrs. Nebitz's age. She'd been living in the building when it was deeded to me and had been for the past century, I'd thought, considering her fixed, rent-controlled payments.

She nodded. "We didn't live there long. My mother, she was ill, you know. Had moved here to America. So we followed so I could take care of her."

I enjoyed listening to Mrs. Nebitz's stories, if only because it seemed to give her such great joy to share them.

"This was our first wedding present."

"Are you sure you want to use it now?"

She handed me the platter and waved me away. "Of course. It's old now. Not much good for anything but serving."

I smiled in response to her unwavering pragmatism.

Five minutes later, the table was set, the roasted chicken and noodles were on the platter, matzo-ball soup in bowls, and we were eating.

Or, rather, Mrs. Nebitz was eating. Given my large, late

lunch, I planned to pick now, take home later. But the soup I could eat. And Mrs. Nebitz's was great, the matzo balls fluffy and tasty.

"So are you looking forward to Halloween?" I asked.

She waved a blue-veined hand. "Jews don't believe in Halloween. We have Purim, but that's not until around March or so. We just celebrated Sukkot, but that doesn't involve costumes."

I nodded, pretending I understood. I didn't. I'd heard the words before and thought the latter holiday had something to do with purity and the harvest, but that could be because of the time of year.

Instead of asking, I said, "The Greeks don't believe in Halloween, either."

Not that it made any difference. We kids pressured our parents so much to participate in the holiday that they'd given in, understanding that it was more about friends and fun and how much candy you could collect and your mother could take away than about worshipping any pagan gods.

Yiayia had yet to get used to it, however. I remember when I was nine and my parents had been catering a special event and it had been up to her to man the door.

"Ti theloune e diavoli stin porta? Zitane karameles," my grandmother muttered, saying that the demons were at the door and they wanted candy as she got up from her chair with a bowl of sesame-seed-and-honey candy every time the doorbell rang.

But even that had been an improvement over the homemade halva she'd tried to give away the year before when we ran out of candy. Thankfully, my mother had been home to stop her then.

"This is really good, Mrs. Nebitz. Actually, everything you give me is delicious. You really should give me some recipes sometime."

She reached over to pat my hand. "I plan to be around to make food for you for some time to come, Sofie. No need for recipes. I'll show you."

I nodded, and talk turned to the weather and how I'd called in a handyman to see to the furnace and duct maintenance, as well as caulking around some of the windows, including Mrs. Nebitz's. She'd thought the handyman was lazy, but he did a good job as long as you watched over him.

"So how's that nice Mr. Porter doing?" she asked me.

I nearly choked on my matzo ball. I wiped my mouth with a napkin and reached for my glass of water. "I don't really know," I said, even as my mind filled with the memory of his grin as he'd sat opposite me at the pizza joint, sexy, suggestive, and downright dirty.

"That's a shame. I like him."

I'd liked him, too. A little too much, maybe.

I'd never introduced her to Dino. Of course, that accounted for little. Mrs. Nebitz probably knew everything that happened in the neighborhood, much less this building and particularly the single Greek girl that lived across the hall from her.

I'd brought Muffy with me, and he sat at Mrs. Nebitz's feet, happy to accept scraps from her. I hoped she hadn't saved him chicken liver.

Me, he ignored.

I stared at the little mongrel and then down at my plate, which was almost empty. I raised my brows. I hadn't meant to eat that much. Hadn't even been that hungry when I'd come over.

So how, then, had I eaten so much without realizing it?

I sat back. "I wonder, why haven't we done this before?"

Mrs. Nebitz stacked the bowls, waving away my attempts to help clear the table. "You're always so busy, you are. Going here, coming back from there. And then there's that handsome young Greek man who comes over."

I stifled a groan. So she was familiar with Dino. Probably she hadn't mentioned him directly because they'd yet to be officially introduced. Or she'd been waiting for me to mention him.

Probably everybody knew I'd been seeing Dino.

I realized I was thinking in past tense and grimaced.

Mrs. Nebitz got two fresh plates from the cupboard. "Sofie, dear, why don't you bring in that *mohnstrudel* from the dining room table for me?"

I recognized the "strudel" in the word she'd used and was all too happy to bring in the fresh pastry from the other room. Dessert, there was always room for. Especially Mrs. Nebitz's desserts.

Then again, it could be said that I've never met a dessert I didn't like.

"Thank you, thank you."

She began cutting small pieces and I had to stop myself from moving her hand to cut a larger piece. Until I realized that she was putting two slices on each plate.

"What's the *mohn* in the strudel?" I asked.

"Poppy seeds."

I should have guessed that, but still, it was better to ask. I took a bite and hummed in approval.

"My grandson Seth is afraid to eat my *mohnstrudel*. Says the seeds might make him test positive for drugs."

I slowed my chewing.

"Drugs, shmugs, I told him. Besides, why would he have to worry about being tested for drugs? He's a good boy. Who would want to?"

"That depends on his profession. The city regularly and randomly tests many of its employees nowadays. You remember that number four train accident? The engineer was drunk, people died, the city paid out millions to the surviving families."

"Ah, yes. I understand."

I tried to catch her eating her strudel. Funny, I couldn't remember seeing her take a single bite of anything. The fact that there was nothing on her plate told me she had indeed eaten. And I'd witnessed her chewing. I just hadn't seen her put anything inside her mouth.

I looked down at Muffy. Nah.

"But my Seth doesn't work for the city. He's completing his medical internship now, you know."

"No, I didn't know."

"Going to be an ear, nose, and throat specialist."

I noticed that she'd picked up a paper napkin and was worrying it in her fingers.

"That was wonderful, Mrs. Nebitz," I said. "Thank you so much for inviting me for dinner."

"You're welcome, Sofie."

"You really should let me return the favor sometime."

"That's all right. I know how busy you are. Besides, I prefer to eat a meal prepared in my own kitchen."

I smiled.

"I'm sorry, Sofie, but I must admit that there's an ulterior motive for my inviting you over."

"You mean more than for the joy of my company?"

She either didn't hear me or ignored my attempt at humor.

"I need for you to do something for me. A favor."

I'd folded my hands on top of the table and turned them palms up. "Sure. What is it?"

"I need for you to find out the name of the shiksa my grandson Seth is dating. . . ."

Fifteen

MUFFY AND I RETURNED TO our apartment a little while after Mrs. Nebitz's surprise request, him retreating to his chair, me sitting on the couch staring at the television without really seeing it.

"I don't understand," I'd said to my elderly neighbor and hostess. "If you want to know who Seth is dating, why don't you just ask him?"

"That's something a grandmother doesn't ask a grandson, Sofie. Usually by now he brings a girl he's been dating for a while around to visit. You know, like a good Jewish boy."

I took that to mean that she'd asked, he hadn't told. "Are you sure he's dating the same girl? How can you be sure?"

"Because I know my Seth. His mother tells me he goes out all the time but won't tell her where or with whom. And whenever I ask if he's met any nice Jewish girls, he clams up on me like an old woman's change purse. Me. His *bubbie*."

I'd pretty much guessed at that point that the girl Seth must be seeing must not have been a nice Jewish girl. She could very well have been nice, but not Jewish.

And Mrs. Nebitz wanted me to find out who it was.

I hadn't actually said I would. But I hadn't said I wouldn't, either.

I sighed heavily and earned a growl from Muffy. I looked in his direction to find him sound asleep.

Great. Even the dog was growling at me in his sleep. Probably he was dreaming about growling at me. Probably he was dreaming about biting me.

What had I done to the little mutt, anyway?

The ten o'clock newscast came on. I reached for the remote to turn up the volume. I half expected the impending jury selection in the Laughton case to be featured somewhere. I was surprised when a picture of a girl not Valerie Bryer flicked on in the upper-right-hand corner.

"Seventeen-year-old Hannah Greenberg went missing two days ago after she left a group of friends at a local coffee shop sometime after seven P.M. She was wearing jeans, a white top, and a yellow jacket. . . ." The anchor went on to state her height and weight and shared that she had a small tattoo of a sunrise on the inside of her left wrist, then gave a number to call if anyone had any information on the missing girl.

Great. Another missing girl. Just what I needed to hear. At least I knew Johnny wasn't responsible for this crime.

I squinted at the screen. Could it be that the killer behind Valerie's disappearance could be the same guy?

My cell phone chirped loudly on the coffee table, and I jumped.

I cursed under my breath. Probably I'd spent too much time with my cousin Pete, the conspiracy theorist, today.

I looked at the display on the cell: Waters.

"Mission accomplished," he said simply. "You want the phone, come down and get it."

"Where are you?"

"Double-parked in front of your building."

"So bring it up."

"Uh-uh. I already been towed once this week for double parking. I ain't going nowhere. 'Sides, you live on, what, like the tenth floor?"

"The third."

"Same difference."

"I'll be right down."

Muffy lifted his head from his paws.

"You stay here."

A growl was his response.

I jogged down the three flights of stairs and out into the cool autumn night, wishing I'd thought to grab my jacket. Then again, I didn't plan to be outside long.

I walked behind my Mustang, rounded Eugene's Caddy, and rapped on the driver's-side window. He jumped, grinned when he recognized me, then the window slid down.

I coughed at the smoke that hit me full in the face.

"For a minute there I thought you was the fuzz."

Fuzz? Did they even call the police that anymore?

"Is that weed?" I asked, sniffing.

His grin widened. "Hey, I'm not on your dime no more. Knocked off the minute one of my guys unlocked that damn thing." He looked at someone in the passenger seat that resembled Waters right down to the polyester shirt he was wearing.

Why didn't it surprise me that they were listening to George Clinton?

I held out my hand palm up. He put Papadakis' cell phone in it. "The code's 987123."

I tried it and immediately gained access. "Thanks."

"Don't mention it."

There was a blast of a police siren along with a flash of blue and white lights. I looked to see that an NYPD squad car had pulled up behind Eugene.

"Oh, fuck," he said, dropping the roach in his hand. It landed between his legs and he jumped around, trying to find it and put out any possible fires.

I smacked the top of the car. "Get out of here. I'll handle this."

Eugene didn't need any more incentive than that. He sped away down the street even as I stepped into the spot where his car had been and crossed my arms, staring straight into the lights as if they didn't feel like they were piercing the backs of my eyeballs.

The squeak of a speaker. "Get out of the street, Metro, or I'll arrest you for obstructing justice."

"Knock it off, Pino," I called. "It's ten o'clock at night and you've probably woken the entire block."

The lights went off and moments later Pino got out of the vehicle, hiking his pants up to his rib cage.

I winced.

"I ought to run you in, Sofie."

"For what? Talking to a friend in the street?"

"A friend with expired temporary tags."

Were Eugene's tags expired? I hadn't noticed. Then again, I didn't make a habit of reading a car's license plates unless I had to as part of a job.

It would be just Eugene's luck. Get nailed for expired tags and hauled in for illicit drug use and DUI.

I'd have to talk to him tomorrow about the tags.

"Don't you have anything better to do, Pino?" I asked.

"What you got there?" He gestured toward the cell phone in my hand.

If I found it awfully coincidental that he should happen to pull up at the same time that I gained access to Papadakis' cell, I wasn't saying.

"My phone. Why? Is it illegal to make a call in the middle of the street?"

"Now you're sassing me."

Sassing. Fuzz. Two words not normally a part of any vocabulary I drew from.

"Good night, Pino," I said, walking toward my door.

"Sofie?"

I stopped and sighed. "What?"

"Anything new on Papadakis?"

I tightened my fingers around the cell. "No. And given your presence, I'm guessing you don't have anything, either."

"I didn't say that."

I indulged him and turned around. I stepped to within two feet of him. "So what do you got, Pino?"

"I didn't say I had anything." He shrugged. "But I didn't say I didn't, either."

I leaned closer to him. "You know, Pino, there's a little advice I'd like to share with you."

His jaw tightened.

"First off, you might try giving me a call sometimes instead of hanging out around my apartment waiting for me to come outside."

"That's not—"

"Second, you might want to upgrade the size of your uniform and probably your civilian clothes as well." I hadn't seen him in anything other than his uniform, but I suspected his lack of fashion sense extended to his personal life. Or else he wouldn't spend so much time on his professional one.

"What's the matter with my uniform?" he asked, hiking up his pants again before taking a look.

I surprised even myself by grabbing the front of his belt. "See this? Pull them up any further and it won't be just gum you're chewing."

"Take your hands off me, Miss Metropolis." He gripped the billy club he had tucked into the back of his belt.

I stepped back again. "Every time you hike your pants, you make even me cringe, Pino. Not to mention that you also look like you came fresh from wading through a mud puddle."

"I'm not following you."

I bent down and tugged on the hem of his slacks, pulling them down until they rested where they were supposed to.

"Hey, you're an inch away from pulling them off."

I stood back up straight and realized he was right.

"You need to get new pants, Pino. At least two inches longer." He reached for the waist again, and I pushed his hands away. "And stop doing that already. You look like an idiot."

He blinked at me, very much resembling the pimply kid with whom I'd gone to St. D's.

Crud.

"Never mind," I said, stalking back toward my door.

"Hey, Sofie, you're not exactly a fashion plate, you know? You could probably do with one of those, you know, makeovers."

I stopped dead in my tracks. Had he really just said what I think he had?

I began turning slowly back in his direction.

He quickly rushed for his car, then got in and slammed the door. Moments later, he was speeding down the street.

I released the breath I was holding. What was I doing? Surely I wasn't listening to a guy whose pants were so far up his crack that he was in danger of splitting himself in two?

I stalked back toward the building and up the stairs. I gained access to my apartment and started to slam the door. Then, re-membering Mrs. Nebitz, I caught it in time and shut it quietly instead.

I really needed to get a life. Or at least decide one way or an-other in which direction I wanted it to go.

AN HOUR LATER, I STRETCHED across my bed and entered the code Eugene had given me into the cell phone. I'd switched on the clock radio on my nightstand. Specifically, I'd tuned in to *Coast to Coast AM* with George Noory, a show Pete had reminded me of and that I listened to occasionally when I couldn't sleep and there was nothing I was really interested in watching on TV. In honor of Halloween, the topic of tonight's show was vampirism.

Oh, great. Just what I needed to be listening to just now.

Then again, I could always call Rosie and tip her off about the show.

No. I was already hearing enough about people of the night from the excitable Puerto Rican. I could only imagine what lengths she'd go to if she was listening to the show.

"So what you're suggesting is that vampirism didn't begin with Vlad the Impaler in Romania, but that, instead, the origin resides in Greek history," George Noory was saying to one of his callers.

I perked up. Oh, my mother would love this. Efi would love it even more.

"That's right, George. Beginning in the nineteenth century . . ."

Lord Byron.

I rolled over and stared at the cell phone screen. The damn thing had relocked itself while I was listening to the asinine show.

I entered in the code again.

What was it about the human condition that we felt an unquenchable need to scare ourselves? From roller coasters and fast car rides to horror movies and practical jokes, if we weren't scaring ourselves, we were scaring others.

Hey, even though Greeks didn't believe in Halloween, the night when the dead were said to return to walk the earth, I got the creeps a good week before the scheduled event. Like now. I didn't feel the same at any other holiday. Not Easter, not Christmas, not the Fourth of July. No, the end of October was when I was afraid that ghosts and vampires and zombies lurked around every corner.

I don't know. Maybe injecting a little fear into your system made you feel more alive somehow. Feel things more acutely.

I could understand that. For the longest time after my wedding that almost was, I'd felt numb. I'd kept myself busy with my new job tracking cheating spouses of all things, not taking a vacation or even going out with friends. Well, I hadn't done the latter because my ex had inherited most of my friends, most notably my best friend.

Still, while I appreciated the odd roller-coaster ride, and had been known to run Lucille hard when I had a stretch of open highway in front of me, and even listened to Noory and his guests talking about the difference between gray and white aliens, and government conspiracies and ghostly visitors, I'd always thought myself above the fear they inspired.

After several menu attempts, I finally got somewhere with Papadakis' expensively technical cell phone. I browsed through his phone book. Nothing but numbers with no names associated with them.

Figured.

Didn't it stand to reason that the guy would have at least one number in there with a name attached? Someone I could call and pretend to know?

My thumb froze on the down arrow button. Now there was a number even I recognized.

To make doubly sure, I bounced off the bed and went back into the living room, forgetting for a moment to look for any vampires that might be hiding in the shadows, and picked up my cell from the coffee table. After a couple of clicks, I obtained the info I was looking for.

Bingo.

I stared at the number on Papadakis' screen, closed my eyes

briefly, and then dialed, in that one moment understanding that need to feel alive a little too well.

Jake Porter answered on the second ring. "What are you doing calling me on a dead man's phone, Sofie?"

Sixteen

"I'LL PICK YOU UP IN fifteen."

Those were Jake's words to me when I didn't answer his question.

He hung up, and I merely stood there staring at the cell phone before looking for a place to hide it. I could use the online reverse directory to look up the other numbers at the office in the morning. But right now I didn't want to lose custody of the phone.

I stopped when I caught myself about to hide it in the mountain of still wrapped wedding gifts stacked against the far wall of my bedroom. What was I doing? I didn't have to hide the phone from anyone. I had a right to have it in my possession, seeing as my aunt had claimed the body and by extension claimed the right to Papadakis' possessions.

Still, I didn't feel entirely comfortable putting the phone in my pocket. Instead, I put it on ice—literally, because I put it in the freezer and hoped the damn thing wouldn't explode or anything—rushed to the bathroom to freshen up, and then stood staring at my old jeans and sweatshirt.

I rushed back to my bedroom and changed into a new pair of jeans (okay, I liked the comfort of jeans, so sue me) and a stretchy sweater, then I pulled my new pair of leather boots back on. I checked myself out in the full-length mirror. Damn hot if you asked me.

But no one was asking me.

I grabbed my barn coat and my purse complete with Glock and cell phone inside and hurried out the door.

I hit the outside curb at the same time Jake pulled up in his black monster truck with tinted windows. I heard the lock mechanism give, and I hesitated before opening the passenger door. It was nearly midnight and I was definitely tempting fate.

Oh, damn it all to hell. I wanted to know what he wanted from me.

And at the same time, I hoped that it was the same thing I wanted from him.

The truck cab smelled of warm leather and even warmer man as I awkwardly climbed inside and closed the door. I made out the strains of a country-and-western song (was that Johnny Cash?) on the stereo that flashed "CD" even as he pulled away from the curb.

I found myself swallowing hard as I finally looked at him.

"Do you ever sleep?" I asked.

He glanced my way, his eyes seeming to glow from under the shadow caused by the brim of his leather cowboy hat. "I could ask the same of you, luv."

I made a face and crossed my arms over my chest.

I was so engrossed in my own thoughts of the man next to me, I didn't realize that neither of us had said anything until a good five minutes had passed and we were near Astoria Park and the East River. When he'd said he was picking me up, I'd assumed he wanted to warn me against pursuing the Papadakis case any further—again. But if that was all he'd planned to do, he was taking the long way around.

To my surprise, he parked the truck, shut off the engine, and got out, all without sparing me a look.

I sat in the truck cab watching as he rounded the front and then walked down the street a bit before turning right toward an apartment building.

Okay, this was a new one.

Up until now, my relationship to Porter had been limited to him tinkering with my sheila and his tailing me by way of protection or his popping up when I landed a case he didn't think I should be working on.

This new tactic threw me for a loop.

I looked behind me. We weren't that far from Ditmars. Although it would mean a long walk, I could always get out and hoof it back to my place.

I glanced back at him where he'd stopped midway to the building. Was he picking his nails with his keys?

Okay, so I'd figured out long ago that curiosity not only killed the cat, but usually got the better of me. And while I'd managed to stay alive until now, I'd gotten into more than my fair share of hairy situations. I stared at Hell Gate Bridge not too far away and shuddered, that memory one I could have done without just then.

Finally, Jake looked in my direction. I couldn't see his eyes. Then he tipped his hat back and I made out the suggestive expression he wore.

I swallowed hard, thinking of every last reason why I shouldn't go with him. Dino's sexy smile flashed through my mind, trailed quickly by the image of him hunting for a lash in Efi's eye, and followed even more quickly by the thought of my mother mailing out wedding invitations.

I was seized by the desire to press my thumbs against my eyelids until I heard a satisfying pop. Something, anything, to release the pressure of indecision building within me.

I never used to be like this. Seven months ago, I knew exactly who I was and where I was going. Up until I had the flokati rug pulled out from under me. That's when I found myself going from a warm, woolly virgin white cushion to lying on top of a grate staring at the rushing waters of life below, not quite sure how I got there and not knowing how in the hell to get back up.

Would Jake help me find the way?

I smiled. No. But he might help me forget about that damn grate for a little while.

As I opened the door and hopped down onto the sidewalk, I realized what I was feeling was fear. In spades. Funny that I should describe my emotions in that way, considering my previous meanderings on fear and the desire to feel alive.

And oh, boy!—at that moment I wanted to feel one hundred percent, exhilaratingly alive. And I knew Jake was just the person to do that.

"Second thoughts?" he asked as I drew even with him, taking in the old apartment building in dire need of renovations rather than the tall man next to me.

"First thoughts."

I glanced up to find that sexy half grin on his rugged face before he led the rest of the way to the front of the building. After unlocking the door, he opened it for me. I stopped just inside to allow him to pass. He went down instead of up, stopping at the second apartment to the left. Another set of locks and a flick of a light switch and he held open the door into a small, neat apartment sparsely furnished.

"Looks oddly familiar," I said, holding my purse tightly to my side.

"Oh?"

Since we both knew I'd never been there before—in fact, I'd imagined Jake moving from motel room to motel room, leaving fast-food wrappers and empty beer bottles in his wake, not staying in an apartment—I supposed I owed him an explanation.

"Yeah," I said. "Looks a lot like Papadakis' place." I walked around, taking in the black leather couch, the recliner, the no-frills television. "Looks like a home, feels like a home, but it's not really a home, is it?"

I looked over my shoulder to find him watching my bottom. His gaze flicked up to my face, and he grinned. Whether it was in response to my comment or my catching him staring, I couldn't be sure. Not that it mattered. His grin had always done funny things to my stomach. And now was no exception, no matter how much I tried to convince myself otherwise.

His hands moved to rest against my shoulders and skimmed over my jacket, down over my arms, then under them.

"What, are you frisking me?"

His fingers squeezed my bottom. "Figured it couldn't hurt." He finished and started taking off my jacket. "What is your stand on cavity searches?"

"That the gun you didn't find on my person will exit my purse quicker than you can blink."

His chuckle washed over me like a cool spring shower on a hot summer day. "Shame."

Damn, but the man was insufferable. Just when I thought I'd moved on from him, was over him, he came swaggering back into my life like an Australian cowboy who had spent the day working in the sun and wanted me not only to run him a bath, but to crawl into it with him.

I moved my purse from one hand to the other as he removed my jacket. He tossed the coat to the recliner and indicated that I should have a seat on the sofa.

"Can I get you something?" he asked, heading toward the kitchen.

"Yes, some answers."

"Sorry. Beer's the best I can do. Swan?"

"Yeah, sure, okay."

I'd never heard of the brand, but I figured beer was beer no matter what it was called.

As soon as he'd disappeared around the corner, I craned my neck to try seeing into the bedroom just off a hallway to my right. I made out an unmade . . . was that a water bed? I was pretty sure it was. And the size of it guaranteed that it took up much of the space.

Of course, Jake was like six feet five if he was an inch, and he probably needed a pretty good-size bed to accommodate his height.

If only I didn't suspect that the bed had been chosen for more than just sleeping.

"Get a good look?" he asked, appearing at my side and holding out a bottle of Australian beer.

"Not as good as I'd like."

He sat next to me and gestured toward the hall with his own

beer, his grin filthier than a cowboy's chaps after a long haul. "Have at it."

My spine stiffened. I had to stay away from the cowboy analogies or I'd end up getting myself into trouble. "No, thank you. I've seen my share of bedrooms."

"Have you now?"

His arm snaked along the couch, and I felt his fingers on the back of my neck before I could prepare myself for the touch. I shivered, torn between wanting to move away from him and the desire to lean into him.

I already knew that Jake kissed better than any man had a right to. But kissing and a few hot caresses were as far as we'd gotten. My gaze fell to his full mouth, riveted as he took a long pull of his beer. I licked my lips.

"So . . . have you called any other numbers on that new phone of yours?"

I made a face and turned my attention to my own beer. "I wondered when you'd get to the point." I shifted on the couch so that my bent leg was between us and I was facing him more fully. "Tell you what, Jake, we can play that game. But this time you're going to offer up as much as I give."

He hiked a brow and reached up to take off his hat, giving me another glimpse of the cowboy character he resembled.

The guy must have watched a few too many movies growing up.

Yeah, look who was talking.

I ran my fingers through my own hair.

"So who goes first?"

I felt oddly as if we were playing a game of Truth or Dare? and the bottle had just pointed squarely in my direction.

"Okay. No, I haven't called any other numbers in Papadakis' cell phone."

"Good girl."

"I'm neither a dog nor a pet, so I'd appreciate you not calling me that."

He dipped his head forward. "Fair enough."

I spun the bottle in his direction. "Tell me, Jake, why all the attention all of a sudden?"

His finger budged from my neck to the line of my jaw. I swallowed thickly. Who knew a simple touch could be so sexy?

"You've always had my attention, luv."

Luv. Now that was much better than "girl" any day of the week. Especially when spoken in his Australian accent.

But I wasn't giving up the ghost just yet. I might be easy, but I wasn't that easy. "Why'd you bring me here?"

He didn't say anything for a long moment. Merely took his time looking me over. I waited until his gaze met mine again. "Isn't it obvious?"

I crossed my arms, partly to communicate my unhappiness with his evasiveness. Mostly to hide the goose bumps that had just run up my skin. "Two months ago if I'd thrown myself at your feet, naked, you would have stepped over me in your hurry to leave."

"I never hurry anywhere."

He had a point there. Even in tense situations, the guy was as graceful as a cat.

Was that what was behind the long courtship?

I cringed inwardly at my word choice.

Seduction probably better fit the bill.

Especially since he had moved his hand to my back and was slowly pulling me closer to him.

"Any objections?" he asked, his attention flicking from my mouth to my eyes and down to my breasts and back again.

"Not a one," I said, and kissed him.

Seventeen

MMM . . . MMM . . . MMM.

If kissing Dino was like eating chocolate, kissing Jake was like sampling spicy wings. Almost too hot, but so good you couldn't help risking tongue burn in order to get just one more taste. And that one led to another and then another. . . .

I lifted my arms, allowing Jake to peel off my shirt even as I yanked at the hem of his, anxious to finally, finally have my skin resting against his. I half expected him to pull away, to put the brakes on our activities as he had a thousand times before.

Instead he plunged full speed ahead.

"Tell me something, Jake," I said between hot, tonsil-reaching kisses. "How come we haven't done this before now?"

He popped the back clasp on my bra and tossed the scrap of material across the room before cupping his large hands over my breasts. I shuddered straight down to my toes at the feel of his rough, callused palms against my hypersensitive nipples.

"Jesus, woman, do you always talk this much?"

I smiled. "Always. Got a problem with it?"

He shook his head slightly, kissing me again. "Not at all."

I got up enough to allow him to strip me of my jeans even as I stared deep into his blue eyes and reached for his fly. "Sounded like a complaint to me."

"No complaints here, luv."

"Then maybe you won't mind my asking about Papadakis and your connection to him."

He'd leaned me back against the cushions of the couch, both of us stripped of clothing and breathing heavily.

He paused, hovering above me, his biceps well defined and making my mouth water with the desire to run my tongue along the skin there.

For a moment, I thought he might stop. And feared that he would.

Damn, damn, damn. Why had I gone and asked an idiotic question?

Then again, I was getting a little tired of asking vague questions and getting even vaguer answers.

A small part of me wondered if I'd done it on purpose. I mean, even though Dino and I weren't officially a couple, wasn't there at least a conversation coming before I had sex with another man? Even if that other man was Jake and he pre-dated Dino by a good couple of months?

"Your call, Sofie: Do you want to talk? Or have sex?"

He'd fit himself nicely between my waiting thighs, and I bit on my bottom lip. "Mmm . . . both?"

He drew his head back slightly and chuckled. Then bent in to give me a kiss that robbed me of breath and set fire to my limbs.

"Sex . . . sex," I whispered between deep kisses, finally giving in.

The question that went unanswered this time was, for how long?

I AWOKE TO FIND SOMETHING heavy lying against my leg. Muffy. I gave a little nudge and snuggled deeper into the bedding . . . only to have the bedding move back against me.

Holy shit!

I bolted upright and was almost catapulted from the water bed for my efforts. I quickly realized that it hadn't been Muffy up against my leg, but Jake, who appeared to be fast asleep next to me.

I clutched the sheet to my breasts like a virgin who'd awakened without her clothing. I was not amused with the image as I tried to make sense out of the situation I was smack-dab in the middle of.

Seldom was the time I'd fallen so deeply asleep at a guy's place. Lord knows I'd never done it with Dino. Okay, mostly because he had to get up at an ungodly hour at his bakery, but still, that gave me little comfort.

I rubbed the heel of my hand against my eye socket. What in the hell was I doing thinking about Dino at such a moment?

Then I remembered sex with Jake. . . .

My tension melted and I began to snuggle back into the bed . . . slowly, so I wouldn't make any further waves and eject a sleeping Jake.

It wasn't all that long ago that I'd have given my eyeteeth for an hour in bed with this guy. And, boy, would it ever have been worth it.

And I'd finally gotten what I wanted.

Of course, I was ignoring that he'd finally chosen for it to happen on his terms. His call, his place, no stack of unopened wedding gifts or ring-eating garbage disposals anywhere in the vicinity.

I looked at him next to me. What was it about watching a great-looking guy sleep that made you hot all over again?

A sound came from near the window.

I froze where I lay, listening carefully.

I had family in Greece that wondered how I could sleep in such a big, busy city. I explained to them that there were times when even a big, busy city had to sleep. And that in the middle of the night it was probably as quiet here as it was in some small country villages in Greece.

Okay, maybe I was stretching things a bit, but not by much. And if I needed any reminder of that, I was getting it now. It was so quiet that I swore I could hear a tenant in the building three blocks up breathing.

Another sound.

I wasn't the only one who moved. Jake rolled quickly off to one side of the bed while I rolled toward the other. He moved quicker and the water bed compensated, pretty much throwing me off the other side so that I landed on the floor with a thud.

Ow.

I lifted to peek over the bed, at the same time rubbing my tailbone, staring in the direction of the high window.

Movement!

I ducked down again, and several soft poofs were followed by a hissing sound. I found out quickly what they were when spray from the punctured water bed hit the top of my head, much like the Roman fountains my grandfather said were good for nothing but having a fat cherub piss on you.

Had someone just shot at the bed?

Someone had just shot at the bed.

Both thoughts came to me at once.

My purse . . . my purse . . .

Everything was in the other room. Underpants, jeans, boots, purse with the gun in it.

Glass shattered and I yelped as I scrambled quickly from the room. I felt something under my knee as I peered around the doorway back into the bedroom to find Jake standing and shooting back at whoever was shooting at us. Where in the hell had he found a gun? Then my attention was drawn elsewhere as I realized he was still as naked as I was.

Nice ass.

He ducked, and another series of holes opened up across the water bed and then took a chunk out of the wood molding next to my cheek.

I jerked back, sliding on whatever was under my knees.

My underpants!

I quickly put them on, then found my jeans and top and did the same. The only thing I couldn't find was my purse. There! I'd left it on the couch next to me. Jake must have gotten up in the middle of the night and gone through it, because now it lay on the recliner under my coat. As I stuck my hand inside for my gun, I wondered what he'd been looking for. I was reasonably sure he hadn't been looking for money. Then again, nowadays you never really knew, did you?

Papadakis' cell phone, I realized. He'd probably been looking for the cell phone.

The same one that was on ice back at my apartment. Literally.

I pulled out the gun just as Jake stumbled into the living room, still shooting. Somewhere along the line he'd put on his jeans, although they were unbuttoned, slid into cowboy boots, and thrown a shirt over his shoulder.

Yum.

The thought registered just as he ran out of ammo and his gun made a dull *click*. He turned around, immediately spotting where I crouched behind the recliner, gun aimed at the open doorway.

"I think this is the part where we run, babe," he whispered.

I felt his hand on my arm. He hauled me from my hiding place and shoved me toward the front door. I didn't need much more incentive than that. Keeping my gun stretched out in front of me, I ran toward the front stairs and the building door. A shadow emerged just beyond, and I took aim and pulled the trigger. A man wearing a ski mask shouted in pain and fell to his knees, grasping his right upper arm.

I'd been aiming for his chest.

But rather than concentrating on the fact that it had been a few days since I'd visited the firing range, I ran flat out for Jake's truck. I was ten feet away when I felt Jake's hand on the back of my shirt. He yanked me backward just as the truck exploded, throwing us both to the ground.

As I lay there, struggling for air, feeling as though my skin were on fire for reasons having nothing to do with sex, I resoundingly decided that this middle-of-the-night rendezvous had produced a little more fear than I'd been looking for.

The world went black.

———

I WOKE SLOWLY, A FAMILIAR weight against my calf. I groaned and burrowed further into the bedding, only to bolt upright a moment later, my heart racing as I frantically looked around the safety of my own bedroom.

Swallowing back the fog of fear that clouded my sleepy brain, I lifted the blanket. I was sans jeans and shirt and boots and was now wearing a sexy purple nightie, one of my wedding gifts. The fact that I had it on was material enough to figure out what must have happened the night before, after Jake's truck exploded. I'd passed out, either a result of the explosion or from fear. He must have brought me home, changed me out of my clothes, and put me to bed.

A quick check of the other pillow told me he hadn't joined me.

Surprisingly, I felt relieved.

Muffy growled. I stared at the little ragamuffin. He got up, sniffed my leg as if checking to make sure I was all right, and then jumped off the bed, his toenails clicking against the wood, each step amplifying his growl.

I gave an eye roll and got up, grabbing a change of clothes before carefully checking the apartment to make sure no one was there. My coat was hanging on the wall hook by the door, along with my purse. I took out my gun, checked the clip, and then put the firearm on the table. Since I'd shot it, I would have to clean it of any possible residual debris.

Coffee. I needed coffee.

I ignored that it was after nine A.M. and that I was late. Hey, coming so close to death the night before had that effect on a girl. I padded into the kitchen still wearing the nightie and began mixing the ingredients for my frappé. As I shook the ingredients, I opened the freezer to get ice cubes for my travel cup. I froze midcube.

The cell phone was gone.

Shocker.

I slammed the freezer door, finished making my coffee, and then stomped toward the bathroom, where I did my business.

Damn Jake and his outdated sense of chivalry.

Or should I be saying, "Damn Jake and his set of chivalrous objectives"?

Either way, what had been a great night had turned into a certifiable nightmare in more ways than I could count.

I caught myself scratching the area above my right breast. I looked down to find that the lace of the nightie was irritating my skin. I quickly peeled it off and fashioned it into a slingshot, then flung it across the bathroom and into the living room where Muffy was passing. He stopped, sniffed it, showed me his teeth, and then stepped on top of it and made as if he were wiping his feet.

"My sentiments exactly," I mumbled, and climbed into the shower, wondering exactly what this day held in store for me.

And whether or not it might be a better idea just to go back to bed.

Eighteen

THE AGENCY WAS PACKED TO the brim when I finally made it in. Given the time of day, I decided it was probably better to walk the short way to work rather than drive and hunt for a parking spot. Now I weighed the option of keeping on walking rather than going inside to confront whatever was happening. The problem lay in that Rosie was out front with a broom.

"What are you doing sweeping the sidewalk?" I looked up at the roof of the place. Was it possible that someone had jumped? I couldn't fathom another reason why the picky Puerto Rican would be sweeping the walk when she absolutely refused to clean anything else in the place for fear of ruining her nails.

Rosie looked so relieved to see me, I was afraid she might hug me. "Thank God you're here! It's a madhouse in there."

"Is that why you're out here?"

She did that bobble-head thing. "No. I'm out here chasing that damn cat away again. That makes the third time in so many days."

I supposed I should be glad she was chasing it away on her own rather than standing on her chair waiting for me to chase it.

"You know, I was just reading about how cats know . . . you know?"

I blinked at her.

She *tsk*ed. "They know when someone's about to die, I mean. And cats that aren't even friendly start getting really buddy-buddy with that person ready to go you-know-where."

"Where?"

She pointed to the sky with an orange fingernail. "Heaven."

"There is no heaven."

"Uh-huh, there is, too. Because I know there's a hell. And if there's a hell, then there must be a heaven."

"So now you're afraid that the presence of the black cat means you're going to die?"

The bobble-head thing again. "Me? Oh no. I take precautions." Her word usage made me think of birth control, which made me think of last night, which made me mentally calculate the reliability of condoms. "I'm not the one who should be worried. You are."

I stared at Rosie. How could she know that I'd spent the night with Jake?

Oh. She didn't. I was projecting my own thoughts onto her words.

I said, "Me? You think I'm at risk of dying?"

She leaned closer to me. "I heard that there was an explosion last night. Somebody's truck. Not just somebody's, but that bounty hunter guy that was hanging around here a while back."

"Oh?" I managed to push out of my closed throat.

"Uh-huh. His license plate landed in somebody's flower bed five blocks away. That's how I know. My cousin lives three doors down from where it hit. I ran the number this morning, although I remember . . ."

Rosie continued rattling on as I opened the agency door and she followed me inside. I recognized two clients who had hired us to follow their spouses, likely there for the money shots or updates or even to pay on their bills. Eugene Waters was also there, along with Pamela Coe, both probably accepting their daily summons to deliver. And my cousin Pete, wearing a suit, was leaning against my desk as he shuffled through what looked like messages meant for me.

I said hello to everyone, then took the messages from Pete's hand as I continued on to my uncle's office.

"Did you hear the news that there's another missing girl?" Pete asked as he followed me in.

I put the messages on the desk, stowed my purse under the desk, and then turned to face him. "Yes, I did."

He didn't say anything for a long moment, merely stared at me. "And?" he prompted.

"And, what?"

"And don't you see the connection? Same day, one year later. Girl from the same neighborhood—"

"Forest Hills and Bayside are not the same neighborhood."

"Excuse me," he said. "Same class division. Same type of circumstances."

"This girl was out with her friends, not with her boyfriend."

"Because she'd recently broken up with him."

I twisted my lips. Was that true? Given everything that had

happened last night, I hadn't had a chance to follow up on the original news broadcast I'd caught. "Really?"

Pete nodded, and the conspiracy theorist that resided in him went into overdrive. "One of the papers also reported that there's some evidence connecting the girl's disappearance to her boyfriend."

I scratched my head, just then realizing a dull ache had lodged itself between my brows. A result of last night's explosion? Seemed likely.

"They pulled the kid in for questioning this morning."

I leaned against the desk and crossed my arms. "She might not be dead."

He gave me a long look.

I sighed. "Okay. Let's say that she is declared dead, like Valerie Bryer. The best we have is that two different guys killed their girlfriends after an argument, breakup, whatever."

"On the same day?"

One of my uncle Spyros' top rules—along with never leave home without your galoshes if it looked like rain—was that there was no such thing as coincidence. But I was pretty sure he'd meant that in relationship to cheating spouses. If a suspected cheating spouse was at the same hotel as a suspected floozy, there was no coincidence, he was banging her.

When it came to murder cases, however . . .

I tried to remember if my uncle had worked on any kind of high-profile case like the one currently weighing down my workload. Actually, there was at least one that I knew about. About a year and a half, two years ago. He'd been asked by Detective Sergeant Tom McCurdy of the 114th to consult on the suspected assassination of a Greek politician, an Astoria assemblyman who'd been found dead in his bathtub. The original cause of death had been ruled suicide . . . until electrocution had proven to be the cause of death and not the postmortem slashes on his wrists that hadn't produced much blood. This and there hadn't been a small or large appliance plugged in found anywhere near the tub.

I rubbed my brows, trying to ease the pounding behind them. "Okay, Pete, this is what I want you to do. . . ."

I proceeded to tell him to compare the details of yesterday's case with the details of Valerie Bryer's. Victims' ages, backgrounds, if they shared anything in common such as education, friends, the works. And I wanted him to get back to me by day's end.

My cousin looked as if it were Christmas morning and I were the bike he'd always wanted sitting next to the tree bearing a big red bow. He hugged me and gave me a loud kiss on the cheek.

"Thank you, Sofie. You won't regret this."

He started to walk out of the office and then turned. "Oh, and I'm not sure, but I think this warrants a salary increase."

"You're paid by the hour."

"Exactly."

I shook my head as he continued on and left the agency.

"What, you calling me a liar?" Rosie's voice carried loudly through the open doorway. I looked to see her waving a sheet of paper at an angry young woman. "If the spot tail says he ain't doin' nothing, then he ain't doin' nothing."

I walked to the door and closed it, leaning against it for long moments before walking to stand in front of the whiteboard. At some point yesterday I'd written, "The person you least suspect is usually the one who done it."

I considered the list of suspects, with the addition of Valerie Bryer's convicted sexual predator uncle.

I picked up a marker, uncapped it, and then recapped it, the clicking sound doing little to jump-start my thinking processes. Truth be told, I was having a hard time not thinking about last night. So shoot me, I wasn't used to spending the night with a guy and then having it end in such a dramatic way.

Speaking of which . . .

I collected my purse from under the desk and then opened the office door. If I'd been expecting the hubbub to have let up, I was sadly mistaken as I watched Rosie console a spouse who'd just gotten a look at the money shots.

"It's okay, honey," Rosie said. "You don't need that low-down, cheating bastard nohow."

"But I love him!"

Rosie gave me an eye roll over the woman's head. "Then why did you have us follow him? If you were going to stay with the rat anyway, don't you think it would be better not to know?"

That was Rosie for you. Always the honest pragmatist.

The woman snatched the photos and stuffed them inside her purse.

"Would you like to pay the invoice now?" Rosie asked, rounding her desk even as I checked my own for more messages.

"Bill me," the woman said, getting up and charging the door.

Rosie planted her hands on her hips. "I never. I swear, some of these women need to look into some major therapy or something." She waggled her finger in the direction of the door. "I just know I'm going to have trouble collecting on that one."

"Yeah, well, if you were a little nicer, maybe that wouldn't be the case."

"Nicer?" She huffed. "She's the one who hired us."

"Yes, but in my experience, there's a big difference between suspecting your spouse and sitting there looking at it in black and white. Or worse, full eight-by-ten color glossies."

Rosie focused her attention on me instead of the door. "Well, look who's become the little expert already. I'll have you know I've been here a lot longer than you have, Miss Thing. And I haven't failed to collect on a debt once."

I shrugged as I put on my jacket. "Just making a little suggestion, is all. No big deal."

"Yeah, well, keep your suggestions to yourself."

I hid my smile. "Watch it, Rosie. You forget, I'm the one responsible for the new love in your life."

She blinked at me. "How did you figure it out?"

I stared back at her.

She smacked the heel of her hand to her forehead. "Oh, you mean my computer," she said, laughing. "Here I thought you were talking about . . ."

"Who?" I couldn't resist prompting when it probably would have been better to stay quiet and let her continue on her own steam.

I cringed when my question seemed to bring her back around. And verified that we hadn't been on the same page and I'd almost gotten the information I'd been looking for for over two months. Namely, the lowdown on the guy she was dating.

"Uh-uh. I told you. He's going to meet my family this weekend. Then after I'll bring him by here to meet you."

I made a face as I headed for the door.

"Where you going?" she asked.

"Anywhere but here." I turned just inside the door. "Unless you want to tell me."

"Nope."

"Fine."

"Great."

"Terrific."

I stepped outside and listened to the door *whoosh* closed behind me.

Steinway Street wasn't called the World's Longest Department Store for nothing. It was busy at almost any time of day, but now it was bumper-to-bumper traffic, crammed with people jockeying for parking spots so they could shop at any one of a hundred stores like Shoenique or Indigo. Or eat at any one of the countless ethnic restaurants. I took a deep breath, regretting it when my nose filled with exhaust fumes. I turned in the direction of my apartment where I'd left Lucille parked and nearly tripped over something.

I stared down at the black cat that had been terrorizing Rosie as of late.

I considered the feline that appeared to be purposely blocking my path, then glanced through the agency window. Rosie was sitting at her desk with her back to me, busy at her computer. Figured. Then again, it was just as well. A panicked Rosie I could do without just now.

"Hello again," I said to the cat, crouching and holding out my hand.

What was I doing? I didn't think cats were like dogs. Then why was I offering my hand for a sniff? I shook my head and tried to pet it instead. It hissed at me and stepped back out of reach.

Ooookay.

I snapped upright. "Well, I guess I should be glad you didn't try to scratch me."

I pushed my purse strap up my arm and considered the scrap of black fur. It didn't look hungry. And its coat was shiny and full. So what did it want from me?

I looked around, as if expecting the answer to come to me. Or perhaps the owner to come rushing around the corner, looking for her lost pet.

Nothing.

Hunh.

I was used to being asked to find people's pets. This was the first time a pet wanted me to find its owner.

"You know I can't help you unless I get a look at your collar."

The cat seemed to shake its head and then followed with its body until even its tail seemed to shake.

Fine.

I moved to the left and then to the right, weighing the risks of passing the animal. Not just the immediate physical threat, but the long-term, superstitious one.

What was it they said about not letting a black cat cross your path?

I shuddered and passed the damn stray anyway. Hey, it was either that or walk all the way around the block. And since I wasn't about to do that, I figured I'd take my chances.

I felt around in my purse for my cell phone and clicked it open, finding the number I was looking for and dialing.

"G'day, luv."

"Jake, I want some answers and I want them now. . . ."

Nineteen

BEYOND THE SMELL OF CAR exhaust, the scent of autumn hung heavy in the air as I walked up Steinway toward my place. The street was jumping with everyone rushing to and fro. Mothers with their kids in tow, bags overflowing with Halloween stuffs clutched in their hands. Older ladies doing their shopping. Older men out watching them all.

I moved my cell phone from my right ear to my left and asked, "Mind telling me what happened last night, Jake?"

I could virtually hear the smile in his voice. "Simple. I took you home and tucked you in and called it a night."

Now that was just like a man for you. Gloss over the important details and focus on the trivial. "Ha, ha."

"By the way, that purple number looks good on you."

"That purple number is in the garbage can. It gave me a rash."

A soft chuckle. "Shame."

"What's a shame is that Papadakis' cell phone wasn't where I left it when I got up."

Silence.

"Jake?"

"What, luv?"

I gritted my back teeth, surprised at how I'd gone from orgasmic to annoyed in such a short span of time. And wondered how much our history played a role in that. It stood to reason that more time resulted in more ammo. And I certainly had plenty on Jake. Yes, he'd saved my ass. But he'd also stolen my cell phone.

"Are you planning on answering any of my questions?"

"No."

I stood in the middle of the sidewalk and considered his response. Figured.

I grew aware that I wasn't alone and looked down to find that the black cat was following me.

Great. Not only had a black cat crossed my path, it was on my heels.

I thought about what Rosie had said about cats being able to detect when a person was about to pass over and stopped breathing for all of two seconds. I think that some sort of mythology said that cats were the guardians of the underworld.

I had a feeling all this cat wanted was some tuna.

"Okay, forget the cell," I said reluctantly, accepting that I probably wasn't going to see it again. "But I would appreciate at least two answers."

"I'll see what I can do."

I started walking again, noticing out of the corner of my eye that the cat did the same. Great.

"Do you know where Papadakis' body is?"

A pause, and then, "No."

Good. At least I'd gotten that much.

"One more . . . since I already know that the chances of your telling me what happened last night are between nil and zero, can you at least share whether or not I'm in imminent danger?"

"You're clear, luv."

I exhaled deeply. "And you?"

"I think that makes your two." Obviously one of those questions he wasn't going to answer.

"Of course."

"Anything else?"

I shook my head even though he couldn't see me. "No. That should about do it for now."

"Okay, then."

"All right."

"G'day."

"Jake?"

He didn't say anything, but he hadn't hung up, either.

"You be careful, you hear?"

"Careful is my middle name."

"Right." I clicked off the cell phone. It wouldn't be so bad if I actually knew what his middle name was. Or was sure that his real name was Jake Porter.

But at this point I had to settle for the reassurance that what had gone down last night had been directly related to him and had nothing to do with me.

Somehow I didn't think it was going to help me sleep any better tonight. . . .

I STOOD OUTSIDE THE FRONT of my apartment building, considering the black cat that had followed me the entire ten blocks from the agency.

"If I didn't know better, I'd think that something was on your mind," I said.

Merely saying the sentence aloud made my skin crawl.

"But of course that's ridiculous, isn't it? Because you're a cat and I'm a human, and we don't even speak the same language, much less exist on the same level."

The fearless feline seemed to regard me with boredom as it plopped its bottom down on the sidewalk and bit and then licked its hind leg.

"Okay," I said. "I'll give you some food. I don't know what I have in the house, but I'll find something. But then you've got to go."

It took me all of three minutes to go upstairs, stare at a growling Muffy, open a can of sardines in oil, then make my way back downstairs.

"Here . . ." I put the can nearer the grassy area next to the steps.

The cat didn't budge from where it was still sitting in the middle of the walk.

Great. A finicky cat. Go figure.

I picked up the can and held it close to its nose. It seemed to take interest.

I put the can back down near the grass.

The cat remained sitting, looking at me expectantly.

"Fine." I sighed heavily and put the can down directly in front of it.

It began eating.

I took the opportunity to pet it gently, all the while inching around the collar it wore so I could see the metal tag.

"T," it read on one side. Nothing on the other.

Well, that was helpful. The letter *T* could stand for just about any name, male or female. And since I wasn't about to look up the cat's furry butt, I decided to make him male.

"Hey, Tee?" I said, running my fingers down his coarse fur. "Where do you come from?"

There wasn't a license number or any other identifying marks on the tag, only the letter. Which would help me not at all in locating his owner.

He sidestepped my touch and began growling.

I snapped upright.

I wasn't sure how I felt about having two animals I fed growling at me.

Yes, I did know. I didn't like it much.

"Okay, I'm going to go now. So once you're done . . . scoot. Go back home. Return to where you came from, all right?"

The cat sat down and began licking his paw and cleaning his face.

Aw.

I tried to pet him again, and he batted at me.

So un-aw.

"Right."

I took the can away, put it near the grass, and then stalked toward my car, having had it with growling animals and unresponsive Australian bounty hunters with exploding trucks.

A while later, I sat outside the Bryer house in Forest Hills.

I went through my notes even as I waited for movement at the Bryer house. Only I didn't get far because a black BMW pulled into the long driveway and stopped next to the walk to the front door rather than driving around to the garage.

I got out of my Mustang, affixing my fake reporter credentials to my belt, hoping that I'd get something out of Valerie's father. . . .

Twenty

"IF YOU DON'T GET OFF my property now, I'll call the police and have you forcibly removed."

I stared at Richard Bryer as if he had a monster mole under his left nostril. "You don't understand—"

"I don't understand? Don't insult my intelligence. From day one the media has pretended to care, but you don't. It's all about what will sell more papers, commercials, anything and everything to make money. But when we needed you, you were nowhere to be found."

Maybe it hadn't been such a good idea to impersonate a reporter in this case.

Then again, I don't think I'd have gotten any further had I identified myself as a PI hired to clear the defendant accused of killing his daughter.

Still, I figured it was worth a try.

"Mr. Bryer, please. I apologize for misrepresenting myself, but I'm not a reporter." I held up the fake ID and then tucked it into my pocket. "My name's Sofie Metropolis, and I was hired by Melinda Laughton to independently investigate the case."

If I'd thought he was upset before, the high color that rushed to his face told me I just might be in physical danger now.

Ooops.

"Get out of here. Get out of here now or I won't be responsible for what I do next."

He took an ominous step forward, and I followed by taking one backward, casually aware of the weight of my firearm under my jacket. "Look, Mr. Bryer, I'm sorry for your loss. But have you ever considered that Johnny might be innocent?"

He took another step forward, and I noticed the curling of his hands into fists.

"Did you know that another girl, who shares a lot in common with your Valerie, has just gone missing? A year to the day?"

He blinked bloodshot eyes as if I'd thrown a McDonald's cup of ice over his head.

"That's right, Mr. Bryer. The girl just went missing."

I didn't know what I hoped to accomplish by sharing the information. I wasn't even convinced that the two occurrences were linked. But at this point, I'd say whatever I could to get more information. Information the prosecution didn't have and the defense might not know.

All at once Richard seemed to crumple in on himself, putting his hand back just in time so that when he dropped, he sat on the low brick wall surrounding the front shrubs rather than in the shrubs themselves. His head was bent low, and his shoulders seemed to be shaking.

This was a new one.

I'd known when I'd accepted the case that it would be unlike any other I'd worked until that point. And if visiting Little Johnny in the county lockup weren't enough of a reminder, watching this man, this father, collapse certainly was.

I hesitantly reached out and touched his shoulder. "I'm sorry, Mr. Bryer. Is there someone I can call? Is someone in the house? Your wife, maybe? Son?"

He didn't respond for a long moment, and then he shook his head. "No. There's no one. We haven't been much of a family since Valerie . . . disappeared."

"I understand," I said, but I wondered if anyone could truly understand the depth of grief of a parent that had lost a child. Especially in such an indefinite way. There had been no body to identify. To bury.

"Maybe we should go inside?" I asked. "Get you something to drink. A glass of water, perhaps?"

"Yes, yes," he said, as if suddenly realizing we were outside in public where the neighbors might see.

I looked around as he unlocked the front door and motioned for me to enter, then I followed him to the kitchen. I was struck by the number of framed photographs everywhere of Valerie. In the expected places like the fireplace mantel and in unexpected places like on the wall next to the kitchen table.

I rubbed my arms against the autumn chill that existed between the changing of seasons and the time the furnace was switched on to chase it away. I looked through a couple of cupboards next to the sink, found a glass, and filled it with filtered tap water. I handed it to Richard Bryer where he had sat on a stool next to the large island.

"I keep thinking it will get better," he said, taking the glass but not drinking from it. "That I'll wake up one morning and remember only the good, and the bad will have faded away." He shook his head, staring at something I couldn't see. "But it doesn't. It only seems to get worse."

"The grieving process works differently for everyone," I said softly, taking the stool next to him.

"Johnny was a good boy," he said long moments later. "We all loved him. He was like part of the family. That day . . . it was like we lost two children instead of one."

I was surprised by his words. Surprised he'd have anything nice to say about the boy . . . man accused of killing his daughter.

I didn't know what to say, so I said nothing.

"Is it true? Has another girl gone missing?"

I nodded.

He closed his eyes tightly. "God, I remember when my wife and I called the police to report Valerie's disappearance." He swallowed hard, and I motioned for him to drink his water. He took a sip.

"Where is your wife, Mr. Bryer?"

"I don't know. I came home to pick up some papers I forgot this morning. I didn't expect her to be here. The first few months after it became clear Valerie was dead, she wouldn't come out of our bedroom. Now . . . now she won't step into it."

A little more information than I was looking for. Or, rather, not the type of information I needed.

I took a card out of my pocket. "Do you have a pen?"

Richard appeared not to recognize the item I'd asked for, then he felt around his jacket and took out the pen I'd seen in his front shirt pocket. I accepted it.

"This is my business card. I'm writing my cell phone number on the back. Call me if you can think of anything you think might help."

I slid it across the counter along with his pen.

I knew that asking a man who couldn't seem to help himself to help me—and by extension Johnny—likely wouldn't yield results, but I felt compelled to do something.

I rose from the stool. "Have you and your wife considered grief counseling?"

He dropped his chin to his chest again. "No."

"Maybe you should."

I rested my hand against his shoulder again. He didn't shy away. In fact, he seemed to take some comfort in the simple touch.

"There's nothing wrong in asking for help, Richard. Nothing at all."

He nodded.

Since there wasn't anything else for me to say, I let myself quietly out of the house, taking in all the photographs of young Valerie again as I went. Once I'd closed the door, I paused, realizing that the house had felt more like a mausoleum than a home. The pictures indicated that hadn't always been the case.

As I walked back to my Mustang parked on the street, I thought about how the Greeks handled grief. Usually there was much wailing over the body of a loved one. So much so that if you were an outsider, you might think that kind of emotional depth was impossible and that perhaps the display was orchestrated. I know that I once did. Until I came to understand that somehow over the millennia, the Greeks had learned to tap into the grief and allowed it escape. There was the initial burial, then the forty-day observation, when it was believed the soul actually left the body. The women wore black out of respect for the deceased—for months when the lost one was a sibling, for life when it was a spouse—and the men wore black armbands.

I'd thought the traditional arcane. But I was beginning to understand that perhaps it was a step-by-step process for grieving. By creating milestones and guidelines and setting aside time designated specifically for mourning, perhaps the process was made a little easier. "Easy" being a relative term, of course. Because I didn't think the word should come anywhere near what Richard was experiencing.

Speaking of forty-day observances, I recalled that Uncle Tolly's should be coming up soon.

I climbed into my car and closed the door, feeling oddly distanced from my own life. But as I started the engine and drove away, I began to feel better. Almost as if Richard Bryer's grief had manifested itself in some sort of invisible cloud and had caught me up in it. And the farther away I moved from it, the better I could breathe.

I WAS HALFWAY BETWEEN THE Bryer house and my next stop when my cell phone vibrated in my jacket pocket. I fished it out and looked at the display. My mother.

I sighed and answered. "Hi, Mom."

"Hi, Mom? Hi, Mom? I haven't heard from you in two days and this is how you address me?"

I grimaced and flicked on the blinker to turn left onto Northern Boulevard. I could have taken Grand Central, but I thought I was too distracted to be driving in fast-moving traffic.

Besides, I needed the extra time to shake off the emotions inspired by my visit with Richard Bryer.

"I've been busy, and I'm busy now. What do you want, Mom?" I asked.

Silence.

Okay, I knew I was being abrupt with her. I put it down to my ignoring my original reaction to Efi's telling me that my mother had tried a matchmaking sleight of hand. That pretty much worked.

As well as the fact that I had yet to confront that particular part of my life.

I bit my lip to keep from apologizing.

"I need a ride to the *saranta* tomorrow," my mother said.

I was surprised that she didn't try to play the guilt card in regard to my behavior. Instead she was asking me to take her to Uncle Tolly's forty-day observation.

I sighed, thinking of a million other things I could do with my time. Then I remembered Bryer and said, "What time do you want me to pick you up?"

She told me, and I was about to end the call when she asked, "Sofia, are you all right?"

I paused.

Was I all right? I was functioning. So I supposed in that regard I was okay.

So I told her, "I'm fine."

I didn't ask her why, partly because I was afraid of what she might say. Mostly because I didn't want to hear what she might say.

"Look, Mom, I've got to go. I'll see you tomorrow, okay?"

She told me it was, and I ended the call.

I tossed the cell to the passenger seat and then tightened both hands on the wheel. Right about now I might have conversed with Muffy, who had been more with me than not over the past few months. But now he didn't even seem to register when I came back to the apartment, much less try to follow me out.

Merely having him with me often relieved whatever pressure I was feeling. I supposed because with another person—or in this case an animal—present, it was hard to hide from yourself. One cock-headed look from him, and I realized how ridiculous I sounded or was acting and would adjust accordingly.

Now I was without such a mirror or filter. Which meant I was free to marinate in whatever ridiculous juices I wanted to.

I found myself in East Elmhurst near LaGuardia, the scream of a landing plane passing overhead making me duck, I was so out of it. I mumbled something as I caught a couple of kids in a neighboring car laughing at me. I repressed the urge to stick my tongue out at them—or worse, flip them the bird—and tried to remember what I was doing over here.

Oh, yes. The witness list.

Since my interview of the pizza joint waitress had gotten me little more than I already knew, I didn't expect my conversation with the next witness to go any differently.

I parked near the address listed and got out, squinting at the high, chain-link fence that bordered the commercial property that stretched at least half an acre. I could barely make out the words SACKETT LANDSCAPING on the dented, faded white sign with red lettering attached to the open gate.

"Hello?" I called out, hesitant to enter the open gravel parking area without permission.

A machine was running in the far left-hand corner of the area next to lines of saplings and shrugs, some planted, some propped up, revealing burlap-covered root-balls. A shed that spanned about the length of a two-and-half-car garage was to my right, the double doors standing open, revealing various pieces of lawn equipment. I guessed that whoever was present was probably running the noisy apparatus and couldn't hear me. I shielded my eyes against the watery sunlight. Yes, there. The same man I'd seen working at the Bryers' place earlier in the week.

I took a step closer, stopped, and then looked around. Oh, well. If my choices were to wait for him to finish or to trespass, I'd choose the latter and take my chances.

"Hello?" I tapped on the guy's shoulder.

The gears on the machine made a sickening grinding sound as he looked at me. I smiled, since words were pretty much useless given the racket.

After a few moments, he finished feeding a branch about eight inches in diameter into what I figured was a wood-chipping machine and then switched it off and turned to face me.

"Hi," I said, extending my hand. "I'm Sofie Metropolis, and I'm following up on a few things on the Laughton case. I was wondering if you wouldn't mind answering a few questions?"

"I know who you are," he said, taking off his gloves one by one and then pointedly ignoring my outstretched hand. "You're trying to get that boy off for killing his girlfriend. Personally, I think that what happened to her should happen to him."

Okay, so the guy was creepy. Certainly that wasn't against the law. Was it? I mean, if it were, a good percentage of the city's denizens would be candidates for a spot behind bars.

He was maybe forty-five, fifty, his hair shot through with strands of gray, and it looked as if he hadn't shaved for a good four, five days.

And what was that smell? Extreme body odor mixed with the scent of chipped wood and . . . was that cat spray? Or maybe the combination made him smell as if he'd been doused by a dozen stray felines.

"Excuse me?" I said.

He'd begun walking away from me toward the metal shed some thirty feet away.

"I'm not sure I heard you correctly."

"Oh, you heard me just fine," he said. He turned inside the shed and shook his finger at me. "Mr. Thompson told me I should steer clear of you."

Great. The assistant DA knew who I was and that I was asking around and had warned his witnesses not to talk to me. Probably Gwen Stefani had called him right after I left yesterday.

I rubbed the back of my neck as I looked around the place, trying to figure out where I went from there.

"So you're convinced Johnny is guilty, then?" I tried.

"Hell, yes, he's guilty. He killed that poor girl as surely as I'm standing in front of you."

"How can you be so sure?"

"Because I saw him do it."

Twenty-one

"WHAT DO YOU MEAN, YOU saw him do it?" I said, pretending to refer to notes that I didn't have.

Was he serious? Was he an actual eyewitness to the murder? Or to the abduction?

Given the attention I was paying to everything that crossed my desk lately, I found it incredible to think that this guy had slipped through my fingers. Surely if he was an eyewitness, his name would be at the top of somebody's list. At the very least, Gene Shipley's. And there would have been some mention along the way in the media pieces I'd reviewed.

Floyd washed his hands at a large, industrial-size aluminum sink with an attached counter and began drying them with an old gray towel. "I saw that boy put his hands around her neck and give her a good shake. I saw him talk to her without respect. I saw him yelling at her the night she disappeared."

"Did you see John Warren Laughton abduct Valerie Bryer, Mr. Sackett? Did you bear witness to her murder?"

He didn't answer me right away. His avoidance was enough to inspire a slight breath of relief.

Just a blowhard who wanted to see the murderer pay and was convinced John was that man.

Which explained why no one was taking the guy seriously. He might not even make a great prosecution witness if he went off at the mouth the way he had with me.

"I see," I said, flipping my pad closed.

"What exactly do you see, Miss Metropolis?" he asked me as he wiped the towel over his grizzled face. "I've worked for the Bryers for over three years. I watched that little girl grow into a young woman. And now she's gone."

"And you've already tried and convicted Johnny for a crime he may not even have committed."

He leered at me, revealing teeth that were in just as bad shape as the rest of him. Blech. "You said 'may.'"

"What?"

"You said 'may not have committed.' So even you believe that boy did it."

"I didn't say that."

"You didn't have to."

Maybe. But I didn't like that he'd gotten the jump on me. I was there to get the jump on him. If indeed there was any jumping to be done.

"So you'll be testifying for the prosecution, then?" I asked, stepping farther into the shed and pretending an interest in the tools hanging on the walls. Despite his disheveled personal appearance, he kept a neat shop.

"Of course I'll be testifying."

"I trust they're coaching you."

"I don't need no coaching."

I gave him a long look.

He grumbled and made a lot of racket as he tossed a tool to the table he stood in front of.

I suspected that the prosecution team had already led him through what they intended to ask him as well as anything the defense attorney might confront him with. I wondered if Shipley knew how volatile the witness was. How easy it would be to trip him up and have him do more damage than good to the prosecutor's case, even though the opposite was intended.

I scratched my arm as I stepped closer to the corner.

"I wouldn't take another step if I were you," Sackett said.

"Oh?" I did just that. "Why not?"

"Because this is an old place and the flooring needs to be re-done over there."

I stared at the boards under my feet.

"I heard about you," Sackett said. "Shot your own client in the knee, if I remember correctly." He shrugged as he sharpened a pair of shears. "I'm not saying he didn't deserve it. Probably did. But you might want to be a little more careful which snakes you poke around at."

I found it interesting that he used the same terminology Porter had when he'd warned me away from the Papadakis case.

"Yes, well, I've always fancied myself a bit of a snake person," I said, coming to stand across the table from him. I took a business card from my pocket and put it on the rough plank of plywood that was laid on top. I didn't bother writing my cell phone number on the back, and the only information on the front was the agency's. "Should you, you know, feel like talking about any actual evidence you might have, or remember any real events, give me a call."

I exited the shed and blinked at the bright light. I hadn't realized it was so dark in there.

"Hey, sweetheart," Sackett called. "That boy should be going to the electric chair for what he did."

Maybe, I thought as I continued walking without acknowledging him.

If Little Johnny had indeed killed his girlfriend, then he should go to prison for life without the possibility of parole, at least. Which was the maximum he could get since New York no longer had the death penalty.

The trouble I was having was proving either way if he had or hadn't done it.

Twenty-two

MY MOTHER WAS HER USUAL chatty self when I picked her up to go to Uncle Tolly's *saranta* the following evening. I told myself that was a good thing.

In all honesty, I wasn't really ready for the coming confrontation. And I didn't fool myself into thinking I'd skate through tonight without running headlong into it. I'd been working nonstop on the Laughton case since yesterday, poring over materials, working out possible motivations, and even calling the police detective in charge of Johnny's arrest. (Now that had been a lesson in futility. I hadn't expected him to roll out the red carpet for me; nor had I expected the cold shoulder I'd received. It seemed word was definitely out that I was working on the defendant's behalf. And those who'd already made up their minds as to his guilt weren't about to help me prove otherwise.)

I was tired and overworked, with little to show for my efforts. The combination didn't bode well for the next hour or so I would spend in my mother's company.

"Sofie, you're not even listening to me."

"Huh?"

"My point exactly." Thalia gave a heavy sigh and readjusted her purse in her lap. "Head of stone, that's what you have."

I gaped at her even as I parked the car. "What did you just say?"

She looked at me unblinkingly. "You know, don't you?"

I pretended I didn't have a clue what she was talking about.

"About Dino. You know." She held up a hand as if to stop me from saying anything, but I was genuinely speechless. "Don't ask me how I know you know, how you might have figured it out, but . . ."

She sighed heavily, as if she were the victim of her meddling scheme to match me up with somebody else not even six months after my disastrous wedding day.

"Yes, that also means that I know about you and Dino." She smiled wistfully. "It was written all over your face that first day at dinner. Not that you would have ever admitted it, mind you." She shook her head. "You've always been a stubborn child."

I knew she was using the word *child* as in I was one of her children, not that I was immature, but I still couldn't help but feel that it could have done double duty.

"*I'm* stubborn," I repeated. "*I'm* stubborn? This from the woman who could have been separated at birth from her twin the Energizer Bunny, because you keep going and going and going no matter the consequences."

"My poor dead mother had a difficult time birthing me." She crossed herself three times in quick succession as she whispered the Holy Trinity.

I gave an eye roll. "Oh no, you don't. You're not going to make me feel guilty now. Not this time. I was speaking metaphorically about your long-lost twin."

I shut off the engine and pocketed my car keys.

"Do you have any idea how angry you make me?" I asked her. She blinked, as if surprised at my words.

"Yes, that's right. Angry. Frustrated. You interfere in my life constantly. You're completely incapable of allowing it to unfold on its own."

"Let me ask you one question, Sofia."

"No. No more questions. Haven't you asked enough already? Haven't you done enough?" I was gesturing with my hands as if the mere act of doing so would stay her. "You've always tried to control my life. Always. If not outright, in obvious ways by forbidding me from doing something, or trying to sway me to your way, then by covert actions. Do you know how frustrating it is to think that I have absolutely no control over my own life? That even when I think I'm making a decision for myself that I'm afraid that somewhere, somehow, you had a hand in it?"

I discovered I was out of breath. I'd never been so upset with my mother. And perhaps that fact was enough to keep her quiet. At least for a couple of moments.

"I swear, sometimes I think I hate you."

I wanted to retract the words the instant they exited my mouth. The trouble was that like birds, once words flew away, you could never catch them again.

And this particular bird had just dumped a load on my mother's head.

The expression of shock and disbelief and pain she wore twisted my stomach into one gigantic knot.

I groaned inwardly. Hell, I didn't need my mother to manufacture things to make me feel guilty. I was quite capable of doing that all on my own.

Still, I bit my tongue to keep from offering up an apology. I hadn't said I hated her. I'd said that sometimes I felt as though I hated her. And that was true enough.

I stared through the window at passersby, feeling detached from them and the world at large as I waited for Thalia's response.

I don't know how I expected my mother to react. Perhaps by saying something to deepen my guilt, like she wished she had her mother to love, much less hate. Or berate me for using such an ugly word.

Instead she stayed quiet.

A new tactic that was proving very effective.

I closed my eyes and sighed. "What? What do you want to ask me?"

That appeared to be what she was waiting for. "Do you love Constantinos?"

I felt as if someone had just shoved me headfirst into an ice machine. "What?" I whispered.

"You heard me, Sofia. Do you love him?"

I didn't know what to say. I only knew that she'd found a way to cut right to the heart of the matter. Or, more accurately, find my heart.

I felt her hand on mine. "What I'm trying to say is, what does it matter who did what? What does it matter that I'm the one responsible for your meeting and that I'd meant him for you all along?"

"You made me feel like I was a *yerotokori*," I whispered. "Told me those men were for Efi."

She patted my hand. "I know, I know. I'm sorry for that. But it was the only way I knew how to make you open your eyes. Because once you get an idea into that head of yours, it's impossible to get it out. And if I'd introduced Dino as a possible match for you, you would have found a way to chase him away, make him not like you, and you would never have seen the potential he has." She smiled. "And he has such wonderful potential."

"Because he's from the same area of Greece that Dad's family is?"

"Because he's a wonderful man with a great smile, a good business, and a warm heart. And, you have to admit, he's . . . what is the word you kids use nowadays? Macho."

I tucked my chin into my chest and laughed. "Hot, Mom. The word is hot."

"Mmm."

I looked over to find her smiling warmly at me, although a smear of her earlier pain remained.

I turned my head away. "I'm not seeing him anymore."

She took a deep breath and let it out slowly. "Like I said, stubborn."

"Maybe," I said. "And maybe not. It's more . . . complicated than that. It's not really something I can discuss, but . . . well, there are some things I need to work out."

Thalia nodded. "I understand."

I squinted at her, getting the uncanny feeling that she did.

"Let's get this over with," she said. "The sooner we go in, the sooner we can leave."

I was all for that.

GREEK FUNERALS AND DEATH TRADITIONS might help immediate family with the grieving process, but for secondary people they were trying at best. Don't get me wrong, I had been very fond of Uncle Tolly. Well, up until he almost got me killed, anyway. And even then I hadn't been able to stay mad at him for long. But despite the violent way he'd died, I'd moved well on down the road in the forty days since his death. So having to revisit a time I would just as soon forget was a little disconcerting. Especially in light of my conversation with my mother in the car.

Since the Pappas house had been destroyed in the explosion, the Widow Vardis had agreed to host the *saranta* following the traditional visit to the cemetery to pay our final, final respects to the deceased. Tolly's wife, Aglaia, was seated at Mrs. Vardis' side on a couch as people milled past. Coffee was being served, and memorial bread was being handed out.

The *saranta* was generally reserved for close family members, but since Uncle Tolly and Aglaia had no family in the States, the women of the church had made sure that there would be a presence. And they'd done a good job. In addition to the women, a few older men that had known Uncle Tolly wore black armbands and sat sipping their Greek coffee. All in all, a respectable turnout.

I offered my prayers to Aglaia and moved on to allow the next person in line to approach. The young male voice surprised me. I looked back and saw that it was Panayiotis Rokkos, Tony DiPiazza's Greek second in command and the one responsible for bringing so much chaos to my life a few months back.

He'd *really* wanted to see me in those cement overshoes.

I chose a spot in the dining room well away from him, yet close enough to watch. After the explosion that had claimed Uncle Tolly's life, there were murmurings that I'd been wrong, that the dry cleaner had been laundering more than clothes for the Mob, and that ultimately he'd been made to pay.

I disagreed with them on the why. But on who might be responsible . . . well, let's just say that I suspected that Rokko had a vengeance streak a mile wide and I wouldn't put it past him to act on his own during Tony's yearlong exile to the old country.

I made a face and sipped my own traditional coffee, although I would have preferred a frappé. Rokko caught me looking at him. He gave me a smile that was one hundred percent evil.

Okay, all this was coming to resemble a Mario Puzo novel a little too much. Only there were no characters for whom to root. Except maybe me. But I'd prefer not to give myself a recurring role in this particular story.

And if things weren't bad enough already, I watched as Rokko made his way toward me.

"Hey, Sofie," he said in a low, mocking voice. "I hear you still haven't turned up that stiff."

The missing body had been brought up by nearly everyone I'd spoken to since entering the house, including Aglaia, the topic being more popular than the man we were commemorating.

"Hey, Rokko, I hear you still haven't looked up the definition of deodorant."

I knew it probably wasn't a good idea to antagonize the man I was afraid was responsible for Uncle Tolly's death, despite the ruling of accident, but I couldn't help myself. The guy had always rubbed me the wrong way, even back in school.

The difference was that back in school I could take him.

I probably still could . . . as long as the guns were left at home.

Unfortunately, I feared Rokko slept with an arsenal under his pillow. And had his goon sidekicks present at all times.

I moved away from him to claim another corner in the living room, out of his line of vision.

"Are you ready?" my mother asked at my elbow.

I raised my brows. I'd figured she would have liked to stick around until the event drew to a natural close. Instead, she wanted to leave.

Huhn.

Not that I was complaining. The quicker I put some distance between me and Rokko the better.

"Let's go," I said, putting down my coffee cup and leading the way to the door.

IT APPEARED EVERYONE AND THEIR brother was home on this Saturday night, parked cars choking the streets so that I had to hunt for a space. I found one two blocks away from my place and climbed out of the car, looking around as I buttoned up my jacket. Doors and windows were shut tight against the cold weather . . . and likely the eerie atmosphere I felt like a cloud around me. It had gotten a little warm today, and a light fog now made everything look hazy. Usually warmly lit lamps emerged dangerous beacons. Simple footsteps sounded like the frenetic shuffling footfalls of a stalker or ghoul.

Of course, it didn't escape my attention that I'd parked across the street from the Romanoff house. I stuffed my hands into my jacket pockets, ignoring the old black Lincoln Continental with its suicide doors that was parked out front and that there appeared to be no lights on in the place. A curtain moved in the front window. I sucked in a breath and quickened my pace.

Okay, I knew it was the fact that Halloween was only a few

days away that heightened my manufactured fear of things that go bump in the night. But that wasn't helping to smooth my gooseflesh any.

Or erasing my brief exchange with Rokko earlier that evening.

I didn't for a moment think that he or the rest of Tony's goons had anything to do with the missing body, no matter how much he would like me to believe otherwise.

The explosion that had taken Uncle Tolly's life was another matter entirely.

The squeak of a screen door spring made my spine ice over. I glanced over to watch as shadows moved on Romanoff's porch. I ducked behind the trunk of a nearby tree, watching. My imagination? Probably. If someone came up behind me and said "boo," I'd probably jump high enough to clutch the tree's upper branches and scream at the top of my lungs.

There! It had been Romanoff's house.

Three figures in long black coats and old fedora-style hats moved one following the other down the stairs. They appeared to float instead of walk as they made their way to the car. The fog didn't help any. I could barely make out the features of Romanoff, his creepy nephew Vladimir, and . . . I didn't recognize the third one beyond that he was young, like Vlad. The doors to the vehicle opened and closed, *clap, clap, clap,* with the nephew at the wheel. The headlights switched on, seeming to spotlight my position behind the tree. I jerked back, the bark biting my skin through my jacket. Strangely, I was out of breath as I listened to the car switch into gear and begin to move. I chanced a peek to find the car parallel with me, the nephew's eyes seeming to glow red as he looked at me.

Then, finally, it was the red of the taillights I stared at before the car and the three creepy men in it disappeared around the next corner.

I stayed where I was for a long moment, ordering my heart to beat normally.

"Get a grip, Sofie," I whispered as I pushed myself from the tree. "There are no such things as vampires."

No matter what Rosie said and my own unforgettable experience with the coffin/cello crate in Romanoff's basement a few months back.

For two minutes I'd felt like a little kid out by herself late at night for the first time. Now that I was fully back in adult mode, I walked toward my place with renewed confidence.

Or at least feigned confidence.

It was unnerving that I could still conjure up things that frightened me to such a degree. I mean, wasn't there some point when you knew exactly what was what and who was who without jumping out of your skin at every strange sound?

I hoped so.

A car passed slowly on the street as I slid my key into the door to my building. I took notice, waiting until it moved on before hurrying inside and closing the door soundly.

Rokko. It had to be. Not necessarily in the car that had passed, but my run-in with him earlier had me on edge. Hey, being fitted for cement overshoes had that kind of impact on a girl. So shoot me.

Then again, no. Don't shoot me. I still had so much life left to live. So much to look forward to. Take the whole Dino situation, for example. I mean, did I love him, as my mother had asked? Was it possible that I had fallen for a guy that I probably

wouldn't have looked at twice had I known about the truth behind our "chance" meeting?

And then there was Jake. . . .

I climbed the stairs, so not ready to consider that angle just
now. I mean, didn't I have enough on my plate? Did I really
want to go piling more on top?

I punched the button to switch on the hall lights. Nothing. I
stood staring up the stairwell. Oh, I so did not need this right
now. I punched the button again, then again and again, to no
avail.

I sighed heavily, the sound filling the otherwise silent stairwell. There wasn't even music coming from the DeVry students'
2B apartment. And there was always music coming from their
apartment.

My eyesight adjusted to the dimness, and I gripped the
handrail, suppressing the urge to take my Glock out of my purse.
Okay, so there was a short in the lines or something. I'd call the
electrician and have him come take a look first thing Monday?

I'd cleared the first staircase and punched the button there.
Again nothing. Not that I expected a different result, but you
never knew.

I turned to walk up the final flight when someone grabbed
me from behind.

If I'd thought my heart had been beating loudly on the street,
now it practically knocked a hole through the wall of my chest.
One gloved hand covered my mouth, the other squeezed my
waist so tightly that I could barely breathe. The smell of something pungent filled my nose. Bleach? Fingernail polish re-
mover? I didn't know.

Chloroform, my mind settled on. But I couldn't be sure. The

only place I'd known the chemical to be used was in old movies. Where did you even buy the stuff? Could you make it at home?

I dug my boot heel into the top of the foot of the guy holding me (I was reasonably sure it was a guy because of his height and the solid wall of his chest against my back and was pretty sure I also felt something else a little lower that I wasn't equipped to consider just then). He growled and held me closer.

"Let sleeping dogs lie," a low, male voice said into my ear. He jerked my head back farther. "Drop the case."

Then the world went black. . . .

Twenty-three

"MAYBE YOU SHOULD GO TO the hospital."

I sat on the front stoop, my head in my hands, just glad for the fresh air filling my lungs. I didn't know how long I was out, but when I came to, Pino was standing over me, Mrs. Nebitz behind him, along with every resident in the apartment building. For a moment, I'd thought I was trapped in a bizarre nightmare where everyone's toilets had overflowed at the same time and I'd lost the number to the plumber.

I shook my head and then regretted the move when it aggravated the throbbing at my temples. Why did I have the feeling aspirin wasn't going to take care of this one?

"No . . . no. The paramedic says I should be all right, but that if I start to feel worse—experience acute dizziness or nausea—then I should call an ambulance."

Pino crossed his arms.

It was then I realized that he had yet to hike up his pants once during the half hour since he'd first arrived on the scene.

Not only that, but he appeared to have gotten longer slacks. He looked almost . . . normal.

I raised my brows and looked into his face.

"You still haven't said who you think it was," he said.

"No, I haven't."

And I wasn't going to, either. Not if what I feared was true and that Rokko was playing renegade Greek Mob heavy and was collecting on outstanding debts.

I shivered and looked over my shoulder at the apartment front. Thankfully, all the residents had gone back inside, including Mrs. Nebitz, although I was pretty sure Pino had paid a price for making her do so. I wouldn't be surprised if she'd whacked him with her walking cane as he said, "Fun's over, everyone. Go back to your apartments."

This wasn't anywhere near what Mrs. Nebitz would call fun. It wasn't exactly my definition of the word, either. But there you had it. Another ugly night in the life and times of Sofie Metropolis, PI.

"Anything more on the missing body case?" he asked.

I shook my head. "Nope. Nothing."

I was reasonably sure my attacker had been Rokko. The events leading up to the hallway meeting were too much of a coincidence. I'd run into him at Tolly's *saranta*. He'd made a crack about the missing stiff. And then assaulted me in the hallway of my own apartment building to warn me away from the case.

I took a deep breath and immediately started coughing. I could still smell the chemicals in my nostrils and tasted them at the back of my throat. I hoped a nice long hot shower would get rid of it. Along with the chill that had settled into my bone marrow.

"You sure you don't want to go to the hospital?"

"I'm sure, Pino. Are we done?"

He looked around and appeared ready to hike up his pants before he caught himself. "Yeah. I guess we are."

I pushed myself up. "Good night, then."

"Good night."

The door had been propped open, and I removed the stop so it would close after I went in.

"Metro?"

I sighed. "What?"

Pino reached around me. "Here. That's my personal cell phone number. If you need anything . . . well, you know."

I squinted at the slip of paper, half-afraid to take it. Personal numbers usually were attached to personal relationships. And I wanted absolutely nothing of a personal connection to the man behind me.

Still, I took the number. Given my recent experience, I seemed to have temporarily lost my sarcasm button.

"Thanks, Pino."

I went inside and let the door close behind me, slowly taking the stairs up to my apartment. I wasn't surprised to find Mrs. Nebitz's door open.

"I think maybe you should have gone to the hospital, Sofie," she said, coming out into the hall.

"I'm all right, Mrs. Nebitz. Really, I am." Or I would be, right after a shower and a long night's sleep.

"Here," she said. "I made you a cup of tea. Old Jewish remedy."

I tried for a smile and accepted the glass. "Thank you."

"You'll let me know how you're doing in the morning?"

"I'm sure I'll be fine."

"Just the same."

I nodded and started unlocking my door, an awkward move without the use of both hands.

"This wouldn't have anything to do with the favor I asked of you, would it?" Mrs. Nebitz asked.

It took me a moment to remember what favor. My muddled brain came up with at least five, ranging from taking out her trash for her to being present when the cable repair guy stopped by to make sure he wouldn't try to hoodwink her by talking her into getting a hundred extra channels she didn't need.

Then I realized she was talking about her grandson Seth and his mysterious girlfriend.

"No, I'm sure it doesn't, Mrs. Nebitz." I finally managed to open the door. "Good night."

"Good night, Sofie. Get some rest."

"You, too."

"Rest. That I've had plenty of. What I'd like are answers."

Wouldn't we all? I responded silently.

I closed the door and searched blindly for the light switch on the wall to my left. The sound of Muffy's growling from across the room gave me pause.

The feel of something brushing against my ankle gave me reason to jump.

I flipped the switch and found myself staring down at the black cat named Tee.

CRIPES. WHAT WAS I GOING to do with a cat?

I glanced at where Muffy sat in his favorite chair. Correction:

He wasn't so much sitting in it as he was guarding it, probably from the trespassing feline.

I stood in the middle of my living room, mulling over the dilemma as I took in the dining room window that I'd left open ten inches so Muffy could have access to the fire escape and the roof behind to do his business. I had little doubt that's how the cat had gotten inside. But how? The fire escape didn't go all the way down to the ground unless the last ladder was released.

Of course, my brain was in no condition to work out the hows and the whys. Only to accept that there was a cat in my apartment and I had to decide what to do with it.

I walked into the kitchen and opened the freezer, taking out an ice tray and dumping the contents into a towel hanging on the stove handle. I must have hit the back of my head but good when I fell because a goose egg . . . well, the size of a goose egg had popped up. The paramedic said I didn't have a concussion but that I should be careful anyway. I lifted the back of my hair and gingerly pressed the ice pack against the lump, cringing as I did so. The sound of crunching caught my attention, and I found that Tee was making quick work of Muffy's food bowl.

Huhn.

Could dog food hurt a cat? Then again, considering that the black cat was the same size as the Jack Russell terrier, and the food I bought for him was of the small nugget variety, I supposed it couldn't hurt. I mean, how different could the animals be physiologically?

Another question I was ill equipped to answer just then.

"How long have you been here, boy?" I asked as I attempted to peer up the cat's behind, failed, and then scratched him behind the ears instead. He pulled away slightly. When I removed my hand, he went back to the food.

Muffy continued growling from his Barcalounger. With any luck, the two would keep a good distance from each other while I took that shower I was longing for and crawled into bed for what I hoped would be sleep that was scent and bogeyman free. The rest . . . well, the rest I could deal with in the morning.

As Scarlett O'Hara had said, "Tomorrow is another day."

I could only pray that it would resemble today not at all.

"NO CONNECTION WHATSOEVER," MY COUSIN Pete said the following morning.

He'd been waiting for me at the agency when I got in at eight and tailed me into my uncle's office. Normally, the office was closed on Sundays, but I'd requested that everyone report for at least a half day, what with the Laughton case still active. And apparently Pete—the man who'd never worked an honest day in his life prior to my hiring him—was turning into a regular workaholic.

"Wait a minute," I said, holding up my hand. I shrugged out of my jacket and holster and put both on the office chair before going out into the other room to fix myself a frappé.

I'd woken up that morning with two animals in my bed that were not of the human variety. Unfortunately. Then again, given my experience with Jake Porter, maybe it was just as well.

I'd expected to find Muffy in his usual place, but instead I'd looked down to find that Tee had claimed it, chasing Muffy to the other side of my legs. If I'd been a thinking woman, the sight might have caused me concern. Instead, I'd clapped my hands, chasing them both off the bed, got dressed, filled the dog bowls with food and water, and then left the apartment to them to do with what they would.

I stuck a straw into my travel cup and sipped deeply. Ah, yes. There were few things that could rejuvenate me faster than a nice cold frappé, no matter how chilly the weather.

"Did you hear what I said?" Pete asked when I reentered the office.

"I heard you. I don't know what you're talking about, but I definitely heard you."

"There's no connection between the Bryer girl and the Greenberg girl that went missing the other day."

I frowned. "Are you sure?"

He stared at me.

"Right." Had I really just asked the biggest conspiracy theorist I knew if he was sure there was no connection between two strangers? I'd half expected him to come back at me with some sort of "six degrees of separation" hypothesis.

Instead, he'd told me there was no connection whatsoever.

"No school? Distant relatives? Hangouts?"

"Nope, nope, and nope." He dropped a pad full of notes on the desk. "I looked everywhere. Even got a list of their doctors and dentists all the way back to booster shots. Nothing."

I put my frappé on the desk. "I guess that takes care of any idea that the two crimes are connected, then."

Pete was quiet for a long moment.

"Pete?"

He shook his head. "I don't know. I keep remembering what

my dad says, you know. That there are no such things as coincidences. . . ."

I snapped my head to look at him. I didn't know if he'd just had a genuine memory of a conversation with his father, my uncle, or whether he'd read my notes on the whiteboard, the one at the top of the right-hand corner bearing the same message.

Or maybe he'd seen the note and connected it to the memory.

At any rate, in that regard we were on the same page.

"Doesn't matter," I said. "It doesn't do us one bit of good."

"I'd still like to pursue it, if that's okay with you?"

"You mean, try to make a connection?"

He nodded, looking altogether too earnest.

I grimaced and went through the notes on my own desk. "Sure, if you want. But I was hoping that maybe you could look into a couple of other things for me, too. If you don't mind?"

"I don't mind. Maybe the busywork will help give me fresh ideas on where to look."

I handed him a sheath of papers. "I want you to go through these depositions. Highlight any contradictory testimony."

"Sure thing, boss."

He accepted the papers and left the office, thankfully blind to the way my shoulders had pinned back and my chest had puffed out.

Boss. I liked the sound of that.

Rosie came into the room. "Nash is in his office," she said.

So much for feeling like a boss.

Lenny Nash was my uncle Spyros' silent partner. "Silent" being the operative word. I doubted we'd exchanged more than a handful of words in my time at the agency. And I never knew when he might pop up. Either he was in his office or he wasn't.

He'd never really acted like my superior or tried in any way I could tell to contribute to the day-to-day running of the agency, but the fact that he was my uncle's partner, and that he was so silent, made me überaware that he was, in some roundabout way, one of my two bosses.

Rosie continued, "Oh, and I have to leave on account of I need to get my nails done for a date."

Her words succeeded in deflating my artificially puffed-out chest. Not only had she just reminded me that there was another authority figure above me, currently on the premises, she was disobeying my request that she work this morning at double time.

"Date? On a Sunday morning?"

Rosie beamed, making both her dimples pop. "Yeah. I'm taking him to meet my mother."

"Who?"

She *tsk*ed and put her hands on her hips.

"Oh, yeah. *Him,*" I said, putting extra emphasis on the pronoun. I waved my hand. "Fine. I'll see you in the morning."

"Great."

I focused my attention on the whiteboard.

"Oh, by the way, I hear that five-oh was called to your neighborhood last night. Anything interesting happening?"

I absently fingered the goose egg that was now little more than a bad memory. "Nope. Nothing."

"Okay, then. Later."

"Yeah, later," I said.

After I heard the outer door close, I went out and locked it and then went in search of my cell phone. I needed to make a call. . . .

Twenty-four

"G'DAY, SOFIE." JAKE PORTER ANSWERED my call on the first ring.

I squinted. How did he do that? I almost never got to my phone in time to answer on the first ring. I was pretty sure he didn't wear one of those Bluetooth earpieces because I would have noticed it. Usually it took me at least three rings to find the damn phone and another one to actually answer it.

"Do you know anything about my midnight visitor last night?" I asked.

Silence, and then, "It was eight o'clock. And no."

I sighed heavily.

"You okay?"

"Yeah, I'm fine. Just trying to trace my attacker back to one of my cases."

"Maybe it was a pissed-off husband."

I shook my head. "No. The guy warned me to let dead dogs lie, or something like that. And told me I should drop the case."

"Dead dogs lie . . . is that like letting sleeping dogs lie?"

"That's what I'm guessing. Do you think it's tied to the Papadakis case?"

"Maybe."

I rubbed my forehead. "Have I ever told you what a big help you are, Porter?"

"Once or twice."

"Thanks."

I rang off and then tossed my cell phone to the desk, wondering why I'd even bothered with the call since I probably could have written the dialogue of our exchange in my sleep.

I walked to the whiteboard, erased a couple of ill-chosen words, and then swung the whole thing over altogether, hoping the change in scenery would help my thought processes. I stared at the blank corkboard and backed away from it until I was standing at the desk again. I opened a couple of case folders until I came across some photos I'd compiled.

"Now, where did I put those pushpins?" I wondered aloud.

I heard a sound in the lobby of the office and froze. Pete and Rosie had both left. And I had locked the front door.

I soundlessly slid my Glock out of the holster on the back of the chair and clutched it to my chest as I flattened myself against the wall. Listening for other sounds, I scooted toward the door.

Whoosh, click, whoosh.

The sounds were familiar, but I didn't know how. Swallowing thickly, I swung around the corner, gun drawn toward the sounds.

"Hold it right where you are!" I said to no one.

I looked to the left and the right even as I drew closer to the Xerox machine. The light under the lid flashed and then went dim.

"What do you think you're doing?"

I swung in the direction of the tiny bathroom, my gun nearly touching Nash's chest where he'd just come out, doing up his fly as casually as if I were holding out a flower instead of a loaded Glock.

"Jesus, Nash, you scared the hell out of me."

I now recalled Rosie saying something about his being in the office before she skipped out the door to get a manicure. I figured my reaction was due to a mixture of leftover fear from the night before and the subject matter of my latest cases.

Nash's owlish eyes looked at the gun muzzle and then me.

"Oh," I said, dropping the firearm to my side. "Sorry."

"Good reflexes, Sofie. Your uncle will be glad to hear it."

Nash passed me and collected whatever he'd been copying from the Xerox bin and then lifted the top and took out the original.

"You've talked to my uncle?" I asked, putting the gun on my desk and leaning against it as if my question were of no consequence. Truth be told, the guy never failed to unnerve me.

Nash gave me a long look and then disappeared back into his office, closing the door after him.

I sighed and looked at the freshly painted ceiling. I hadn't spoken to my uncle since last month. All I knew was that he was still in Greece and called in once a week to talk to Rosie. I tried to be in the office for the scheduled calls, but something always interfered with my being there on time. Then there was the time Rosie had taken the call while she was talking to her sister and I'd been none the wiser.

At any rate, I had a few questions for my mentor, mostly having to do with the office that I could probably have Rosie ask.

But call me mulish, I wanted to talk directly to the boss every once in a while.

I heard my cell phone ring in the other room. I ignored it as I sat considering the closed door to Nash's office. One of these days I was going to have to aim my investigative skills at the two men in my life that had nothing to do with sex. Hey, I figured it couldn't hurt.

The telephone extension next to me rang, and I jumped.

Sure. I'd investigate my uncle and Nash just as soon as I could sit next to a ringing phone without it scaring the bejesus out of me.

"Metropolis Agency," I said, picking up. "Sofie Metro speaking."

"Metro? Metro? What's this Metro?"

I winced. "Morning, Mom. How are you today?"

Silence.

I wasn't used to that. She usually went into a full litany of what was right and what was wrong, and seeing as it was Sunday, she was probably calling to try to strong-arm me into attending church.

"It's Aglaia," my mother said quietly.

I grimaced. I'd forgotten that it was tradition for the Saturday fortieth-day commemoration to be followed by a Sunday church visit.

"Mom, I'm sorry, but I can't go."

"No, no, that's not what I'm talking about."

I moved the phone from one ear to the other. My desk was littered with more than the usual suspects. I began sorting through the three neat piles there.

"Mom?" I said, signing off on a couple of closed cheating

spouse cases and putting them back on Rosie's desk for final filing. "You still there?"

"I am. But Aglaia isn't. She died last night. In her sleep at the Widow Vardis'."

I SUSPECTED THAT LIKE MANY Greek-American households across Queens, the immediate family gathered to absorb the latest news to rock the community. While all the Metropolises usually made it for regular Sunday dinner, today was different. A kind of reflective hush had fallen over the house. Even my father and maternal grandfather seemed distracted from their ongoing feud where they sat in the living room in their respective recliners, pretending to read the paper.

"Where's the feta?" I asked from where I was helping prepare dinner in the kitchen.

"Shhh . . ." Yiayia, my paternal, black-clad grandmother, nudged me aside, reaching across the counter on the other side of me so she could pick up the item I was looking for, a container of barrel feta and its milk.

"Thanks," I whispered, although I had no idea why I had lowered my voice.

Every once in a while, my mother would shake her head and whisper something while she put the finishing touches on the roast beef in red sauce and cloves on the stove behind me.

Personally, I'd gotten over my own initial surprise about an hour ago. It seemed to be taking everyone else a little longer.

Okay, so Aglaia had died. It wasn't that I hadn't been fond of the woman—I hadn't—but you'd think someone close to us had kicked the bucket rather than a crotchety old woman who'd insulted nearly everyone she'd come in contact with.

Shock had brought me to my parents' house. Boredom threatened to chase me out. Right now I could be back at the office working on the latest of my projects, putting together a pictorial flowchart on the Laughton case and perhaps uncovering something that would definitively prove Johnny's innocence or guilt.

"Forty days to the day," my mother murmured. "Almost to the minute."

"You can't possibly know that. Widow Vardis didn't find Aglaia until this morning." I cut feta into the salad. "Besides, the official forty days isn't until this Tuesday, remember?"

It was Greek tradition that *sarantas* be observed on Saturdays, so if the day fell during the week, it was observed the Saturday before. Apparently, my mother preferred to forget the facts.

"She died of a broken heart," my mother said, ignoring both me and the facts.

"She probably died of a clogged heart."

"Clogged with emotion from losing her Tolly."

I made a face, beginning to feel sick to my stomach. The way I remembered it, when Uncle Tolly had come up missing, Aglaia's only concern had been about finding his body so she could declare him dead and sell his brand-new Mercedes. Nowhere had there been mention of love or affection. Or even the intent to bury him.

"Clogged with bitterness, more like it," I muttered.

"Sofia!"

I stared at my mother. "What?"

Had I said the words aloud? Yes. Yes, I had. And I'd meant to.

"Come on, Mama, stop being so dramatic. There was no true affection between Tolly and Aglaia. Only bitterness and resentment."

"That's not true! When he miraculously returned from the dead, they rekindled their love for each other."

"Right."

Thalia pointed a wooden spoon dripping with red sauce in my direction. "I think you're the one spoiled by bitterness and resentment, Sofie."

I blinked.

Okay, I suppose I'd left the door wide open for that one. Still, the accusation caught me unawares.

I attached the top on the feta container and put it in the refrigerator, where Yiayia retrieved it to finish it off.

"Say all you want, Mama, but I know the truth. I'm not going to stay around here listening to you romanticize the life of a woman whose middle name was 'Miserable.'"

"She's dead, Sofia."

"So I've heard." I sighed heavily. "Look, I don't mean any ill will. I just think it's stupid to walk around here like it's some kind of huge loss. Because outside of not having a good place to take our dry-cleaning—which actually happened last month—it's not."

Yiayia gasped and smacked me with the wooden spoon she was using.

"Ow."

"No less than you deserve," my mother agreed.

I pushed aside the salad. "I'm going upstairs."

Neither commented on my leaving as I took the back steps.

Which was just as well because I'd likely have said something else to piss them off.

I reached the second-floor landing and listened. I wasn't particularly interested in running into either my brother—whose camera I'd borrowed, broken, and replaced but had yet to return—or my sister—for obvious reasons.

I went quietly down the hall to my old room. Kosmos' door was ajar. I peeked in and saw him reading one of his university tomes at his desk, oblivious to my presence. Efi's door was closed tightly, but I could hear her talking to someone, presumably on the phone because none of us had visitors on Sunday. Actually, none of us had invited many non-Greek friends over, period. It kept things simple. As well as kept us from having to explain what a boiled goat's head was doing on a plate on the table or something else equally unpalatable.

I quietly opened the door to my old room, entered, and then stood taking everything in.

Not a thing had been changed or moved. I smiled. I had been out of the house for seven months, but my mother had kept everything exactly the way it had been. My twin bed still bore the hot pink comforter and heart-shaped pillows from my teen years. My vanity bore photos from various high school events as well as body sprays I hadn't used in eons. I felt as if I'd walked into a time warp, although it really hadn't been all that long ago that I'd lived there.

I walked around slowly, touching this, remembering that. There was a framed photo of my sister and me taken on Christmas, both of us wearing reindeer horns and red noses. I picked it up, running my thumb along the glass, and then put it on the bed, planning to take it with me.

I crossed to the closet and opened the double-shuttered doors. Old dresses still hung in plastic bags bearing the Pappas Dry Cleaners logo. I moved each hanger, looking through them. Most could go to the church. What's the saying? If you haven't worn it in a year, get rid of it?

"Not thinking about moving back in, are you?"

I glanced at where Efi was leaning against the doorjamb.

"Not a chance." I finished with the hanging clothes and then reached for the boxes on the shelf above them. I nearly fell backward with the first one. Efi stepped forward to steady me and then accepted the box and put it on the bed.

"Thanks."

"Don't mention it."

I concentrated on getting the next box, being a little more careful this time.

"You're ignoring my calls again," my sister said.

"Am not."

"Are too."

I grimaced as I opened the first box. Violà. Sweaters. I pulled out an old cardigan I hadn't worn in years and put it on, automatically checking the pockets. I slid out a folded slip of paper with a phone number on it. "I've been busy with my latest case. You know, the Laughton one."

The name didn't seem to faze Efi. Not that I expected it to. I'm sure she was familiar with the case if only because it was hard to live in Queens and not know something about it. As a general rule, few things fazed my sister. Like my mother, she was able to stay staunchly on topic.

"Cop-out," she said, as if to prove my point.

I shrugged as I put the number back into my pocket. I had no idea whose it was, but you never knew if it might be important.

I decided to take the entire box with me. "Maybe."

"You know, you could at least let Dino know where things stand. He's been going out of his mind with worry."

"He shouldn't."

"That doesn't change the fact that he is."

I gave her a sidelong glance. "Talking to him often, are you?"

"Only because you're not."

I shrugged as if it were of no never mind to me.

The truth of it was that it did matter. A lot.

"Dinner!"

I'd never been so relieved to hear my mother's voice.

"Avoidance isn't going to get you anywhere, you know that, don't you?" Efi asked quietly.

"Get that, will you?" I asked, gesturing toward the box as I held the other and the hanging clothes. "As for avoidance . . . well, that's my decision, isn't it? You live your life as you see fit, I'll live mine my way."

"Whatever."

"Fine."

I led the way out of the room, knowing that wasn't going to be the end of it. But glad to have dodged the proverbial bullet. At least for now.

Twenty-five

BACK AT MY UNCLE'S OFFICE later that afternoon, I wondered if my sister was right. I did owe something to Dino. A simple conversation, maybe, to let him know where I was coming from.

I'd pinned up all the photos I had on the cork side of the board, along with everyone's names, and had connected them to Johnny with a length of purple ribbon that I'd found in the supply cabinet. What we were doing with purple ribbon, I had no idea, but I was glad to have it.

I leaned against the desk and considered my handiwork, waiting for something to jump out at me.

Nothing.

I pushed my hair back from my face. Was I too close to the case? My imaginative blinders had been fixed on the same facts for so long that I couldn't see anything that lurked just outside my immediate view. Maybe what I needed was to take a step further back. Better yet, change the view entirely.

I approached the board and flipped it over. Then flipped it again. Nothing.

Okay.

I gathered my notes from my uncle's desk, along with my gun and holster, jacket, and purse, and then stood in the open doorway for a long moment, taking in the room I'd spent the better part of the past week in. I silently shut off the light and closed the door, feeling better the instant I did.

I sat at my desk in the open area, glancing at Rosie's side and then outside the windows at the quiet street. If not for dinner at my parents' earlier, I'd have forgotten it was Sunday altogether. I methodically went through everything on my desktop, separating items related to the Laughton case from the rest. When I finished, I had a towering pile on the left-hand corner and a much smaller pile in front of me. I spent the next half hour clearing out paperwork and moving it to Rosie's in-box and then sat back to consider what else I had.

The missing body was what jumped out at me.

Well, not literally, of course. Although despite whatever scare the action would inspire, it would make my life a whole hell of a lot easier. I mean, how many places were there that a dead body could hide? He certainly hadn't gotten up by himself and walked away. Which brought me back to the fact that someone had taken it.

The Mob?

I remembered Porter and his warnings. When paired with what had gone down at his apartment, someone—likely the Mob—had taken Nick's body.

I tapped my pen against the desk. But that didn't really make sense, did it? I mean, aside from the sick intention of displaying the stiff as a souvenir, what point was there in keeping it? The coroner had already had a stab at it, and the autopsy report showed he'd died of natural causes.

I rummaged through the documents, coming up with the one in question. The weight of all his individual organs (did a liver really weigh three pounds?), down to the last detail, all the information surrounding his death had already been recorded and he'd been mere hours away from being buried forever. So why, then, would the Mob—or any shadowy government agency, for that matter—want to take his body?

Because they didn't.

I sat back in my chair, causing it to squeak.

So who else might be interested in taking an embalmed body hours away from burial?

I jotted down possibilities.

A disturbed cult of teenagers.

A hungry homeless man.

Neighborhood vampires.

Only the first option made any kind of sense. And would be almost impossible to follow up on until, when, and if the body popped up somewhere. As it would, inevitably, because I'd learned during the time I'd worked at my aunt Sotiria's that while embalming preserved the body, it only did so through the viewing to the burial, usually within three days. By now, while the skin would still appear smooth and unmarred, the internal organs would be decomposing and the smell would escape from any orifice.

Surely soon someone would call in a god-awful stench and it would be investigated. Case solved, my life made that much easier.

I picked up the phone to call Pino when I realized that it was late on a Sunday night. While I expected that he was probably working—in my experience, the guy lived for the job—I didn't want to have to owe him anything. Being in debt to Pino would be a fate worse than death.

Then I remembered the phone number I'd found in my old sweater pocket.

I looked for another number entirely and picked up the phone again.

I DIDN'T MUCH LIKE SNOOPING around by myself in the house of a dead man, but at this point I didn't know what else I could do. I mean, it wasn't as though I could look up "stupid teenage cults" in the Yellow Pages. So I was reduced to continuing to look for clues in the disappearance of Nick Papadakis' body.

I'd called his landlord, Dottie Grear, from the office and she'd offered to leave the door to Nick's old place unlocked for me. Now I stood in the living room, much as I had a few days before, looking for anything I might have missed the first time around. I put on a pair of rubber gloves I'd found in the supply cabinet. (Okay, so messing around in a dead guy's things gave me the hee-bies. During my earlier visit, I'd poked. Now I intended to in-vade.) No missing change in the couch cushions. No grocery lists behind or under the refrigerator. No old receipts in the empty garbage bin out back.

I stood on the steps of the back porch and looked around the small yard that was attached to the town house next door. I took a deep breath. I detected the scent of rotting vegetables maybe, dead leaves definitely, but nothing similar to rotting flesh.

Yes, unfortunately, I did know what that smelled like. During my brief stint at my aunt's when I was seventeen, a two-day-old corpse had been brought in (it was an elderly woman who had died alone at her house), and the smell had chased everyone out of the funeral home, leaving my aunt to wheel it into the freezer until she could talk the woman's niece into cremation.

I went back inside, locked the door, and made my way upstairs, looking through the medicine cabinet, checking behind the neat stack of towels in the linen closet, and then I finally found myself in front of his closet again.

I opened the doors. Thankfully, Dottie hadn't yet taken my advice and sent out Papadakis' suits to a consignment shop. Although I didn't know if I'd feel the same way once I was through. I searched through side jacket pockets, inside jacket pockets, methodically pulling out the pants pockets to make sure I wasn't missing anything.

Twenty minutes later, I stood staring at the wardrobe, feeling ridiculously like the pants were sticking their tongues out at me.

Well, so much for that idea.

I left the suits as they were and closed the doors before peeling off the gloves and sticking them inside my own jacket pocket. My hands felt powdery, so I went to the bathroom and quickly washed and then dried them on a hand towel. A pink hand towel with little pink appliqué roses, the type that were hand-sewed on.

Huhn.

When had my mother said Nick's mother had passed? Ten years ago? This towel looked newer. I reluctantly gave it a sniff. Recently laundered, as if waiting for the occupant to come home anytime.

I switched off all the lights as I went and locked up before going to the town house next door. I knocked.

It opened immediately.

"Hi, Miss Grear," I said.

"Dottie, please," she said, pulling her pink robe closed.

I wrinkled my nose at the scent of mothballs. It wasn't a smell with which I was unfamiliar. My paternal grandmother's apartment had reeked of mothballs before she'd come to live with us. And every now and again, my mother had to confiscate a box or two my grandmother had picked up at the market, should she feel compelled to make my parents' house smell the same.

"Okay, Dottie, then." I smiled, glad she wasn't inviting me in, where the mothball smell would be worse. "I just wanted to tell you that I locked up."

"Any luck?"

I shook my head. "Unfortunately, no. But thanks just the same." I put my hands in my pockets, feeling the rubber gloves there. "I do have one question for you, though. Did you make the hand towels in the bathroom?"

She appeared puzzled for a moment.

"You know, the pink ones with the roses."

"Oh, yes. Yes, I did make them." She smiled. "I was getting the town house ready for showing and wanted to spruce up the place, you know?"

"Ah. Yes. Of course." I noticed the way she held the door closed against her back. "So you didn't make them for Mr. Papadakis?"

"What? Oh, no. Why would I do something like that?"

"He was a nice-looking man, Dottie." I tried to look beyond

her again, and she pulled the door tighter so I couldn't. "Am I interrupting something?"

"No. No, of course you're not." Her cheeks pinkened. She lowered her voice. "I have a . . . man in the house," she whispered.

"Not a bad thing to have," I said, amused by her almost adolescent behavior.

She came farther outside and closed the door completely. "I'm sorry. I'm new at this. I spent most of my life taking care of my elderly parents, so I didn't get much of an opportunity to date and whatnot."

"So you're taking full advantage now."

She flushed again. "Yes."

"Good for you." I turned and walked down the stairs. "Good night, Dottie. And thanks again."

"You're welcome."

She quickly went inside and closed the door. I shook my head as I climbed into Lucille. Funny, the things we did for love.

Speaking of which, I pulled out my cell phone and dialed a familiar number. . . .

"I WOKE YOU," I SAID to Dino after he'd unlocked the shop door and let me inside. "I'm sorry, maybe I should come back tomorrow."

He shook his handsomely disheveled head. "No, no. Now is fine." He looked at me and grinned. "Now is perfect."

I'd forgotten how sexy his Greek accent was and what kind of effect it had on me. Actually, I was beginning to think I was an accent-loving kind of girl, because the two men in my life both spoke with one.

I cleared my throat and stepped inside the shop.

"Do you want to go upstairs?" Dino asked, locking the door again after me.

I shook my head as I took in the display case of pastries before me. My stomach immediately growled as I homed in on a triple chocolate torte smack-dab in the middle, nothing separating us but a sheet of glass.

Truth was, I couldn't go upstairs. If I went upstairs, we'd end up in bed together. And right now that wasn't a very good idea.

"So," Dino said, clearing his throat as he rounded the counter. "How are you?"

"Fine," I said as I slid onto a stool. "You?"

"Not so good."

"Oh?"

I realized that I had yet to look him straight in the face. His hair, his smiling mouth, but not his deep brown eyes.

And I found that I was having a hard time doing so.

"Coffee?" he asked, as if it were the middle of the day and this were a casual stop-in, like many we'd experienced over the past month.

"Yes, please."

"Decaf?"

"Full octane."

He smiled as he went about making me a frappé.

Call me soft, but there was something about watching a man making me coffee that turned me on beyond words. Especially considering that the man in question wore little more than a snug white T-shirt and gray drawstring pants that clung to all the right parts, his feet bare, ten o'clock shadow darkening his jaw.

Mmm.

I wiggled on the stool. I wasn't there to sleep with Dino. We'd already done enough of that.

I was there to break things off.

Of course, I'd known all along that that's what I'd come to do. But admitting it openly to myself was another matter altogether.

Okay, so I liked the guy. A lot. What was not to like? It didn't bother me much that it was ten o'clock and he'd likely been asleep at least an hour or so while I craved coffee over bed at the same time. After the other night with Jake . . .

My cheeks felt as if they were on fire.

"Everything all right?" Dino asked as he put the frappé in front of me.

I took a long pull from the frosty glass and nodded, keeping my gaze averted.

So sue me, I hadn't really thought of my time with Jake as it related to whatever Dino and I had. The rugged, Australian bounty hunter . . . well, he existed outside of time for me. He didn't reside in the real world. At least not in my real world.

God, I can't believe I hadn't thought about my being with Jake as being unfaithful to Dino.

And to think it was my fear of his unfaithfulness to me that had proved to be the wedge that came between us.

I wished the Greeks had never created the word *irony*.

"So," Dino said, leaning his hands on the counter. He looked a breath away from touching mine where they clutched my frappé. I pulled my hands back.

"So," I agreed.

Silence, then Dino said, "It's nice to see you, Sofie."

I nodded, drinking my frappé. "Nice to see you, too."

Ugh. Okay, this small-talk stuff had to stop.

"Look, Dino," I began, twirling the coffee in my glass with the straw.

He seemed to pick up on something in the way I spoke and pulled away from the counter.

"I know that nothing happened between you and my sister . . ."

I was so busy trying to formulate what I had to say in my mind that I wasn't paying attention to what he was doing beyond that he was moving around. My eyes widened as he put a slice of the triple chocolate torte in front of me.

I inwardly moaned at the unfairness of it all.

Here I had a great guy—a hot, funny, sexy great guy—who not only fed me chocolate torte, but made it with his own two hands. So what if he went to bed at nine so he could get up at four A.M. to start baking? So what if he had to work ten hours at the shop and his life was predictable? As far as I could tell, unpredictable was overrated. And if I needed a reminder of that, all I had to do was recall my explosive night with Porter.

"Sofie, please," Dino said, touching my hands with his while I wasn't looking. "Let's not have this conversation now."

I blinked at him. "You've been calling me twice a day for the past week."

He looked down and nodded. "I know I have. But now that you're here . . . well, I'm scared to death you're about to say that you can't see me anymore."

I looked down at our hands as well. "It's not you . . . it's me."

He winced. "Ouch."

I gave him a bittersweet smile. "That didn't come out quite the way I intended. . . ." I swallowed hard. If given a choice between the torte and the Greek, I'd take the Greek any day.

But I couldn't have him. At least not right now.

I met his gaze full on for the first time since he'd let me inside the bakery. And my heart plunged to my feet and then bounced back up at the intently suggestive look in his dark, sexy eyes.

"Do you have any idea how much I want to have sex with you right now?" I whispered, without realizing that's what I was about to say.

"So what's stopping you?"

I shook my head as if to clear it. "Me . . . you." I sighed heavily and slid my hands out from under his. "When I first spotted you and Efi . . . well, while I know that nothing personal happened between you two, there's not a time when I blink my eyes that I don't see the image of you both standing so close. . . ."

I took a deep, steadying breath.

"Sofie, I know you've had a tough time of it. Efi told me what happened at your wedding. . . . I just want you to know that I'd never do that to you."

I laughed humorlessly. "You know what the most absurd thing about this entire experience is? We, you and I . . . we weren't even officially dating."

"Oh? And what did you view it as?"

"A series of one-night-stand encounters."

He chuckled. "Wonders are many, and none is more wonderful than man." He nodded in my direction. "Or woman, in this case."

"Sophocles." The quote was one of my father's favorites.

"Yes." Then he asked, "Have you ever stopped to think about how often we all lie to ourselves? Close our eyes to something that's staring us right in the face?"

I shook my head. "Dino, please—"

"No, Sofie. You've had your say, now it's time for mine."

I had the feeling I wasn't going to like what he was about to tell me.

But I was helpless to stop him.

"What you saw as sex, I viewed completely differently. You and me . . . we fit." He gave a wry smile. "I don't mean physically, although you have to admit, there wasn't a problem in that area, either. But in every way. You get my humor, I get yours. I never feel put out by you, and I think it's the same with you."

My throat grew tight.

Run, said a small voice inside my head.

Stay, another answered.

"I guess what I'm trying to tell you is that what you view as strictly chemistry . . . I see as love."

There. There it was. The four-letter word I'd been avoiding like a gang of flesh-hungry zombies.

"I think I'm falling in love with you, Sofie," he said. "No, there's no thinking involved. I know I am. And . . . and I think you would discover you felt the same way, too, if you'd stop overanalyzing yourself and us for one minute and look at the situation objectively."

I shook my head. "Well . . . that's the problem, isn't it? I can't look at it objectively. I have to see it subjectively. And on the subject of love . . . well, I'm striking out more than I'm hitting."

I slid off the stool, curiously feeling as if someone had just ripped my heart out of my chest.

"I've got to go," I whispered so quietly that I almost didn't hear the words. "Thanks for the, um, coffee."

Twenty-six

AND HERE I THOUGHT I couldn't possibly feel any worse than I already did when it came to Dino.

Oh, how very wrong I'd been.

I lay in bed with my arms straight at my sides, staring up at the ceiling. I'd come home right after my conversation with Dino, taken a shower, and gone directly to bed—I did not pass Go, did not collect two hundred dollars, and did not turn on the television to browse through the channels to see what might be on to take my mind off the issue at hand.

He was falling in love with me. . . .

Of course, I'd known that. Well, I hadn't *known* it known it, because that would suggest some sort of conscious thought on my part, and I'd gone out of my way to be incognizant of anything beyond temporary need for longer than I cared to remember.

I did, however, recall what Jake had said when I'd tried to bulldoze him into my king-size bed: "You come with too much baggage, luv. And I'm not talking about the wedding gifts you have piled up in your bedroom, either."

Or something to that effect.

He'd also said he hadn't been interested in the role of rebound man.

The question was, why not? I mean, for all intents and purposes, what had transpired between us had "temporary" written
all over it. Rebound man, one-night stand . . . call me stupid,
but didn't they have the same ring?

Why, then, the drawn-out game of cat and mouse?

And why, then, when it was obvious he knew that I was
seeing someone ("seeing" being used in the loosest sense of the
word), did he pop out of the woodwork and welcome me into
his water bed?

Okay, so the fact that bullet holes were shot into that same
water bed, and the gunmen responsible for them had chased
us both out of his apartment, might have something to do with
the temporary nature of our liaison. But still, I couldn't see dating Jake regularly, you know, dinner and dancing, anywhere in
the picture.

I sighed. Another glaring difference between Jake and Dino.
Dino was capable of telling me just how he felt even in the
middle of me dumping him, while Jake would probably never
utter the words even if the thought of jumping off Hell Gate
Bridge was preferable to living another day without me.

No, Dino hadn't told me that. But I had the feeling that he
would if given half the chance.

Only I hadn't had the chance to give him.

I felt a weight on the bed next to my legs. I figured it was
Muffy, even though we weren't on speaking terms as of late. I
nearly jumped out of my skin when Tee nuzzled his head against
my arm.

"Hey there, sweet stuff," I said, scratching him behind the ears, his vibrating purr bringing me a measure of comfort in the swirling chaos that was currently my life.

Who'd have thought a cat so wild would be so affectionate?

Another weight near my feet. Muffy, it had to be. Unless another animal had gained access to my apartment via the fire escape. Which was certainly not beyond the realm. I shuddered to think that a squirrel had gotten inside and was settling on my bed to gnaw at my toes while I slept.

Did squirrels gnaw on people's toes? Or was I thinking of a rat?

Now *that* thought did get me up.

Both the dog and the cat followed me to the dining room window. I put my hand on the sash and then looked at them both. "Do either of you have any business to see to? Because I just creeped myself out and am going to have to close this for the night."

They both just looked at me, Muffy's tongue lolling out of the side of his mouth, Tee curving around my ankle.

"Okay, fine. Just please don't go waking me up in the middle of the night because you suddenly have to go."

I moved to close the window when a high-pitched screech filled my ears. I jumped as something flapped its wings and tried to gain access to the apartment. I swatted at it without thinking of the consequences, glad when it went back outside. I quickly closed the window and then leaned against the wall next to it, surprised to find myself out of breath.

I stared back at where both Tee and Muffy stared at me, their ongoing feud momentarily forgotten.

"Please don't tell me that was a bat," I whispered.

I ran toward my bedroom, not stopping until I was back in bed with the covers pulled up to my chin. Tee and Muffy appeared to think my actions were part of a midnight game, as they both jumped up after me and began playing with each other (at least I preferred to think it was playing—the alternative was they were out for the kill) across my legs. I folded my feet under me and closed my eyes, praying that the night would get better from there.

I'D FIGURED OUT OVER THE years that people used cologne and perfume for a variety of reasons, not all of them having to do with attracting the opposite sex. My own Greek heritage allowed me a particularly keen insight into covering body odor as one of those reasons. I understood that many of the older Greek immigrants had come from a country where water had been at a premium, so tradition had it that they took baths once a week. Although they did try to wash up every day. Like I'd heard in an old George Carlin routine, "armpits, asshole, crotch, and teeth." Of course, the Greeks hadn't gotten the armpits part, or if they had, they didn't follow up with a really good deodorant. (My aunt Sotiria was convinced that it wasn't that the Greeks merely smelled, that's the way they were designed to smell. Too much lamb intestines in the diet or something.)

At any rate, I thought about this when I entered the agency late the next morning to find Rosie swimming in perfume. Which was nothing new, really, except that she appeared to be wearing two different brands, because even I coughed at the overwhelming mix of scents. And, curiously, garlic wasn't one of them.

She also had her head down on her desk. Which wasn't like

her. She was usually either angry or happy, one of the two. I don't think I'd ever seen her that tired or dejected.

"Everything all right?" I asked.

A long, drawn-out Puerto Rican moan was the answer. (I wasn't exactly sure how a moan could have a Puerto Rican accent, but there you had it.)

Rosie said, "I just want to die."

"Is it Carlos?" I asked about her colicky nephew.

"No, no. He's doing okay. Most of the time, anyway. Either that or we're just used to the crying by now."

I shrugged out of my jacket and hung it on the back of my desk chair and then put my purse with the Glock in it in my drawer. "Probably you should have passed on that last margarita last night, then."

"If only I could blame it on liquor." Rosie turned her head toward me from where she was facing the opposite wall. Her cheek bore a crease created by the papers she was lying on. "Last night was a disaster."

I blinked at her. How could she know anything about my night?

Then I remembered. She was to have taken her new boyfriend to meet her family.

She groaned again.

"It couldn't have been that bad," I told her.

"That's what you think." She pushed to an upright position and sipped from a mug that had a faded decal of Enrique Iglesias on it. "First it started with my mother calling him by the wrong name. Understandable, you say. It could happen to anybody, I admit. Only she made a point of doing it all night long. I mean something like twenty times, no matter how many times

I corrected her." She shook her head. "Then there was the baby incident."

"The baby incident?" I wasn't sure I wanted to hear this, but I was hoping she would casually drop the name of the guy she was dating in her explanation. Of course, I should have known better. I was coming to understand that Rosie could keep a secret better than anyone I knew.

"Yes, the baby incident. My guy seemed . . . I don't know, a little uncomfortable taking the baby from my sister. He—the baby, that is—is only a month old, you know. Hell, I was scared of breaking him in the beginning. Then the instant he had him, the baby spit up all over the front of his shirt. Even I smelled it throughout dinner no matter how well I cleaned it up. And I could tell he didn't like it."

"Doesn't sound like something to get all bent out of shape over."

Rosie gave me the mother of all eye rolls. "That's because you don't know what happened next."

"What?"

"I specifically asked my mother not to serve pork. And what does she do? She puts the whole damn pig on the table."

A small alarm went off at the back of my head. "Why not pork?"

"Why do you think not pork? Because he's Jewish, stupid."

Jewish.

The alarm got louder.

"I mean, I know a lot of Jewish people eat pork nowadays, but not him. It's not that he's against it, it's just that it was never served at his house and he's never eaten it aside from trying bacon, and he doesn't see a reason to start now." Rosie dropped her head back to the desk and chewed her gum for a few moments. "Then my mother filled his plate with it. I, naturally, took it off, only she put even more." She groaned. "So we got into an argument right there in front of God and everybody."

"Who?"

"Who do you think?"

I prayed she'd say his name.

"My mother and me, that's who."

Damn. "I guess you're right. It does sound like it was a disaster," I said, an image of Mrs. Nebitz emerging in my mind.

It wasn't the first time I'd considered that Mrs. Nebitz's drop-dead-gorgeous Seth might be dating Puerto Rican hottie Rosie. But the possibility hadn't really started taking root until my dinner with Mrs. Nebitz when she requested I find out whom he was dating. Up until then . . . well, as long as it didn't involve children or small animals, they were free to have all the fun they wanted without worry of my sticking my nose into it.

Now, I mentally connected the dots that might take me from remote possibility to firm probability.

Number one, I remembered all too well when they'd met a couple of months ago. After Tony and Rokko had broken into my house and duct-taped Muffy to the commode. Yummy Seth had been dropping his grandmother off after their weekly meal out, and Rosie had rushed to my rescue. Then we all had left them alone in my apartment while I ran off to identify a floater that had popped up in the East River.

Number two, I couldn't think of a single reason why Rosie wouldn't tell me the name of the guy she was dating, unless there was a very good reason. One beyond her fear of jinxing the relationship.

Number three, the guy she was dating was Jewish.

Oh, all right. That didn't necessarily mean it was Seth. But when combined with the first two musings, I was pretty sure I had my woman.

Or, rather, Mrs. Nebitz's woman.

Rosie groaned, and I joined her.

I cleared my throat as if I still weren't sold on her story of woe. "I'm sure everything will be fine, Rosie. I mean, Seth is a great guy. I'm sure he'll see beyond all this."

I pretended an interest in the messages on my desk.

"Seth? I didn't tell you his name was Seth. Why would you call him Seth?" Rosie said in what came out as one long sentence.

I stared at her.

She drew in a deep breath, puffing out her chest even farther. "Ohmigawd! Did you have one of the guys tail me? You did, didn't you? You had me followed."

"I did not have you followed," I said quietly.

"Did you get pictures? Oh, God, tell me you didn't get money shots."

I gaped at her. Eeuw. "Number one, why would I want to watch the two of you having sex?" I squinted at her, absently accepting that I seemed to be on a number roll this morning. "You guys have had sex?"

She grimaced at me as though I had to be the dumbest thing this side of the East River.

"Of course you've had sex." I swallowed hard. "Number two, it makes no never mind to me who you're dating." Liar. "Number three . . . it doesn't take a rocket scientist to figure out that the looks the two of you exchanged that night at my place weren't of the 'Hey, how ya doin'?' variety."

Rosie chewed on the inside of her bottom lip for a few moments. "Bullshit. You just figured it out."

"Okay, I just figured it out."

While Rosie might be a pro at keeping secrets, we both knew that I couldn't keep from blurting out a movie spoiler even with a hand over my mouth.

"So it is Seth, then?" I asked.

Rosie gave that Puerto Rican groan again and laid her head back on her desk. "Yeah." She closed her eyes tightly. "Things were going so well before last night. It's been a long time since I've wanted to bring anyone home to the family. What a grade A, unqualified, freakin' disaster." She opened her eyes. "I didn't even want to get out of bed this morning. Didn't brush my teeth." She ran a finger across her front teeth to demonstrate. "Hell, I didn't even want to take a shower."

I'd noticed.

She glared at me.

Had I spoken the words aloud? I had to be more careful.

"Sorry," I said.

Then it occurred to me. Another reason why people used perfumes. Or sent flowers to a funeral. To cover the smell of a decaying body.

"Where you goin' now?" Rosie *tsk*ed and whined.

I'd grabbed my jacket and was heading for the door. "To finally close one of these damn cases for good."

Twenty-seven

FUNERALS, MISSING DEAD BODIES, AND murder cases, oh my.

My life seemed to have turned into some sort of cautionary tale. You know, something along the lines of, "See, she's the reason why you should stay in school. Learn a trade. So you have something to fall back on. Do something important with your life."

As I drove to Middle Village, I wondered what, exactly, I had to fall back on if this whole PI gig didn't pan out. More specifically, something that didn't involve a tip jar and an apron and bunions and crotchety old Greek men.

Nothing.

The thought caught me by surprise.

One of my biggest guilty pleasures was watching reality TV shows. Okay, I admit it. And, trust me, that's not very easy for me to do, because even as I'm watching a girl from the backwoods of Kentucky sing like an angel, or a guy kiss up to Donald Trump in order to make half of what he's already making in order to apprentice for the real estate mogul, there's always a small voice in the back of my head that's telling me I should be doing something more constructive with my time. You know, like reading the newspaper I'd merely skimmed through that morning. Or buying important novels from the bookstore. Or even viewing PBS.

Instead I was vegging on my couch with my junk food of choice, living vicariously through someone else's dreams.

Somewhere down the line, I'd come to figure out that part of the reason I was drawn to that form of entertainment was that while my parents and their families had come to America because they had a dream and this was the land of opportunity, they didn't know how to instill that very American inspiration in their children. I'd never been told that there was nothing out there I couldn't do. That even if I wished to be president, it wasn't outside my reach.

Instead I'd been constantly told what I should and shouldn't do. Encouraged to bow to Greek tradition. Given a completely separate set of rules to abide by than my brother, who was a year younger than me.

"I don't understand," I'd told my father when I was seventeen and watched as my brother came home at two in the morning after a night out, while my own curfew was midnight. "Why are the rules different for Kosmos than they are for me?"

"Because he's a boy and you're a girl," he'd said simply, and then turned the page of his newspaper.

"And you're sexist."

The gender debate was one my father and I had participated in ceaselessly, especially throughout my teenage years, you know, when I was rebellious enough to verbally challenge his archaic, chauvinistic beliefs. Long before I'd finally accepted that I wasn't going to change his view on life no matter how blue in the face I got.

I'd been so busy questioning the restraints on my life, I hadn't had a chance to focus on the possibilities.

My parents' fault? Or my own?

The jury was still out on that one. Although the verdict wouldn't matter. Not now that I was twenty-six and had full control over my life and its direction.

Now it was up to me to convince myself that there wasn't a thing out there I couldn't do.

Yeah, right. Just like when I thought being a private investigator was a good idea.

I turned onto the street I was looking for and found a parking spot that would put Lucille's nose dangerously near the corner, but hey, I didn't plan to be long, and it would be worth the ticket. I got out of the car, squeezing my left arm against my body, reassured by the weight of the Glock there.

Not that I expected a threat from a dead man. I just wasn't up to taking any chances.

Of course, the entire trip was probably unnecessary. But better I should eliminate the possibility than dismiss it outright. While I had seen a lot in my career so far, not even I had seen everything. And I wasn't looking forward to seeing what I was afraid I was about to. But if I could solve but one mystery in my life right now . . . well, I'd be a much happier camper than I had been recently.

I bypassed the front of Nick Papadakis' town house and instead went next door and knocked. I stood back and waited for Dottie Grear to answer. Nothing. Huhn. I rapped my knuckles against the screen door again with the same result.

That's funny. I'd gotten the impression that she didn't work. Had I been wrong?

I looked up and down the street, trying to spot which car might be hers. My gaze caught on a white-and-blue car with the words *Grear Ambulance Service*. Interesting. . . .

I squinted at it, then moved in the direction of Nick's old town house, but rather than approach the door, I went around back. Thankfully, the two-unit building was at the end of the block, and an alley ran between the side of his place and the back of the multilevel apartment building that faced the next cross street. I considered the tall wood fence surrounding his small backyard, pushing against the boards around the locked gate until I found one that was semi loose. I reached for my gun, then changed my mind and looked around for a large rock instead. I used it to one-two-three bang the slat from its mooring and then reached inside to unlatch the gate.

While breaking and entering wasn't my thing (even though I had bought myself one of those lock-picking kits and gun mechanisms a while back, I hadn't had much of a chance to try them out yet), I was banking on my lack of skills not mattering.

Where before my hunger for trivia had included the first and last names of every player on *Survivor*, now I inhaled crime statistics as my drug of choice. Like the one that said that the majority of burglaries didn't include forced entry, meaning the home owner or tenant had left something unlocked, essentially hanging a neon sign above the door that read, ENTER HERE.

I didn't stop at Nick's door. Instead, I crossed the postage-stamp yard to Dottie Grear's back steps, thankful that the two yards had been left open so as to give the tenants the illusion of more room. (Frankly, I thought it was an invitation to disaster.

I mean, what happened if both wanted to have a barbecue with friends and family at the same time?)

I opened Dottie's screen door and wrapped my hand around the doorknob.

Of course, it only stood to reason that my cockiness about crime stats would end in a sigh of defeat.

Locked.

This, and I hadn't brought my lock-picking gear. Mostly because I hadn't expected to feel the urge to do some exploring before confronting the nice effusive Dottie directly with my thoughts.

I quietly shut the screen door and stepped down to the minuscule brick patio. There was a small window about two feet from the door. If the layout of the place was the same as Nick's—and I was sure it was, since the connected town houses were mirror images of each other—then that window was above the sink.

And it was cracked open.

Bless useful trivia.

I picked up a plastic lawn chair, moved it under the window, and then climbed up on it. The screen easily popped out, and I lifted up the lower section. Now, how was I going to get in there? My hands were above my head, which meant I'd have to rely on upper body strength to hoist myself up.

I think we've already established that I'm not very big on exercise. I figured whatever I got walking around—which wasn't as much as many New Yorkers but was enough—put me in good physical stead.

Unfortunately, it did absolutely nothing for my biceps, triceps, or any other muscle ceps that had to do with my arms.

I managed a pretty tight handhold on the windowsill and

gave it a shot. I barely lifted myself up an inch, felt as though my face were going to explode from the effort, and then hit the chair in a way that almost toppled it and me to the brick patio.

Damn.

At this rate, not only would it take me all day to get inside, I'd probably be spotted by either a neighbor or Dottie herself when she returned.

I pushed my purse up and then waved my arms to loosen them up and tried again.

After about ten times, I managed to get my head inside and balanced precariously on the sill, my face inches away from a decorative sink faucet, my legs dangling outside.

I wiggled and scooted and pushed until I was finally able to sit on the counter and swing my legs the rest of the way in.

Whew. I was sweating.

A fact I quickly forgot as the strong scent of mothballs hit me straight on.

I quickly unlocked the back door and left it ajar just in case I would have to make a fast getaway, then moved cautiously toward the hall leading to the living room. I heard the sound of a television somewhere, but it wasn't on the first floor. I hesitated. Was Dottie home? Was she upstairs doing something and hadn't heard my knock?

I felt for my gun, just to make sure it hadn't fallen out in the sink, and then unsnapped the protective strap just in case. I didn't think I'd be needing it, but as some of my more interesting cases had proved, you never knew.

The smell of mothballs combined with something else, reminding me of Rosie's unsuccessful perfume mixing. Probably she had a nighttime perfume, a daytime perfume, a hot date perfume . . . Probably her bedroom dresser was filled with perfume bottles so that she could pick and choose at will.

Only I didn't think eau de mothballs was one of them.

And neither was . . . was that the smell of a pine auto freshener?

I slowed my steps toward the stairs, spotting a metal gurney that probably belonged to the ambulance out front, collapsed and propped against the wall. Oh, God.

Okay, call me a coward, but I really didn't want to know why a woman obviously as neat as Dottie Grear felt it necessary to use such strong air deodorizers . . . or why she had an ambulance out front with her family name on it. But if I hoped to ever get my aunt Sotiria off my back, and by extension my mother, then I had to go up those stairs and confirm my worst suspicions.

If only my frozen feet would listen to me.

The damnable thing of it was that they weren't frozen strictly from fear. The higher I climbed, the colder it got.

I also picked up other scents. Vanilla incense. Or was that a candle? No, the coconut was a candle. And was that flowers? Roses, maybe?

I looked at the stairs behind me, thinking I'd pretty much uncovered enough to bring Pino around for a look-see.

The problem was, I didn't think I'd ever live down coming this far and not going the rest of the way.

I recalled the time I'd thought the same thing when I'd gone down into Romanoff's basement and fallen into a coffin, the lid closing on me with a final click. (It wasn't a cello crate, I'm telling you.)

My throat closed up, the reaction a mixture of the addition

of another pungent scent I didn't want to try to identify and—yes, I'll admit it—fear.

I finally reached the upper hall and stood, shivering, as I took in three doors, two of which were open (to a bathroom and a small bedroom with an empty twin bed), the third closed.

Before I went any farther, let it be said that while I've seen my share of dead bodies (beginning, coincidentally enough, at my aunt Sotiria's and continuing through the East River floater that wasn't Tolly), I didn't think I'd ever get used to seeing them. It was the primary reason I hadn't lasted more than three weeks working at the funeral home . . . and it was also the reason I didn't want to go into that room.

I found myself pointing toward the door, waving my finger as if to drum up the courage to either open the damn thing or get the hell out of there altogether.

Before I knew that's what I was going to do, I was turning the knob.

And the final smell became undeniable. Because it was that of one hundred percent dead and internally decomposing Nick Papadakis. . . .

Twenty-eight

HOLY SHIT.

The scene that met my innocent eyes was so incredible it could have been snipped right out of some B horror flick. I even half expected some sort of obese, sick-looking clown with bad makeup to come charging at me from the closet, a dull hatchet clutched in his hands.

Instead, I found myself alone with the unmoving corpse of Nick Papadakis, who was dressed in . . . I leaned closer—were those navy blue satin pajamas? And he was tucked into bed, his hands folded on top of his stomach, looking as if he were snoozing instead of dead.

Or rather, he would have looked that way had my aunt's embalming job not given him a sickly pale color, despite the spots of rouge high on his cheekbones.

And what was that smell?

No embalming job was meant to keep a body from decaying indefinitely. And I'd learned from my aunt that far less embalming fluid was used nowadays than even a couple of decades ago for various reasons—one of them a question of need, another having to do with possible ground contamination—meaning that by the time a body was buried, internal decomposition was already well under way.

Nearly every surface in the room was filled with an air freshener of some sort, pine tree types hanging every couple of inches from the ceiling. The room was freezing, the reason the window unit air conditioner in the opposite corner was apparently set on high. Probably to keep the body from deteriorating as quickly as it might have otherwise. A television was on across from the foot of the bed, as if to keep Nick entertained, Kelly Ripa's laugh filling the room with life when there was no life to be had.

Holy fucking shit!

I began to back out of the room. Hey, I'd come and I'd seen. It was now long past time I called the boys in blue in on this one.

What was Dottie Grear thinking?

"Okay, darling, it's time for your sponge bath. And boy, do you ever—" Dottie stopped when she spotted me. "Oh!"

Having been in the neighboring twin town house twice, I should have realized there was a connecting master bathroom. And that the door to this one had been closed. But I hadn't, and now Dottie Grear and I stood staring at each other, shocked.

Hands down, I'd have to say that I was the one most surprised.

Words failed me.

She was wearing a winter coat, presumably to ward off the chill created by the air conditioner, and a knit hat was pulled low over her features, giving her an almost timeless, childlike appearance.

Hey, when the guy was dead, you didn't have to worry about what you looked like, did you?

My gaze flicked from her face to the tray she held. It bore a basin of soapy water, a sponge, and a thick white towel. I hated to tell her, but I didn't think all the sponge baths in the world were going to help get rid of the smell, which I feared would be stuck in my nostrils forever.

Dottie laughed nervously. "I bet you're wondering what's going on."

Understatement of the century.

I moved back as she put down the tray on the bedside table closest to Nick. She couldn't possibly be planning to go ahead with the sponge bath in my presence? Could she?

I cleared my throat, hoping to engage her in conversation even as I reached for my cell phone in my jacket pocket. "I'm the last person to judge anyone on their decisions, Dottie."

I eyed the pillow next to Nick's inert body, to find the bedding mussed as if someone had just gotten up.

Had Dottie been sleeping with the rotting corpse?

Yikes.

The very idea was enough to send the two frappés I'd had this morning along with *paximadia*—Greek biscotti—rushing up into my throat.

Dottie sighed and shrugged, moving around the room and blowing out candles. "Honestly, it didn't seem so outlandish to me in the beginning. I mean, do you know how difficult it is to find a decent man out there? You would think it wouldn't be so hard, what with the city being so big, but . . ."

I cleared my throat, glad the smoke from the extinguished

candles briefly masked the smell. "You and . . . Nick were dating?"

Dottie smiled almost shyly. "I wouldn't say we were dating, dating. I mean, I saw him a lot. You know, coming and going. And I'd bake him banana and zucchini bread. He really liked my sweet breads." She gestured toward him, her voice low, as if she were afraid she might wake him. "He came for dinner the week before . . . well, the week before he died." She sighed wistfully. "I lit candles and served him meat loaf, and he proclaimed it was the best he'd had since his mother passed, only without the egg." She shrugged. "I didn't know what he meant about the egg, but I was tickled with his compliment. I mean, a guy's comparing you to his mother is a good thing, right?"

I was beyond speech at that point, although I understood the egg part. Greeks added hard-boiled eggs to the middle of their meat loaf so that when you cut it, each piece held a perfect slice.

"It was a casual thing, really . . . although things have become quite serious between us over the past week."

"I see," I said.

And I think I was beginning to.

"Um, I take it you inherited more than just these two town houses from your father, then," I heard myself saying. "I saw an ambulance out front. . . ."

Dottie nodded. "Yes. Grear Ambulance Service. A private company. Unfortunately, there isn't much business for a private company here in the city. Except for transporting bodies from the morgue to funeral homes. . . ."

I was nodding as if what she was saying made perfect sense. And it did. To some extent. At least between the ambulance and the gurney I'd seen downstairs, I understood how she'd transported the body. No one would have given her a second glace at the funeral home, believing her to be dropping off a corpse when instead she'd been taking one. I didn't know how difficult it had been for her to get Nick inside the house and then lug him up the stairs, but she wasn't a small woman. And I was coming to understand that determination outranked size any time of day.

As for the rest . . .

I couldn't say whether relations between the landlord and her tenant were as romantic as she was portraying—and neither could Nick, for that matter—but apparently she'd grown smitten with him. So much so that she'd swiped his body from the funeral home and taken him home, where she was taking care of him, perhaps even trying to make him well.

I hated to be the one to tell her, but no amount of TLC was going to make Nick well again.

Then there was the whole "quite serious" angle of her story. I squinted at the bedsheet across the corpse's torso and farther down to his crotch area, averting my gaze the instant I did so. Just how serious had things gotten between them?

Double yikes.

"Yes, good men are hard to find," Dottie whispered.

I guess that depended on your definition of good, really. I suppose if "living" wasn't a prerequisite, well, then she had the perfect mate. He never complained, never argued, didn't hog the remote, and was never late for dinner. And snuggling was never an issue.

It was the coital part I was especially having a problem with.

I recalled an old Mae West quote I'd read once: "A hard man is good to find." I shuddered straight down to the toes of my boots.

The line on my cell phone was already ringing as I put it to my ear, blindly pushing the button that would link me directly to the 114th Police Precinct.

"Yes, I need to get a message through to Officer Pino Karras. . . ."

THE REMAINDER OF THE DAY was a whirlwind of activity as news of my find hit the Astoria grapevine, burning up every church telephone tree like Greek lightning. I'd heard from my mother, who'd wanted every detail, only to stop me before I got to the most interesting of them, and then asked me to continue (I envisioned her cringing on the other end much as I had when I'd stood in Dottie's bedroom).

Pino had made it to the town house in record time, along with backup. I'd waited downstairs for him, and when he'd caught up with me, I'd thought the shocked expression on his face might never disappear.

My most interesting conversation had been with my aunt Sotiria, who wanted to know why I had called the police instead of her.

"You were working for me. I should have been the first one contacted."

"Aunt Sotiria, we're talking about necrophilia here. The poor woman needs help, and she probably won't get it unless the court orders her to."

"Still . . ."

"What had you planned to do? Just pretend Papadakis' body had gone missing for eight days and now was back and reschedule the viewing?"

"For heaven's sake, no. I would have gone straight to the burial."

Leave it to my aunt to think solely of her business and how it might be impacted.

"Oh well. I guess you had to do what you had to do," she'd finally said on a sigh. "I do have to admit, it seems the news has been good for business. I had three times the usual mourners at the afternoon's viewing. Most of them there trying to pick up any news they hadn't gotten elsewhere."

I'd bet more than a few had asked to see the body, which had been immediately transported back to the funeral home after the city's forensics team had made quick work of their duties and signed off on it. The burial service was scheduled for first thing in the morning, and I had the feeling that turnout would be better for that than for the original viewing.

Who knew a simple case of necrophilia would make you so popular?

I shuddered where I sat in the restaurant down the street from the agency, sipping regular coffee since Phoebe Hall didn't serve frappés. I'd given up trying to stay at the agency a little while earlier. Every television news crew and newspaper wanted me to give them a good quote, something to run alongside Nick's body being rolled out of Dottie's town house and a shot of Dottie herself being cuffed and put into the back of a squad car.

The incident had even served to relieve Rosie of some of her despair over her nightmarish *Meet the Rodriguezes* yesterday.

Not entirely, but it was nice to see her peel her face from the top of her desk and man the phones with efficient style.

"Uh-huh. That's right. She was sleeping with the rotting corpse," I recalled Rosie telling someone on the phone. "I hear that . . . *it* stays hard like weeks after death. And, of course, you don't have to worry about getting pregnant or anything. . . ."

That's about the point where I'd collected a few things from my desk and made my escape to the restaurant.

Of course, neither . . . *it* nor any other part of Papadakis' body had stayed hard. I knew from working at my aunt's that the rigor mortis that kicked in about three to fifteen hours after death was only temporary and the body went limp again afterward, contrary to popular belief. And while regular embalming gave the body weight and shape, it didn't give life to muscles that were already flaccid.

Although I'd heard that if one was knowledgeable in the embalming process . . .

I placed my hands over my ears. What was the point of leaving the agency if all I was going to do was think about the damn case anyway?

I sighed and tried to concentrate on the file in front of me.

"Hey, Sof."

I looked up to find my cousin Pete taking the chair across from me. "Hey, yourself." I gladly closed the file and settled back to focus my attention on him. After a few no-nonsense questions regarding the missing stiff when I'd called him earlier, he'd had no problem moving on. Thank God.

"Here," he said, pushing an envelope across the table. "Nia left these for you at the agency."

"Thanks." I considered the closed envelope. I'd asked my

cousin to do a few things in connection with the Laughton case, one of them to see if she could unseal a file and translate a couple of legal briefs into layman's terms for me. I wasn't entirely convinced she'd earned the fee she'd quoted me, but I figured that since I'd been working in the dark, the learning experience hadn't hurt me or the agency's accounts any.

Of course, that would depend on the outcome of the case.

I asked Pete, "Do you want anything?"

"Nah. My mom's making dinner for me tonight, and she gets upset if I don't eat everything."

Pete's mother wasn't Greek, and from what I understood from Pete, she couldn't cook well, either, so he'd probably been starving himself since yesterday in order to generate the appetite and willpower with which to eat her food.

"So have you made any more progress on the case?" I asked, tucking the envelope under the file in front of me.

"What, linking Valerie Bryer to Hannah Greenberg?" He shook his head. "No." He ran his hands through his hair, looking a little ragged around the edges. Mirroring pretty much what I was feeling. "Maybe I will have some coffee." He motioned for a waitress, who turned over his cup and filled it and then topped mine off. "But I did some other research, you know, looking for other girls who might have gone missing on the same date over the past few years."

I added sugar to my coffee. "And?"

"And nothing. I mean, there was nothing last year, but the year before that there was a similar case of a missing girl. Only she was found a week or so later saying some guy she couldn't identify had abducted her."

"So no connection there, either."

"None that I could tell."

I sipped my coffee. "Were you thinking that maybe we had a serial killer on our hands?"

Pete leaned forward and then back again, as if weighing his words carefully.

"You're talking to me, Pete, not a prosecutor. Everything's game."

He took a deep breath and then released it. "Yes." He relaxed the moment the word was out, making room for the enthusiasm I'd come to expect from him over the past week. "I still do. I can't explain to you why, can't prove it, but . . . I feel it here, in my gut, that there's one guy behind all this."

"And that guy isn't the one currently on trial."

"Yes."

I couldn't say one way or another if I agreed with my cousin. But if the adage was true that there were no such things as co-incidences when it came to cheating spouses and murder, well, Pete might be closer to being right than wrong.

"Are you ready to throw in the towel?" I asked. "I mean, you won't be doing anyone any good if you give up."

"Yes," he said, holding his cup but not drinking from it. "No."

I smiled and touched his wrist. "I'll let you make that call. Let me know if you come across anything more."

He nodded, recognizing my words as a dismissal.

Simply, there was nothing I could do to help him through this. Partly because I didn't know how to. Mostly because I was experiencing much the same frustration with respect to the Laughton case, despite today's success with the missing stiff.

I watched him leave, thinking again how impressed I'd be-come at his growing interest and dedication to the job. But even as I registered the emotion, I realized looking from the outside in that there were probably going to be those cases that were never solved. Police had cold case files. It only made sense that private investigators would encounter the same thing every now and again.

I stared at the documents in front of me. I just didn't want this to be one of them.

Twenty-nine

AT AROUND SUNSET, I FOUND myself driving to a place I'd had no plans to revisit—namely, Jake Porter's apartment, which probably wasn't his apartment anymore but rather a vacant place that resembled Swiss cheese. I'd tried calling him earlier to tell him the news that his warning against working the Papadakis case had been for naught. To share with him that rather than the Mob being behind the body snatching, a sick, lonely woman had done the dirty work.

And with that out of the way, I'd planned to ask him what Nick Papadakis' job had really been (I had the sneaking suspicion that he hadn't been an insurance underwriter) and who he'd thought might have been behind the snatching.

He usually answered my calls after the first or second ring, so when I was routed straight to his anonymous voice-mail account, I knew he was avoiding me.

I didn't care if he was in the middle of a gunfight; I needed to talk to him.

I didn't, however, think this was the place I was going to find him.

I parked Lucille a ways up and across from where his truck had exploded and put her in park. Although an Accord was now in the spot, I could make out the larger black mark under the smaller car. I gave a shudder and cut the engine, sitting for long moments in silence, without even Muffy as my car mate.

Dottie Grear's words echoed through my mind: "Good men are hard to find."

I drummed my fingers against the steering wheel. It seemed ironic, somehow, that I currently had two good men in my life, "good" being a relative term. Dino was good good, meaning that he was good-looking, a good man, would make a good father, and was a good worker.

Jake, on the other hand, was good in other ways.

He was good at getting my blood up. Good at making me obsess over him day and night. And good at making me wonder whether or not I would ever see him again.

A black truck stopped on the street next to my car. Probably the driver thought I was in the process of leaving the car-choked street and wanted my spot. I opened my window and waved him on.

He didn't leave.

I rolled the window back up and leaned over to peer out the passenger's side to find the driver grinning at me.

Jake.

My heart dipped low in my chest as I rolled down the passenger window. The truck he was in looked exactly like the truck that had blown up.

"You could have gone with a different color," I told him, considering the replacement.

"Like which one?"

"I don't know . . . white?"

His chuckle made my toes curl in my boots.

"Want to go for a ride?"

I squinted at him. "Depends on what you mean by 'ride,'" I said, remembering the last time he took me for a ride.

"Around the block once or twice."

I figured I couldn't get myself into much trouble in a truck with him for only a few minutes. I rolled the passenger window back up, grabbed my purse, and was climbing in next to him within moments.

He gave me a once-over. "You look good."

"Is there some reason I shouldn't?"

"No. Not at all. It's just that every time I see you I'm surprised, that's all."

I put my purse on the floor and crossed my arms. "How so?"

"At how damn attracted I am to you."

I stared at him as he switched his attention to the road and put the truck in gear.

He was attracted to me.

Of course, my reaction was a bit on the ridiculous side. I should hope that Jake was attracted to every woman he slept with. Still, I experienced a little zing at his admission.

"You got my call," I said.

"I got your call."

"And?"

"And I'm glad things turned out the way they did."

"I thought that might be the case." Namely, because it meant he wouldn't have to answer any more of my questions about his connection to Papadakis.

The side of his mouth quirked up. "I'm guessing I can't say the same for you, though. That must have been an interesting scene to happen on."

I gave an inward shiver. "To say the least."

"So all's okay in the land of Sofie, then?"

"The land of Sofie?"

He just grinned.

I gave an eye roll. "Actually, it's not. There's still that other case I'm working. And I've hit a roadblock."

"Ah. The Laughton case."

"Mmm."

He didn't say anything as he drove around the block, just as he'd said he would. In this case, around the block meant around Astoria Park, which made it a long block. Still, I held my breath as we neared Lucille, afraid he was going to stop and I'd have to get out.

He passed the car.

"Are you asking for help on it?"

I gaped at him as if he'd just asked if I'd ever given any thought to entering a convent. "Are you telling me that you can help me out?"

His expression was enigmatic. "I didn't say that."

"No, but you implied it."

"Maybe."

I sighed against the seat. Fabric this time. "I liked the leather seats better," I said quietly.

"Yeah, me, too."

"If you do know something that could spring that kid and

find the real killer, don't you think you owe it to society to do something about it?"

"So you do want help."

"No! I don't want help, Jake. I want the truth from you this once."

He pushed his hat back on his head. "Sorry, luv, but you're unlikely to see much of that. From me or anyone else."

Without my realizing it, he'd pulled over to park next to the East River. The trees of Astoria Park were awash with color, hanging over the bank like a yellow and crimson shower. The western sky was a navy blue and purple backdrop to the Triborough Bridge and the Manhattan skyline beyond.

I thought about what Jake had said and about my own ruminations on the relativity of truth and reality. . . .

He shut off the engine of his truck, and the low sound of country and western filled the cab, the closed windows insulating us from the world around us.

Jake said quietly, "I'm sorry about the other night."

I looked at him.

"That's not exactly the way I imagined everything going down."

I smiled. "You make it sound like you had some sort of long seduction scene planned."

He held my gaze. "I did."

Not exactly what I'd been expecting. Then again, by now I should have come to expect the unexpected from the mysterious Aussie. If that even made any sense.

I looked toward the river but closed my eyes tightly against the beauty. This so wasn't fair. First the whole scene with Dino. Now Jake was making me feel—

"Sofie?" he said quietly.

I didn't respond, merely waited for him to continue.

His finger curved under my chin, and he brought my face to look into his.

"I can only imagine what you're thinking right now, luv," he murmured. "Hell, I didn't plan for any of this to happen. Didn't factor in my meeting you."

He softly stroked my cheek with the pad of his thumb, his skin rough against mine. "Yeah, life has a funny way of doing stuff like that, doesn't it."

A shadow of a smile. "Yes. Yes, that it does."

I recalled Dino telling me how he felt and thinking that Jake would never do that.

I realized that was because he didn't have to. Everything was right there on his rugged, handsome face. Every emotion I felt. My confusion, my need.

A swallow gathered at the back of my throat that I couldn't seem to push down for the life of me.

Jake leaned forward, and I parted my lips in anticipation of his kiss.

Instead he reached around me and opened the door.

"I'd better get going. You don't mind walking back to your car, do you?"

I finally swallowed as I shook my head.

I slid down off the seat and onto the sidewalk and turned to take my purse from him.

Not unlike the darkening sky, his blue eyes shone almost black. "Good-bye, Sofie."

I was incapable of words as I stood watching him close the door and pull away from the curb, clutching my purse to my chest as if it might protect me from the torrent of emotion ripping through me.

Good-bye, Jake. . . .

THE SENSE OF MELANCHOLIA I felt followed me all the way home after I walked back to my car. It was sunset on the eve of Halloween, yet I wasn't afraid of shadowy figures and couldn't have cared less about the neighborhood vampire as I passed Romanoff's house and parked nearer to my apartment building. I was too focused on what was going on inside of me to give half a thought to what might or might not be happening outside.

I lethargically got out of my car. Within the span of a few days, I'd been dumped twice. Well, okay, I guess I had been the one to dump Dino. But directly thereafter, I'd gotten dumped by Jake.

I pushed the strap of my purse up my arm. I suppose you actually had to have been picked up in order to be dumped. And while I surrendered to occasional forays into fantasyland, even I knew that a one-night stand did not a relationship make.

So what did a series of one-night stands make?

I grimaced, the words *series* and *one-night* not fitting together at all.

Dino and I had had a relationship, no matter how hard I'd tried to label it otherwise.

I paused on the sidewalk, staring up at the building I'd been given as a gift. But unlike a toaster, this one would keep on giving well beyond a couple of pieces of toast.

Single, unemployed mom Etta Munson had Halloween decals on her windows of a ghost and a witch. To the right, even the

DeVry students had decorated for the occasion, although I suspected their efforts of a black curtain and a purple light had little to do with being festive.

Above them both, Mrs. Nebitz's windows and mine were empty but for our regular curtains and miniblinds.

I sighed, picked up a ball that Lola Munson had likely left outside, and then let myself into the building, putting the ball outside the Munsons' door as I went upstairs.

Mrs. Nebitz's door cracked open as I took out my keys.

"Hi, Sofie. I heard the news on TV tonight. Did that woman really take that dead body?"

I put my key into the door lock. "Yes, unfortunately she did, Mrs. Nebitz."

She said something under her breath that I couldn't make out.

"I'm sorry to bother you when you obviously have so much on your plate, dear, but I wanted to know if you've had time to look into that . . . matter for me."

I opened my door. I'd forgotten all about that . . . matter.

Funny, it seemed like weeks ago that I'd watched Rosie with her face against her desk. Had it really been only that morning that the matter to which Mrs. Nebitz was referring was solved?

I shook my head and smiled at the older woman. "No, I'm sorry, Mrs. Nebitz, but I haven't had a chance to look into it yet. Have you given any more thought to having that conversation with Seth?"

"No, I haven't." She looked contemplative. "But perhaps I should."

"All right, then. Good night."

"Good night, Sofie."

Both our doors clicked closed. I stood for a long moment leaning against the smooth wood. Only the waning light of dusk illuminated the apartment. I made out the sound of a clock ticking, but just then I was hard-pressed to figure out where it was coming from. Probably some forgotten wedding gift I'd unwrapped and put somewhere without giving it any thought.

For that matter, it might even be a gift that was still wrapped in my room.

I shrugged out of my jacket and let it slide down until I absently caught it with my right hand. I hung it on the hall tree along with my purse and then switched on a lamp and stood staring around the empty place. I'd picked out nearly every piece of furniture, every knickknack, myself. And in recent weeks, it had really begun to feel like home to me.

Only I felt no comfort from it now.

I'd told my mother I'd stop by this evening to share the juicy details on my discovery. While ordinarily I'd shrug it off, get something to eat, settle in front of the television, and ignore her phone calls until it was too late to go over, I instead walked back to the door, put my jacket back on, and called for Muffy where he lay half-asleep on the Barcalounger.

"Hey, Muffster, you want to go to Grandma's house?"

I expected him to ignore me, just as he had the other half-dozen times over the past few days.

I was surprised when he instantly got up and zoomed out the door when I opened it.

I eyed where the cat was asleep on the rug across the room and then followed the Jack Russell terrier's white-and-brown furry butt down the stairs. Probably I should have put out some fresh food and water for Tee, but I figured I wouldn't be gone long and it could wait until we got back home.

I opened the door to the street, and Muffy zipped out into the cool evening air . . .

And kept on going.

"Muffy!" I called.

Usually when I invited him along, he went straight to the passenger side of the Mustang and waited, panting and tail wagging.

He didn't stop. . . .

Thirty

MY HEART POUNDED A MILLION miles a minute, my lethargy vanishing along with one very determined dog.

I ran in the direction he'd gone, thinking about the leash I'd bought and had used only a handful of times because, well, Muffy had tried to guarantee I would never again have hands full of anything but bite scars when I put it on him.

As I jogged down the street, wildly looking right and left and calling out his name, I thought that I should have endured his wrath. Anything not to be feeling the sheer terror I was experiencing now.

What if I couldn't find him?

It was then I realized how much a part of my life the little mongrel had become. I liked having him at the apartment when I came home, his recent foul mood swing aside. Waking up in the morning to his growl. His panting excitement whenever I fixed one of my coffee table picnics and fed him mystery tidbits.

Funny, I'd never really seen myself as a pet person.

I stopped at the first cross street, looking up and down, trying to determine if he'd turned off or had continued straight. It humored me not at all to consider that I, a renowned pet detective, had just lost my own pet.

In that one moment, I knew the desperation owners must feel when they came into the agency begging me to locate their loved ones.

And Muffy was a loved one, wasn't he? No, he might not be my child. Or sibling. Or cousin. But that didn't make him any less important.

And I wondered how much I'd give to have someone bring him back home to me.

"Muffy?" I called out.

I didn't expect him to respond. Partly because he rarely responded on command. Mostly because I knew how upset he'd been with me over the past week or so, for reasons I had yet to fully understand.

Okay, maybe allowing Tee to come and go as he pleased hadn't been such a great idea. But since the sleek feline had chosen me, I couldn't bring myself to reject him.

Was that why Muffy had run away? Had he had enough of having his own needs overlooked?

I'd never before given much thought to why a pet left its owners. This perspective was opening all sorts of new windows. And might be useful when and if I ever personally worked another missing pet case.

"Muffy?" I called again as I crossed the street, deciding to continue on straight.

It dawned on me that I was heading in the direction of my

parents' house. Could Muffy have understood that that's where we were going and decided to walk—or rather run—there instead of drive with me in the car?

Okay, so I should probably consider walking there more often myself. It wasn't as if it were all that far. And sometimes I did.

More often I didn't.

A lot of New Yorkers didn't own cars. With the great Metropolitan Transportation Authority system (aka MTA), you really didn't need to. But my parents had always driven, as did most of the people in my extended family, so I'd inherited my car-loving roots from them, I guess. I took the train when I went into the city, but otherwise, jockeying for parking spaces when traveling in Queens was more than A-OK with me, it was a way of life.

I slid my cell phone out of my pocket.

"Mom, look outside. Is Muffy there on the porch?"

"What?"

"Just look outside, okay?"

She did as I asked. "I don't see him."

The call was unnecessary because in a hundred or so yards I would be at the house to see for myself. But I figured at the rate of speed he'd been traveling when he'd zipped out the door, he would beat me there and maybe Thalia could let him inside the house lest he get tired of waiting and run somewhere else.

"Oh, wait," Thalia said.

Relief suffused my body. I paused on the sidewalk. "He's there?"

"No."

"Then why did you tell me to wait?"

"Because he might not be here . . . but he's next door."

I signed off and crossed the street, hastening my step. I gave a deep sigh as I finally spotted the Jack Russell terrier. Mom was right. He was next door. Specifically, he was barking outside the closed gate to Mrs. K's old place, from time to time leaping into the air as if trying to open the latch himself.

I stopped ten feet away, considering the scene.

It wasn't so very long ago that Muffy had lived in that home with Mrs. Kapoor, my mother's late best friend. I'd thought the dog that once had a seemingly insatiable appetite for Sofie flesh had adjusted well to being my pet after Mrs. K had embarked on her one last journey to Hindu heaven (or did they believe in reincarnation? I couldn't remember).

I guess this was proof positive he hadn't adjusted as well as I'd thought.

"Muffy, honey? Come here, boy." I crouched down and clapped my hands, wishing I had thought to grab some biscuits out of my car.

Then again, I hadn't actually been thinking with a full brain when I gave chase.

I was only thankful I'd found him and that he wasn't wandering the mean Queens streets somewhere.

Muffy ignored me and continued his efforts to open the gate.

A young Asian family had bought the place, of Chinese descent, I think. And right now one of two children I'd spotted so far came outside. He was about ten and looked puzzled to find a dog trying to get into his yard. Usually dogs tried to get out of the yards they were closed into.

"It's okay," I called. "He used to live here."

The kid didn't seem bothered. In fact, he was so unbothered, he came off the porch, down the walkway, and reached for the gate.

"No!" I shouted.

Too late. He flipped the latch, and Muffy nudged his way inside.

I held my breath, expecting a bloodcurdling scream from the kid when Muffy sank his small but very sharp teeth into his flesh.

Instead the dog ignored the gate opener, streaking right by him. I squinted, watching as he barked his way up the sidewalk toward the porch.

Just as he had a thousand times before.

The hair stood up on my arms. It was as if he were being called home by Mrs. K herself.

I neared the gate, coming to stand next to the kid. We both watched as Muffy jumped on top of the lawn chair there, his little tail wagging wildly, his tongue out as if licking something.

Or, rather, someone.

"You know," my mother said quietly, having joined me, "I thought I'd felt Aklima's presence lately."

I stared at her, smoothing my hands over my arms through my jacket sleeves.

Thalia shrugged. "With everything going on, I didn't pay much attention to it. But I can't count the times I thought I smelled curry." She glanced at me. "I've kept the *kadili* lit all week long."

A *kadili* was a religious Greek oil lantern. In the old country, most people lit them every night to keep spirits at bay. Here in the States, my mother lit hers every Saturday night right after she'd blessed the house with the *levani*—a decorative metal decanter used to burn incense.

"Look," Thalia said. "Mrs. Kapoor is saying good-bye to her dog."

I was almost afraid to look. But I did anyway.

Muffy jumped down from the chair, continuing to look up as if at someone, running around and around. My heart beat an uneven rhythm in my chest as he stopped and put his head down. I swore I could see where his fur was being ruffled from being petted.

But that was impossible. There was no such thing as ghosts. Was there?

A passing car's headlights cut through the light fog, and I caught my breath. For the briefest of moments, something shimmered on the porch. Something in the shape of an ancient Bengali woman bent over, petting a dog she'd loved over almost everything else in life outside of her children.

"She's gone," my mother whispered.

I must not have been the only one who thought they'd seen something. Shouting in a foreign language, the boy ran for the house, passing Muffy where the dog walked slowly down the porch steps. The boy cut a wide arc around the terrier and disappeared inside as Muffy came toward the gate. I opened it for him, and he stepped out without missing a step.

My mother looked at me and smiled and then turned to go to her own house.

"Hey, boy," I said quietly, crouching down again. "Are you okay?"

He stopped in front of me, looking back at the porch, then again at me. He made a small plaintive sound and then pushed his head into my waiting hands.

As I gently scratched his ears, I realized that he'd never had a chance to say good-bye to Mrs. K. I'd just recovered him from his kidnapper and was bringing him home when Mrs. K was being wheeled away to a waiting ambulance, Muffy barking like a mad dog in my car.

"Take care of my Muffy, Sofie," she'd said weakly.

It almost seemed as though I heard her words again on the cool air.

Of course, she'd died later at the hospital and none of us ever saw her again.

Including Muffy.

"I'm sorry, sweet pea," I said to the dog who'd growled and barked his way through the past week for no apparent reason.

Only there had been a reason, hadn't there? He'd been anticipating this moment, this chance to get that final shot at saying good-bye to the woman who had brought such joy to his life.

"Are you ready to go home now?" I asked, getting to my feet.

He barked once, causing his furry body to shudder, and then started in the direction of our house. I decided I'd call my mother later to explain.

Then again, I didn't think she was the one who would need an explanation. Right now I had a few questions of my own that needed answering.

If only I held out a hope of having them answered.

Thirty-one

THE FOLLOWING DAY, ROSIE CALLED in sick. And I had to face the music all by my lonesome. On Halloween.

At somewhere after eleven and umpteen phone calls from clients and press, I finally gave up trying to keep on top of everything and was about to send all calls straight to voice mail when first Eugene Waters and then Debbie Matenopoulos, one of my process servers, came in.

I took it as a sign and put them immediately to work at my desk and Rosie's. I figured between the two of them, they could figure out a way to handle what Rosie took care of all by herself, and I disappeared into my uncle's office to take a fresh look at both sides of the crime and witness board I'd put together.

"Yes, Miss Metropolis did find Mr. Papadakis' body. . . . Yes, Ms. Grear was the one who'd taken it."

I listened to Debbie's by now verbatim response, given to her after she'd become chattier than was wise with one print journalist and would probably be quoted as "A source with the Metropolis

Detective Agency reports that the suspect performed all sorts of sex acts on the dead body, redefining necrophilia."

Then there was Waters, whom I banned from taking calls from reporters at all, much to his relief.

"Man, I never seen so many people want to talk about banging a dead guy. Who wants to know about this shit, anyway?"

Lord forbid anyone quote him. Although I think it was a pretty good bet that they wouldn't.

So I was having him take client calls and put all media inquiries through to Debbie, who was putting stickpins on the world map on the wall to indicate where they were calling from.

"India," she shouted.

"Probably he works for the *Times*. Probably they outsourced some poor schmo's job here," Waters said, watching Debbie's ass where she stood on her toes to press the pin into the middle of India.

I gave an eye roll, impressed that she could find the country at all. I'd recently heard that something like twenty percent of Americans were unable to locate the United States on a world map. So I figured that put Debbie a little ahead of the game. I eyed the short shorts she had on. "Little" being the operative word.

I couldn't take this anymore.

I grabbed my jacket and purse and moved toward the door. "Hold down the fort. I'll be back in a half hour."

Hopefully with Rosie.

"Bring back some lunch," Waters said, answering another call.

"Yeah," Debbie agreed. "Something low-fat and low-calorie."

"For her. Something high-fat and high-calorie for me."

I handed the phone to Debbie. "Order in. Just make sure you get receipts."

"Really?" she asked, as if she'd just been given a credit card with no limit.

"Don't go over twenty-five apiece," I said, when I should have quoted a much lower amount. At this point, I was willing to go up to fifty apiece just to keep them there so I could leave.

That deflated Debbie a bit, but not much.

I shook my head as I stepped outside. Didn't take much for some people.

I got into Lucille and pointed her in the direction of Bayside. Then I changed my mind and drove to my place first.

Last night, after picking up a couple of case-solved souvlaki for Muffy, Tee, and me, the quiet dog and I went home and finished out the evening in front of the television, a half-lidded Tee watching the dog and me suspiciously from across the room. Not that I could blame him. Up until that point, he hadn't seen Muffy and me do more than growl at each other. Now we appeared to be best pals.

Well, not exactly best pals, but in a better place now that he'd gotten a chance to say good-bye to Mrs. Kapoor.

And that's all I was going to say on that matter.

At any rate, within a few minutes, I'd gone upstairs to collect Muffy for the ride and found that Tee had left again. I debated closing the window to keep him from returning, then at the last moment decided not to. Since Muffy's attitude had improved and was almost back to normal, I figured the cat could stay as long as he wanted to.

If he came back, that is.

So with Muffy panting through the crack in the passenger-side window, I drove to Elmhurst and Rosie's house.

Simply, I didn't buy that she was sick. Rosie was never sick. And even if she was, I was convinced that she'd infuse herself with massive cold medications and make it into work anyway. So I made a quick stop and a little while later stood at the door to her house and knocked.

"Who's there?" a female voice asked.

I was relieved she was home instead of at her sister's.

"It's Sofie."

No response.

"Sofie Metropolis? The woman you work for."

"You mean the woman I work *with*," Rosie corrected.

I smiled, knowing she'd rise to the bait.

The door opened, revealing that she wore an old T-shirt with a short silk robe with drawings of Betty Boop all over it and big fluffy pink slippers. Her usually flawless hair was a tangled mess around her makeupless face.

I'd only seen Rosie once not looking one hundred percent. But even then she'd held an odd sort of Coke-can-head, cucumber-mask appeal.

"Hey. You look a wreck," I said quietly.

She gave the door a halfhearted push to close it in my face.

I caught it and followed her inside.

"I brought you some chicken soup. Homemade. Phoebe said she'd give me the recipe if you like it."

"Liar. Phoebe never gives anyone any of her recipes."

I looked around for signs that she was sick. Wads of used tissues littered the coffee table and the top of a Mets stadium

blanket that was bunched up on the sofa. A spot Rosie immediately reclaimed, pulling the stadium blanket up to her neck,
causing the used tissues to roll onto the other end of the sofa
and the floor. Not that she noticed.

"I brought meds," I said, shaking a small bag.

She waved me away as she reached for the tissue box, taking
what appeared to be the last one out. She picked up the container, stared inside, and then tossed it to the floor.

"I didn't think to bring Kleenex," I said. "Can I get you a roll
of toilet paper from the bathroom?"

"The hell with the tissues," she whispered.

I slowly crossed the room, half-afraid she'd say the same for
me as I sank into an armchair.

"So . . . ," I said carefully. "When do you think you might be
back in the office?"

She flopped her hands down and glared at me. "Are you serious? I'm dying here and you want to know when I'm coming
back to work?"

I didn't say anything.

She sighed and scooted down farther into the blanket. "I
don't know. Tomorrow. The day after that. Maybe never. I don't
know."

I nodded as if I understood. I didn't. Although I was beginning to get an idea.

I squinted at her. Splotchy skin. Red, raw nose. Indicators
seemed to point to the common cold. But I was coming to learn
that nothing common was able to take Rosie out for long.

"You want I should call a doctor over?" I asked.

She gave an eye roll. "Doctors don't make house calls no
more."

"I know a Greek one that does."

"Does he know how to mend broken hearts? Because if he doesn't, he's not going to do me any good."

Bingo.

I'd had a feeling that Rosie's symptoms pointed not to a virus, but rather to something man-made.

Her big dark eyes filled with tears as she stared at me, her hands fisted at her sides. "Seth dumped me," she said on a long, high-pitched wail.

"Oh, Rosie." I immediately moved from the chair to perch on the edge of the couch, awkwardly moving one way, then another, to hug her.

To my surprise, she hugged me back. Actually, she clutched me desperately, and I winced in pain. It was as if I were the only thing between her and a future of hell on earth.

"I'm sorry, Rosie," I whispered, smoothing her uncharacteristically tangled hair. "I'm so sorry."

She hiccuped, mopping at her eyes with the last tissue. "He . . . he . . . was supposed to meet me last night, you know, after work. I waited and waited. Then I got tired of waiting and I called him." She finished with the tissue and threw it to the floor with the others. "He sent me a text message."

She drew out the last syllable and went into a crying jag again.

I stared at the table behind her couch, taking in the little knick-knacks alongside two bottles of perfume and bulbs of garlic.

Seemed not even being dumped could put a dent in Rosie's superstitious fears that the neighborhood vampires were after her.

"I wouldn't jump to conclusions, Rosie," I said. "Maybe he got caught up somewhere. Maybe he was delayed, and couldn't take your call."

She sniffed heavily and then drew her nose along the shoulder of my sweater.

I winced again.

"Oh, yeah? Then explain this."

She thrust her cell phone at me.

I leaned back and took it cautiously, hoping that she wasn't contagious. Lord knew that I'd had my share of heartache lately.

"Sorry, Ro," a text message read. "This isn't going 2 work. I'm sorry."

Rosie took several ragged breaths and then started crying again. "He broke up with me by text message."

When she began to wipe her nose on my sweater again, I quickly got up.

"Just a second," I said.

I rushed into the bathroom and took the roll of toilet paper off the holder and hurried back to hand it to her.

She busied herself with winding sheets around and around her hand, and I gladly moved back to the chair.

"That's cold," I said. "Really cold."

She nodded. "I was supposed to meet his parents tonight."

I looked everywhere but at her face.

Frankly, I'd been afraid this was going to happen. First there'd been the disastrous meal at Rosie's mother's house that had turned into World War II. Then there was Mrs. Nebitz's asking about her—and probably Seth's mother, too. I knew that Jews were very much like the Greeks in that they preferred their children to marry their own. Probably Puerto Ricans weren't that much different, either.

I shuddered as I wondered what would have happened had I

ever brought anyone not Greek home. In fact, I'd pretty much known what would have happened, so I'd never dared it.

Specifically, the family would have sent me bound and gagged to Greece and married me off to the first widowed goat herder with no teeth.

All joking aside, I thought it odd that in this day and age, matters of race and religion still held such sway. But there you had it. My grandfather Kosmos had told me once it was the only way to ensure a people would go forward. It had been the way the Greeks had survived millennia of war and occupation.

Still, somehow it didn't seem fair. Especially when it came to love.

"The shit," I said.

I blinked at Rosie where she had her right hand swathed in bath tissue. Her tears were beginning to lessen.

"That's right," I continued. "To hell with him if he doesn't know that he's just lost the best thing that ever happened to him."

Her dark eyes sparked at my solidly said defense. "Damn straight."

She sat up, moving the blanket from her legs. But apparently we'd both moved a little too fast to the angry stage and she experienced an immediate relapse.

"I love him!" she wailed.

I got up and pulled her to stand with me.

"Buck up, Rosie. What kind of example are you setting for independent women everywhere by letting one male reduce you to a brokenhearted wretch?"

She stared at me.

"That's right. Have you looked at yourself in the mirror today? Lord, girl, you look a mess."

I was purposely using the Rosie brand of philosophy and talk on her in the hopes that it would get through in a way that my usual approach would not.

I swiveled her in the direction of the bathroom and switched on the light. She gasped in shock.

"That's right. A wretch."

I moved around her and switched on the hot water in the tub.

"Now take a shower and snap out of it, girlfriend. You've got to show him that he can't do this to you. That nobody, but nobody, dumps Rosie Rodriguez, much less does it via a text message."

I watched with some satisfaction as her back snapped straighter.

I took in her face. "You're going to need some major concealer for those eyes."

"I know just the thing," she said.

I had no doubt that she did.

I smiled softly, watching as she went about her business.

I figured out about a second too late that I should have left her to it when she pulled off her T-shirt. I stood looking at what had to be the most perfectly formed breasts I'd ever seen.

"You still here?" Rosie asked me, unaffected by the fact that I was staring at her nude body. And that she'd probably just damaged me for life.

It wasn't fair.

I held up my hands. "I'm going. See you at the agency?"

"Damn right you will. I can only imagine what you've done to the place while I've been gone. Probably it's going to take me a week to straighten everything out."

"Probably."

She climbed into the shower and closed the curtain. I turned to go.

"Hey, Sof?"

I looked over my shoulder to find Rosie peering out from the side of the curtain.

"Um . . . you know. Thanks."

"You're welcome." I cleared my throat. "Just get your ass into work pronto. I don't think broken hearts are covered by sick pay."

I got hit in the back of the head with a loofah as I hurried toward the front door.

Thirty-two

ROSIE WASTED NO TIME GETTING back to the agency and kicking both Eugene and Debbie out of the office, a good deal of Spanish profanity included. She even refused to give them their regular papers to serve, she was so upset, telling them to come back tomorrow, making me wonder if I perhaps had brought her back too soon. That while, yes, she was channeling her emotions into anger, that anger wasn't being limited to occasional Tourette's-like spurts against Seth, but was being directed to the world at large.

It was after she'd read me the riot act for not properly signing off on a case I'd put on her desk that I raised my hands in surrender, gathered my files, and decided to work out of Lucille for the remainder of the day.

Which, I discovered some hours later, might not have been a very good idea, even with Muffy as a car mate.

Especially with Muffy as a car mate.

First of all, it was Halloween. And despite its being the middle of the week, all sorts of kooks and goblins milled around the streets, probably on the way to or from early parties or having dressed in character for school or work.

My original choice of parking spots was down the street from Dino's sweets shop, where I occasionally watched him through the window as I went through my files. But after Muffy barked that he had personal business to see to, I left, ducking when I thought Dino might have spotted me as I drove past. (Not that it mattered. My Bondo-special Mustang would be recognizable even in a sea of like cars.)

Next I went to Valerie Bryer's family's house and watched as her father came home. Minutes later, another car I guessed contained Mrs. Bryer backed out of the drive. Minutes after that, their son left as well. I imagined Mr. Bryer sitting at the empty dining room table, having dinner alone, and had to squelch the desire to see if he wanted company.

Instead, I drove to the house of the family of the latest girl to go missing, Hannah Greenberg, some miles away in Bayside and parked across the street. I pulled out notes Pete had supplied, his having tried to work out a connection between the two girls falling well short.

Muffy barked, and I stared at him.

"Don't tell me you have business again?"

He panted and ran across the files to stand on my lap and then ran back again. Where normally I might be annoyed, now I smiled. It was just so damn good to have him back again.

"All right, all right," I said. "But you have to wear your leash."

He didn't look pleased as I pulled the item in question from the backseat and paused to stare at him.

"Hey, I don't like this any more than you do. But I don't plan on going through what I did last night again anytime soon." I carefully attached the fastener to his collar. "You scared the hell out of me, you know that?" I whispered, giving him an ear scratch.

He growled and nipped at my hands when I pulled them back.

"Fine. I'll take your dissatisfaction under advisement. But I'm telling you right now, you'd better just get used to the leash or else I'm going to leave you home from here on out."

And then where would both of us be?

He seemed to catch my drift and settled down. For a moment, anyway.

While browsing through a mail-order catalog the other day, I'd come across a section of items inspired by literary detective characters. One of them was a Sherlock Holmes cap and pipe made especially for dogs. I'd come close to picking up the phone and ordering them for Muffy. Until I'd realized there wasn't a chance the Mutt from Hell would wear either. I would have given him two minutes to destroy both items flat out.

Not a smart way to spend a hundred and twenty bucks.

But the exercise did go to show that I'd come to view the little fur ball as a partner of sorts. A roommate at the apartment who didn't borrow my clothes or drink the last of the milk; my associate on the road who assisted on missing pet cases. (Okay, he'd probably hurt more than he'd helped in that regard, but when he wanted to, boy, did he ever pitch in. One of the last cases we'd worked together involved breaking a dognapping ring that put nearly a dozen pets back in the loving arms of their owners . . . and left Muffy with a, um, boyfriend.)

I got out of the car and tugged on the leash. Muffy dragged his butt across both seats, biting and growling at the leash.

"Quit it."

I pulled harder, and he was forced to abandon his war and turn his attention to landing squarely on all four paws on the sidewalk. He glared up at me, none too happy.

Hey, I wasn't too happy myself. He was making me get out of my nice safe car at dusk on Halloween.

"Okay," I said, walking him a ways from the car. "Get to it . . . do your thing."

He sniffed and strained against his leash, pulling me forward. I sighed and followed.

The Greenberg place was across the street and up three houses. Like Forest Hills, the neighborhood was nicely residential. There was plenty of room between houses, lots of old trees, and wide sidewalks.

The Greenberg property itself reminded me of England. Not that I'd ever been to England outside Heathrow Airport on a connecting flight to Greece, but I'd certainly seen plenty of movies and PBS pieces of both non- and fictional varieties that had featured the country. The Tudor style of the home, along with the lush green grass, made me crave fish and chips.

Muffy pulled, I followed.

This was my first time casing the neighborhood, although I understood that Pete had questioned the family and the neighbors extensively, trying to find that connection he was convinced must exist. I hadn't asked him how he'd gained access (I wondered if he'd impersonated a news reporter), but he must not have run into any problems or I'd have heard about it.

Muffy finally stopped and I stopped along with him. My new vantage point gave me a clear view of the property. I counted five cars in the driveway. I knew that the family had three kids, Hannah being the oldest and the only one of driving age, so I guessed the remainder belonged to her parents and visitors. Not surprising, I guess. Extended family tended to pull together in situations like this.

I thought of Mr. Bryer again and frowned.

I'd followed up on the angle of his sexual predator brother, only to find that he hadn't left his new home in Iowa since he'd moved there, and he hadn't been anywhere near New York during the time of Valerie's disappearance. I'd considered questioning Bryer about the incident, then chucked the idea. The guy had enough on his plate without dealing with that on top of everything else.

Had I been wrong not to further pursue the lead?

Perpetrator as victim. Victim as perpetrator.

It was said that sexual predators often had been victims of molestation themselves when they were children. Was it possible that sexual abuse had been a part of the Bryer boys' upbringing? If so, could both of them have continued the same sad cycle in their own lives?

Pete and I had already considered and dismissed the father as a suspect in Valerie's disappearance. But could the story be more complicated than that? Could that explain the current stress on the family unit? Or was it, as I had guessed, a sad epilogue to an even sadder story?

I looked at Muffy, who was finishing up a number two on the nice green lawn next to me by kicking grass clippings on top of the steaming pile.

"Great," I said.

I hadn't taken a poop bag from the car because I'd thought he only had to take a piss. After all, he had already done the other earlier in the day.

I must be feeding him entirely too much. Either that or he was making up for lost time given his light eating over the past week.

I sighed and pulled him back to the car, unleashing him and putting him inside. Then I took a poop bag from the door pocket and backtracked alone to collect the pile, hoping no one was watching from inside the house. As I was bent over, a truck pulled to the curb behind me. I looked to make sure I wasn't in danger of being hit and absently read the words on the passenger door.

Sackett Landscaping.

My heart skipped a beat as I made slow work of picking up the poop.

The truck door opened and closed on the street side of the vehicle. I watched from between my legs as the driver took a rake and bag from the truck bed, then walked to the other side of the street.

I quickly snapped upright and walked to my car, tying off the poop bag and putting it on the floor behind my seat before climbing in.

"Please, please, please," I whispered, gripping the steering wheel as I watched the landscaper.

Could this be the break I was looking for? The connection between the two girls?

What was his name, what was his name?

I budged Muffy out of the way and took a file from the passenger seat, ignoring his whine.

Floyd Sackett.

I watched as Floyd stopped on the sidewalk in front of the Greenberg place. I held my breath. He turned and walked back to his truck, doing something in the bed. Gathering more supplies, maybe?

"Scoot," I told Muffy, moving him to the backseat as I rummaged through the various files and information he'd been sitting on. I came across a sealed envelope. I recognized the cheap ink blotter stamp on the upper-left-hand corner as my cousin Nia's name and business address.

Pete. Pete had given me the envelope at the restaurant yesterday. Said Nia had sent it. And I had never opened it up.

I did so now. It was the unsealed contents of Floyd Sackett's juvenile record. I scanned it quickly, suddenly feeling sick to my stomach.

I reached for my cell phone, dropping it twice before dialing the number I wanted even as Sackett returned to the front of the Greenberg place . . . and walked across their lawn to begin raking leaves.

Unholy shit.

Thirty-three

MY MIND RACED FASTER THAN my car as I hightailed it away from the Greenbergs' to where I hoped I might find the missing girl: the landscaper's place of business across town in northern Astoria.

Muffy seemed to tune in to my excitement and barked like crazy, running from the backseat to the front, looking out the window as if to say, "Tell me where he is, tell me where he is! I'll take care of him. He's all mine!"

I'd lived for so long in a state of limbo when it came to the Laughton case that I'd begun to believe I'd never get the break I needed to finally crack the case. In fact, I'd practically given up, period, and had settled into a pattern of waiting. Waiting for Johnny Laughton's fate to be decided by a jury of his peers, a jury that was being impaneled this week. After that, well, I was off the hook, right? I mean, I'd done all I could. Researched until the piles of paper on my desk and my uncle's teetered precariously, threatening death to whoever should be standing nearby when the landslide happened. Pored over that same paperwork until I was afraid my eyes would pop out and roll across the desk and onto the floor. Questioned witnesses, worked out various scenarios, put Pete on the case until he was in the same sad state that I was, fresh out of answers. Worse, fresh out of questions.

Then just like that, something innocuous happened and every last puzzle piece that had been hovering out of reach fit together to make a dazzling, terrifying picture. Not that of a boyfriend killing his girlfriend in a fit of rage. But that of a potential serial killer systematically getting away with taking the life of at least one young woman and possibly another.

I got off Grand Central at 37th and sped north, immediately stomping on the brakes when a group of trick-or-treaters trailed across the street in front of me. The chaperoning mother glared at me as she hurried the kids along. I bit my tongue to keep from yelling, "Get a move on!"

My stomach pitched to my feet as I realized that it wasn't only the life of Hannah Greenberg possibly on the line, but the future safety of the kids before me.

Could Hannah still be alive? If so, where would a sicko like Sackett keep her?

The logical choice in my mind was his lot. It was remote, away from residential properties, and after six even his commercial neighbors shut down for the night, giving him the freedom to do whatever he pleased until the following morning.

And now it was well after six.

I knew a moment of terror for my own safety. What was I doing going to a place that I had essentially outlined as the perfect scene for a crime?

"He's working at the Greenbergs'," I said aloud, as if it would convince me more than if I'd merely thought the words.

Muffy busily barked at the kids through the window as they finally reached the other side of the street intact, and I continued on, this time on the lookout for errant ghosts and goblins trying to double-treat on the same street by weaving back and forth rather than going down the block and then up again.

I thought of the candy at home that I'd bought to give out myself tonight. To guarantee that I wouldn't eat too much of it, I'd purposely purchased items I didn't much care for. What did I do with it now?

I ousted the idiotic thought from my head as I did a little street zigzagging of my own until I finally came to a halt outside the closed gates to Sackett Landscaping.

I checked for my Glock in its holster under my left arm, took my lock-picking kit out of the glove compartment and put it in my pocket along with a few other supplies, and then got out of the car, forgoing Muffy's leash. So sue me, the last thing on my mind was making sure he wouldn't run away. Anyway, I was reasonably sure that he hadn't actually run away at all, but rather had run *to* Mrs. K.

But that's the last I was going to say on that. Seriously.

I hurried to the seven-foot-high double-wide gates, peeking through the privacy slats inserted into the chain links to stare inside the lot as I fingered the industrial-size padlock. I slid the kit out of my pocket and went to work. Although I'd practiced on my own double bolts at home—something at which Mrs. Nebitz had enjoyed watching me fail—I'd never worked on one of these. And it was looking as if I were doomed to fail here as well. Then I remembered that Eugene had gotten me a master key that worked on a large percentage of industrial padlocks. Seems the police department used them to gain access to properties when needed. But where had I put it?

I rummaged through the kit and then remembered I'd put it on my key ring. I took my ring from my jacket pocket, fingering through the keys, briefly touching the Greek eye hanging there to ward off evil, and found what I hoped was the key.

The lock clanked open.

Bless you, Waters.

I slid the keys back into my pocket and pushed open the gate. Muffy ran right in, barking his head off despite my fervent pleas for him to be quiet.

Dogs, I was coming to understand, were a lot like men. In the heat of the moment, they didn't have two brain cells to rub together.

I closed the gate carefully and arranged the chain and lock to make it appear that they had gone untouched, then followed after the maniac canine that was acting as though he'd just entered Doggie Coney Island.

"Muffy!" I whispered. "Get back here. Now!"

A security light in the far left corner slightly brightened half the fenced-in area, leaving the other half, including the shed, in shadow. I shivered, watching as Muffy dove into those shadows just beyond the shed.

I let him go as I wandered closer to the equipment to my left. The industrial-size wood chipper was of particular interest. The lower lip of the feeder stood four feet off the ground and was at least four feet wide and three feet high. I took the Mini Maglite out of my pocket and switched it on, peering into the machine at the corkscrewlike blades inside.

A sound caught my attention. Or, rather, the lack of sound did.

Where was Muffy?

I switched off the light and stepped in the direction of the shed.

"Muffy?" I whispered.

Which was probably the absolutely worst thing to do. I mean, Sackett himself might not be there, but what if he had an accomplice? An assistant who helped him nab young, unsuspecting women to abuse and then feed to the wood chipper when they were done with them?

I was only half joking, but the possibility turned my blood to ice water.

I passed from light into shadow and automatically reached into my holster for my gun. Hey, you never knew what might jump out at you. I also switched the Maglite back on, holding it parallel to the gun. I adjusted the beam to floodlight. Of course, neither the light nor my heightened senses prevented me from nearly tripping over something in the dirt. I kicked at the offending object with the toe of my boot. An old rusty chain with links the size of my fist. I sighed.

"Muffy?" I called a little louder.

Okay, so maybe the gun made me feel a little bolder. Guns had a reputation for changing backwoods geeks and urban street kids into Rambo. Just ask human-hormone-happy Sylvester Stallone.

I grimaced at the unending stream of mental babbling and took a deep breath.

Concentrate. If you were a killer, where would you hide the body?

Of course, I had no idea what it was like to be a killer. And I didn't want one, either.

I passed the locked shed, sweeping the beam of the flashlight ahead of me as I searched for my errant pooch. I rounded the shabby building.

"Shit!" I said, both Muffy and I jumping at the same time as I came right up on him without seeing him. "Scare the hell out of a body already."

I'd dropped the flashlight beam and had to refocus it on the dog.

"What are you doing, boy?" I asked, moving closer.

His little furry butt swayed back and forth, his head thrust into something I couldn't make out. Keeping the Maglite focused on his face, I stretched out a hand and pushed him back slightly, wary about getting too close.

Dog food.

I leaned closer, but Muffy prevented me from getting a closer look.

"Would you stop for a minute?" I caught him by the collar and pulled him away. It looked like fresh, ground-up dog food in a pet bowl. I swung the light to three large, empty cans of a brand-name dog food.

Double shit.

I released Muffy and swung around. If there was dog food, it stood to reason there was also a dog somewhere, right? And a big dog, if the bowl and the amount of food within it was any indication.

If that was the case, where in the hell was it?

I looked down at where my gun filled one hand and the

flashlight the other and wondered where I could work in the portable-size can of Mace I had in another pocket.

Nowhere.

Hey, I was well within my rights to shoot an animal if I felt I was in imminent danger, wasn't I? I swallowed thickly. At least I hoped so.

Of course, I was completely ignoring the fact that I was trespassing.

Which brought me back around to what in the hell I was doing there by myself.

I'd called Pino from outside the Greenberg house and quickly told him what I suspected.

"You're off your rocker, Metro," he'd told me.

"What are you talking about? I'm dead on. . . ."

Despite my unfortunate choice of words, I'd gone on to outline exactly what I'd discovered.

First, there was the juvenile record that Nia had had unsealed. A damning record that had sent a chalkboard screech up my spine.

It seemed that almost twenty years ago to the day, a certain seventeen-year-old Floyd Sackett hadn't attended classes at his private, all-boys school for over a week. Attempts at contacting his parents had failed (it was later determined that they were on a cruise in Alaska). So officers were sent to the home.

Unbeknownst to them, another school had been trying to contact the Sackett family about the truancy of another family member. That of sixteen-year-old Scarlett Sackett.

Police were dispatched to the residence, where they found Floyd in the middle of burying his sister's body beside a wall of shrubs in the backyard, cause of death ruled as strangulation.

Floyd Sackett had spent the next fifteen years in an upscale psychiatric facility paid for by his parents and had been released back into society five years ago.

"That don't prove nothing," Pino had told me when I finished.

"Ah, but I haven't shared the most damning piece of evidence. The day Floyd stopped going to school coincided with the day of his sister's seventeenth birthday. And that date is the same anniversary that both Valerie Bryer and Greenberg went missing."

Pino remained unmoved, but I could tell he was interested. "Why haven't the police or the PD acted on the information if that's the case?"

"I don't know," I said. "The files were sealed because he was a juvenile at the time of his sister's murder. And now he's a witness against the kid, not a suspect. There was probably no reason for them to go through the trouble of unsealing the records."

Pino remained dubious. "Even if the police could get a warrant to search Sackett's professional and personal properties, if they don't turn up anything, chances of their being able to follow up after that will be slim to none."

I was well versed in the limitations of the NYPD. Even in light of the many law changes in the wake of 9/11 made in the name of national security, when it came to crimes on a smaller scale, the police's hands were tied.

I, however, was not bound by those same rules. As a private investigator, I had privileges that afforded me a measure of protection under the law.

Besides, what could I be charged with? Trespassing?

If I was right in that Floyd Sackett had graduated from killing his sister to killing other young women on the anniversary of his sister's death . . . well, I don't think anyone was going to bother charging me with anything.

Of course, that depended on my actually finding something.

"Muffy, back!" I ordered as it suddenly occurred to me that the food could be laced with poison. I mean, if there was dog food out and no dog, it stood to reason that the food was intended for a different reason. Namely, to kill any animals that got into the enclosed area.

But why would someone want to do that?

To keep them from finding something else.

Efi told me I watched too many movies and read too many books, that I saw bears and killers around every corner. I figured it served me well, kept me on my toes.

It also served to scare the crap out of me.

Whether he was heeding my command or he'd stuffed himself, Muffy stopped eating. Then he bolted toward a stand of saplings to the right of the wood chipper.

Christ.

I went after him, slipping between the trees to find him digging in what looked like a low pile of fresh wood chips.

"That's it," I told him, grabbing the back of his collar. "Your title as my sidekick and comic relief is officially suspended until you start obeying my commands."

He came to stand next to me, licking his chops.

To my relief, when I backtracked to the shed, he followed and then stood with me staring at the entrance.

There was a lock on the two doors here as well. I stepped closer to examine it and then took out my lock-picking kit again. This time, my attempts to pick it worked. The hinges creaked as I opened the right-hand side and stuck the Maglite inside.

Why was it that places always looked creepier in the dark than they did in the light? I looked behind me and then edged inside. I was surprised that Muffy not only didn't follow, but plopped his furry butt down in the gravel, apparently content to wait outside.

Fine, I thought. I'll do this on my own.

I stumbled over something on the floor. I quickly moved the flashlight to stare at an uneven floorboard.

It was cooler inside the shed than it was outside. I pulled my jacket a little closer with my gun hand and then made my way to the makeshift table I'd seen the other day. It was covered with a dark stretch of oily cloth. I pulled up a corner and stared at the tools it covered. Only they were unlike any gardening gear I'd ever seen. In fact, they looked exactly like . . .

Oh, my God. It was embalming equipment.

I picked up a trocar, which put any needle an M.D. might come at you with to shame, and nearly swallowed my tongue whole. Christ. What was he doing with all this?

And who was he doing it to?

There was a sound in the far corner. I nearly jumped straight out of my skin. I swung the flashlight beam in that direction, standing frozen for long moments.

There! There it was again. A low, uneven hum and what sounded like rustling.

I started in that direction, slowly, carefully, swinging the beam wide and then narrow. Only when I tried to make out the sound again, I heard another one instead. That of a pickup truck pulling up outside the gates of Sackett Landscaping . . .

Thirty-four

DAMN, DAMN, DAMN!

There was no mistaking it. I peeked through the slightly open shed door to find that the work truck that had been parked at the Greenbergs' was now stopped outside the gates.

"Muffy, come here!" I put the flashlight in my mouth and grabbed his collar, pulling him into the shed and closing the door, hoping against hope that Floyd would believe he'd carelessly left the lock open. I frantically searched for somewhere the two of us could hide.

I found myself in the far corner where I'd heard the sounds and crouched behind a stack of crates. I quickly switched off the flashlight.

If luck was on my side, Floyd would be there only to drop off a few work tools and then would be on his way. He wouldn't even have any need to—

The shed door creaked inward, and an overhead light clicked on.

Apparently, luck wasn't on my side.

I held on to Muffy. I must have been holding him too tightly because he gave a soft whine. My heart stopped beating full out.

I didn't dare look to see if Floyd had heard or what he might be doing. Didn't dare breathe. Didn't dare do anything more than loosen my grip on Muffy and pray that the creepy landscaper was preoccupied with his chores.

How had he gotten back so quickly? Had he spotted me at the Greenbergs'? Had he seen my car and followed me back? Or had I been so slow about my reconnoitering that he'd finished up and was calling it a day?

I had one arm around Muffy; my other hand tightly gripped my Glock. I pointed it in the direction I heard the sounds.

The only problem was, sounds weren't coming only from Floyd's direction.

Icy fingers threatened to rip out my lungs as I realized I was hiding in the exact spot where I'd heard humming and rustling. Only it wasn't happening exactly where I was; rather, it seemed to be coming from a place under me.

Oh, God.

Then it occurred to me: Didn't sheds typically have slab floors? Or, at the very least, dirt? What was with the wood?

Only this wasn't a normal shed, was it? I'd thought it looked more like a car repair garage the first time I'd seen it. If that was the case, then that meant there might be wells dug out so that mechanics could work without having to hoist the cars.

The clang of a tool hitting other tools.

Muffy made a sound. At least I thought it was Muffy. For all I knew, I might have gasped in fear. But that didn't stop me from putting my hand over the dog's mouth. And the risk factor didn't stop him from nipping at my fingers.

I found that I'd pointed my gun toward the floor, but now I aimed it back in Floyd's direction. Or at least what I hoped was Floyd's direction. Truth was, I had no idea where he was in the building. For all I knew, he could be on the other side of the crates holding a crowbar, ready to hit me square on the head.

I leaned slightly to my left . . . slowly, slowly. Inch by inch, the interior of the shed came into view until I caught sight of a man's arm.

I jerked back and bit down hard on my bottom lip to keep from crying out.

Oh, for God's sake, he was across the room. A good twenty feet away, at least, messing with the tools on the table.

My eyes widened. Had I covered them back up with the oilcloth? For the life of me, I couldn't remember.

I slowly leaned to look around the crates again, forcing myself to move farther. I was still protected by shadows as I stared at the face of the man I suspected was guilty of more than just the death of his own sister.

I'd never seen a monster before. Not in the flesh, anyway. An envious brother who wanted to take over his famous brother's life, a client who'd run up more than his share of debts and was willing to sacrifice his wife for insurance money, and an old man who just wanted to open a tiki bar in the Bahamas—but never an outright monster.

The thing of it was, he didn't look that much different from any other person you might come across on the street. In fact, he looked painfully normal. Calm. Possibly even trustworthy.

Which was probably why there hadn't been more evidence of a struggle when he'd taken those girls.

Right now, he was checking the instruments on the table as

casually as if he were rearranging tools in a case. I watched as he covered them with the cloth and then moved toward the doors.

I sat back and swallowed thickly. He didn't appear to have noticed anything out of place. Or as if he'd come back because he'd spotted me and suspected that's where I'd gone.

Another sound from under me. I realized with a start that it hadn't been humming before, but rather the muffled sound of someone trying to scream.

I jumped as a machine started in the yard outside.

Shit!

I put down the Glock and felt frantically along the floor until I found a large round iron pull. Fumbling for my flashlight, I scooted backward while still holding Muffy and gave a heave. And was instantly afraid that I'd just dislocated my shoulder.

I tried again. And again. Even releasing Muffy so that I could use both hands.

Finally I succeeded in opening the hatch about a foot. I released it and pointed the flashlight inside.

As I suspected, it appeared to be a mechanic's well, a three-and-some-foot-wide oblong hole about five and a half feet deep and lined with cement. The muffled sounds were louder now. I poked my head down while shining my flashlight beam around until I spotted what could only be Hannah Greenberg, bound at the feet and hands with thick rope, a gag duct-taped to her mouth.

"Oh my God."

I started to edge inside the open hatch and then hesitated. I've never much been a fan of dark, enclosed spaces. Add a man I suspected had killed at least twice and had kidnapped and was likely about to kill again to the mix, and . . . well, there was no way I was going down there and risking the hatch slamming closed on me.

"Can you move closer?" I asked in a loud whisper, looking behind me to make sure Floyd wasn't about to push me inside with the girl.

I caught sight of a pair of pruning shears hanging on the wall and reached for them. While not the most elegant way to cut through ropes, they would do the trick.

Hannah scooted a foot nearer to me, tears streaming down her grime-covered cheeks.

"I knew you'd reveal yourself."

I gasped, dropping the shears in the well. I quickly scrambled off to the side of the open hatch and stared at where Floyd Sackett stood a few feet away, considering me with smug confidence.

My gun!

Floyd began to walk around the crates just as I spotted my Glock . . . on the other side of the hatch closer to him.

"I saw you in Bayside. There's no mistaking that rust bucket of a car of yours." He smiled in a way that was anything but casual or friendly. It made my skin crawl. "Then there's that ass."

He stepped forward.

I kicked at the crates, thankful to find them empty as they tumbled over, blocking his progress. I scrambled for my gun even as he reached over and grabbed the shoulder of my jacket.

During the last six months of my new career, I was fast coming to understand that while technique trumped strength, you actually had to have a few working brain cells in order to apply technique, while strength required only intent. And my brain had ceased operating the instant I heard his coldly said words from behind me.

Loud barking filled my ears. Muffy hadn't made a sound when Sackett approached, but now that he had his hands on my person, my sidekick showed his disapproval by way of bared, sharp teeth.

Floyd was caught off guard and released his hold on my jacket, intent trumped by the element of surprise.

I palmed the Glock and struggled to my feet, my knees shaking like naked branches in a stiff October wind.

"Back up," I ordered.

Floyd blinked at me as if the image he was seeing didn't jibe with what he expected. Of course, that was because his usual target of choice was a well-to-do teenager whose idea of a bad day up until that point was a chipped nail.

"I said back up!" I motioned with the gun for him to do what I said.

He didn't move.

What was it with people that they needed proof that guns actually worked? Or that the person holding them was not only capable of pulling the trigger, but willing?

I watched Floyd begin to regain his bearings, probably convincing himself that I was neither capable nor willing. I wondered what it was about me that gave people that impression.

I pointed the gun toward the ceiling and squeezed the trigger, the explosion of the round instantly putting all the power back into my hands as I refocused my attention directly on him.

I motioned toward the door. "Go."

I wasn't exactly sure what I was going to do once we got outside, but for some reason I couldn't define, it was important that I get out of that shed and as far away as possible from that makeshift cell. I could see to Hannah afterward.

Muffy ran around and around my feet, barking up a storm, as if asking for me to do that again.

Either that or he was trying to take the gun from my hands so I couldn't.

Floyd was walking so he could keep his sight on me. When he reached the door, I reached out with my left hand and gave him a shove so he was facing forward. As soon as we were outside, I fumbled for my cell phone, "fumble" being the operative word.

I was exclusively right-handed. I'll say that up front. I wasn't even very good at typing at the computer because I'd never given my left hand much attention. So getting the cell phone out, much less trying to dial a number, proved a challenge. But I figured if I was going to focus my right hand on one thing, it had to be the gun.

The metallic grinding of the wood chipper was nearly deafening as I pressed recall.

"Stop!" I called out, figuring I'd taken Floyd far enough. We'd emerged from the shadows and were standing five feet apart in the middle of the yard.

"Sofie? . . . Metro, is that you?"

Pino.

My shoulders relaxed. "Pino, I need you to get over here right away," I shouted.

"What? Where? I can barely hear you. What's that noise?"

Floyd began bending down.

"Stand up!" I ordered him.

"I just need to tie my boot," he called back.

"Sofie?" Pino continued in my ear. "Tell me where you are."

"I'm—"

I watched in abject fear as Floyd pulled on the chain I'd nearly tripped over earlier, catching one of my legs and hauling it out from underneath me. I squeezed off a gunshot that went wild as I fell backward toward the dirt. I hit the ground hard, the gun flying from my right hand even as the cell phone dropped from my left.

Muffy ran around and around me, barking, as if cheering for me to get back up. Ignorant of the fact that Sackett was standing over both of us, that sinister smile back on his face.

"Now what do you plan to do, Miss PI?"

Thirty-five

I LAY BACK ON THE cold, dusty ground, paralyzed with fear and shock as I stared up at a man who had killed at least two women, had a third bound and gagged in this shed, and was looking at me as though he might like to break from tradition especially for me.

It was said that the first time you killed someone was the most difficult. The second time was much easier. And by the third time, you barely felt anything.

I wouldn't know, because I'd never killed anyone.

Of course, my facts also came from reading books and watching movies with Mafia and military themes. But I figured that they must come close to the truth or else the reference wouldn't be used so much. If that were the case, then killing me would be like a walk in the park to a psycho like Floyd Sackett.

My legs felt like lead. I scrambled backward, awkwardly using my elbows and feet. The fall had knocked the wind out of me, and I was having trouble regaining my breath. With a quick glance, I understood that my gun and my cell were beyond reach. I could only pray that Sackett wouldn't try to pick up either one.

"I have to know . . . what gave me away?" Floyd asked, kicking at my foot.

I winced from the hit and inched farther away. Until I realized I was moving back toward the shed. I stopped. There was no way he was going to get me inside there.

"You gave you away," I told him. "You won't get away with this. At least six people know where I am. If anything happens to me, this is the first place they'll look."

Probably I should have tried the ol' "the police are on their way" trick rather than the "if anything happens to me" angle, because I didn't think this guy really cared what happened down the line. He was enjoying himself too much in the here and now.

I swear my bone marrow shuddered.

Muffy finally seemed to understand that I wasn't getting up and I wasn't about to return to my power position anytime soon. He pulled to a full stop near my head, looked at me, then looked at Sackett. And ran to attach the teeth he'd merely threatened earlier directly to the man's flesh.

Sackett cried out, trying madly to shake the dog off. I could have told him that it would only make things worse. The more he struggled, the tighter Muffy's jaws would close.

I didn't, of course. I was too busy getting to my feet, gingerly touching the back of my head where a bump the size of Gibraltar throbbed.

Sackett grabbed the chain he'd used to take over control from me, worked it under Muffy, then yanked up, catching the terrier under the chin.

The terrier yelped, releasing his grip at the same time Sackett grabbed him by the scruff of the neck and threw him across the yard. Muffy's pitiful whine made my stomach ache.

Sackett stepped toward me. I moved to the right. He compensated. I moved to the left.

"Tell me, Floyd, what is it that made you snap? Was there one particular thing that sent you soaring over the edge into crazyland, or were you born that way?"

A muscle in his jaw ticked as we continued our face-off. "You know, my sister had a smart mouth, too. Always criticizing me for this, making fun of me over that. I never wore the right clothes. Didn't have the right friends."

"Your sister Scarlett?"

Floyd blinked, as if hearing her name were unexpected. Probably it had been a long time since he'd heard it or even thought it. During the course of my research, I understood that predators didn't refer to their victims by name. It helped keep a cold distance between them.

"What happened to Scarlett, Floyd?" I asked, moving to the right. My gun sat just outside the circle we were making, but he was too close for me to grab it and get a shot off before he would be on top of me. "Wasn't she a good enough girl for you? Did Scarlett have a boyfriend?" I thought about what steps he must have gone through before kidnapping the girls he had. He must have watched them for weeks or even months or perhaps an entire year before he snatched them.

I cleared the lump from my throat. "Did Scarlett catch you . . . watching her?"

Floyd's face went red, and he made a grab for me. "Shut up! You don't know what you're talking about. It was a lie. I never did anything that Scarlett didn't want me to."

I moved closer to the cell phone, trying to discern whether or not it was still on.

"She wanted me to look at her. Would leave her door cracked open so I could."

He went silent, as if remembering the time so long ago.

Was that what had happened with Valerie and Hannah? Had they made the mistake of leaving their curtains open just a little too wide? Had Floyd stood outside their windows, salivating after what he could not have? What he planned to get? Or had he seen not the girls, but rather his sister while he'd stalked them?

"I highly doubt that Scarlett wanted to die, Floyd."

I had to shout to be heard over the incessant sound of the wood chipper.

"That was an accident!"

"Was it? I don't think it was. Because if you hadn't meant to do it, you wouldn't have tried to bury her in the backyard."

"Shut up! Just shut up!" He put his hands to his ears as if he couldn't take what I was saying.

"And Valerie Bryer? Was that an accident, too? Or how about the others? I suppose they'd wanted you to kidnap them."

His eyes focused on me again. I realized maybe I'd said a little too much.

"I had no idea you'd gotten that far. If I had, I would have killed you the other night instead of warning you." He clucked his tongue. "Yes, you have been busy, haven't you, Miss Metropolis?"

The night someone had fastened a chloroform-soaked rag over my nose and mouth returned to me even as I wondered whether or not he'd just admitted to killing others in addition to Valerie Bryer.

Yes, I'd definitely overstepped my bounds.

Sackett threw himself at me, and I moved right when I should have moved left. He caught me around the neck. I doubled over and twisted around, freeing myself only to be grabbed again.

I was no physical match for a guy like Floyd Sackett, a landscaper by trade. He worked outdoors all day, his body all lean, strong muscle . . . and murderous intent.

He grabbed my arm and swung me toward the wood chipper. My last frappé bubbled up into my throat as my face came within inches of the hopper. I could virtually feel the vacuum created by the swirling blades within.

Sackett grabbed the back of my neck. I gasped, surprised to find a sob escape my throat.

"You want to know what happened to Valerie Bryer?" he shouted into my ear. "I'm more than happy to show you. . . ."

I grasped the lip of the machine tightly, pushing myself away from it with all my might even as he shoved me toward it.

He put his mouth next to my ear. "My only regret is that I won't get to enjoy you first."

I tried to kick out with my legs but realized the action caused me to lose balance. And the last thing I wanted to do was lose balance.

This couldn't be it. The way I went. Could it?

It hadn't been all that long ago that I'd stood up on the Hell Gate Bridge in cement overshoes, reviewing my life up until then, convinced that my last moments on earth were ticking down. Thinking that it was too soon. Bemoaning the fact that I had yet to really live.

But now . . . now I felt nothing but numb, overwhelming shock.

The faces of the families of Valerie Bryer and Hannah Greenberg flashed through my mind. What they must have gone through, not knowing for sure what had happened to their daughters. What anguish they'd endured and continued to suffer.

The truth that I'd learned might not give them comfort, but it would allow them closure.

The problem was, I had to survive in order to share it with them or anyone else.

My arms began to ache. I didn't know how much longer I could hold myself aloft against Sackett's strength.

Then Thalia's face loomed in my mind's eye.

My mother . . .

I squeezed my eyes shut and gritted my teeth.

How many times had she asked me to quit working for my uncle? To go back to waitressing? Just the other day, she'd suggested that I even give thought to opening my own restaurant.

I'd never considered the option. And it was an option, wasn't it? I'd been weaned on the restaurant business. Knew it inside and out. Could have opened up a nice little café of my own. Called it Kalliope's, in honor of the nickname my father called me whenever he was exasperated, or something equally quaint. I could have ordered the baked goods from Dino's sweets shop. Offered up a simple menu of deli items. Hired waitresses of my own rather than working as one. Paid them well and not pushed them too hard.

Funny I should think of all that now. Staring into the mouth of a machine designed to reduce thick tree trunks to mulch.

And what about Hannah? Was she still quivering in the dark, wondering what had happened to the woman she'd hoped was her savior? Would Pino figure out where I was and come with the cavalry? At least save the girl if he couldn't save me?

My right hand slipped slightly, and a whimper escaped my throat.

I slowly grew aware of the sound of barking. I stared up at where Muffy had somehow climbed on top of the running chipper.

No! I wanted to shout. One wrong paw step and he'd end up dog tartar right alongside me.

But rather than fall into the hopper, he launched himself at Floyd. I stared, everything seeming to move in slow motion as the dog fastened his teeth on Floyd's left cheek even as he tried to find a foothold on his shoulder.

Floyd screamed in pain.

Suddenly the hand disappeared from my neck. I stumbled back away from the chipper, dazed, my legs feeling as if the blood had already been drained from them. Muffy's little body twitched as he continued his assault on the man who had tried to make me dead, even as Floyd grabbed at his hind legs, desperately attempting to pull him off.

Muffy made a whining sound and opened his jaws, falling to the ground. He started to get to his feet and then fell back down, his right back leg giving out.

Anger surged up in me strong and sure. Do what you wanted to me, but don't you ever mess with my dog.

I picked up a tree branch and hit Floyd on the side of the head with it. He stared at me, momentarily disoriented, blood seeping from both the bite and the head wound.

"You sick bastard!" I hit him again.

He staggered first to his left and then to his right, his hand reaching toward the lip of the hopper I'd latched on to for dear life mere moments before. But he missed and his hand slipped inside, the weight of his body following after.

His scream curdled my blood as I closed my eyes and looked away, the sound of grinding flesh and bone something I was sure I would never forget as drops of rain speckled my face. Only I was afraid it wasn't rain, but blood. Sackett's blood.

The suck of the machine that had gotten a taste of an item it wanted began pulling him in.

I debated letting the chipper have its way. Who was I to deny something a decent meal when so many of my own had been interrupted over the past week, mostly because of the guy now crying out in desperate fear?

Instead, I grabbed Sackett's foot and hauled him out to safety. He reached to touch his injured arm . . . only to find it wasn't there.

Beyond the nausea that rippled through my every cell, I couldn't help appreciating the poetic justice of it all.

I bent over and undid his belt buckle, pulling it free and using it to fasten a makeshift tourniquet to stop him from bleeding to death, and then I hurried to retrieve my cell phone. Movement caught my eye some feet away to the left.

Hannah.

I remembered that the pruning shears had fallen into the well. She must have struggled to free herself with them. The duct tape still hung from one side of her face, and she was covered in grime from head to toe. While I had gone for the phone, she'd found the Glock. She fell to her knees, holding the gun out in front of her.

"Hannah, no!"

A loud, murderous cry from behind me filled my ears. I twisted to stare as Floyd advanced on me, sans arm, his other arm intent on doing as much damage as it could.

And to think I'd just tried to save him. . . .

A flash of light as Hannah shot the gun.

Another spot of blood appeared on Floyd's face. This time smack dab in the middle of his forehead. He froze midstep before falling to the dirt face-first.

I stood for long moments, taking in the scene. Of Floyd dead, his unseeing eyes staring at the hell he surely faced. Of Muffy wobbling toward me on what had to be a broken leg.

I moved toward Hannah, took the gun from her shaking hands, and then pulled her to her feet, hugging her tightly.

"It's okay, sweetie. He can't hurt you anymore. . . ."

I turned her away from the sight of Floyd's body and stared at him myself, aware somewhere in the back of my mind that the strobe of police car lights was swirling everywhere and the gates were rattling as they were opened.

"He can't hurt anyone anymore. . . ."

Thirty-six

"SOMEBODY TURN THAT GODDAMN THING off!" a uniformed police officer shouted.

A moment later, the wood chipper shuddered to a grinding halt. The sudden silence was deafening where I sat on a wood bench near the fence, watching as a female officer led Hannah to a waiting ambulance. I rubbed my face and then hung my head in my hands, unable to fully absorb everything that had happened in the past half hour.

"Hey, Metro, you okay?"

I looked up to find Pino standing before me. I summoned up a smile, however shaky, as I stroked an injured Muffy in my lap. "Now I am. Thanks for coming."

"Just doing my job."

My smile turned genuine. If there was one thing I could always count on, it was that Pino would do his job.

"Sofie!"

I looked over to where a police officer was guarding the now open gates. My cousin Pete.

Pino waved that it was okay for him to enter, and he rushed over.

"Christ," he said, sitting next to me and hugging me.

I blinked, not sure what to make of his display of affection as Muffy growled his dissatisfaction between us.

"Are you okay?"

He pulled away to look at me, and I nodded.

I listened distantly as Pino related everything that had gone down.

"What is that?" Pete looked at me closely.

Pino took his flashlight out of his belt and shined it on my face. I winced.

"Blood," Pino said.

Pete searched his pockets, but it was Pino who offered up a handkerchief. I was amused as he spat on it and then swiped at the spatters on my face.

"So it was the landscaper. That was the connection," Pete said half to himself.

"Yeah. Turns out he killed his sister twenty years ago. The file was sealed because he was a juvenile at the time and his parents had the type of money and power to seal it."

"That's what was in the envelope Nia gave me to pass on to you?"

"Yeah."

He grimaced, thinking the same thing I was. Had he opened it, he would have been the one to nab Sackett.

I wished he had been. I didn't think this was something I was ever going to forget. I glanced over at the ambulance, where Hannah sat on a gurney inside being checked by paramedics. Pino had seen to calling her parents, and they were going to meet their daughter at Elmhurst Hospital.

I realized that whatever I'd gone through was nothing compared with what she'd experienced. I couldn't imagine the recovery time she would need.

Speaking of recovery time . . .

I gently scratched Muffy's ears, thinking I needed to get him to the animal hospital.

Only I had one more thing to do. I had yet to officially close my case.

While I'd saved a life in Hannah Greenberg, my client Johnny Laughton was still facing a lifetime in jail if I didn't find the evidence I needed to prove Sackett had killed Valerie Bryer beyond my word to his confession. And I suspected I knew just where to look for it.

I got to my feet.

"What is it?" Pino asked, his hand going to his firearm.

They'd taken my gun for forensics purposes. I felt naked without it. "Follow me. I have a hunch about something. . . ."

Holding the Muffster against my chest, I stepped toward the area where the saplings and shrubs were lined up neatly as if waiting to be planted. I shrugged off the blanket over my shoulders and edged my way through two rows of bushes. Pino's flashlight cast a four-foot spotlight on the low pile of mulch there.

Pete crouched down. "What are we looking for?"

Pino neared, moving the flashlight closer.

"I don't know," I admitted.

Pete scooped up a handful of the loosened dirt. "Is that a tooth?"

"Looks like a back molar," Pino said.

I squeezed in between both of them.

"Christ, don't tell me the guy ground up people?" Pete said.

I swallowed thickly as Muffy licked my chin and then stared at the other guys, his tongue lolling out of the side of his mouth in what I thought was a self-satisfied way.

Pete rolled the tooth over in his palm.

"Wait," I said, reaching for it. I held it up to the light. The unmistakable outline of the initials *JL* decorated the enamel. One of Valerie's distinguishable marks, the tooth tat she'd gotten in honor of her boyfriend, Johnny Laughton.

"Valerie Bryer," Pete said.

Pino produced an evidence bag out of his back pocket and held it open, and I dropped the tooth inside.

Case officially closed. Little Johnny Laughton would finally be sprung after having spent the past year in prison for a murder he'd never committed. One girl had been saved. And the Bryer family could now find the closure that had eluded them along with the real killer.

"Can DNA be done on this?" Pete asked, motioning toward the mulch where Sackett had presumably buried the blood-drained, ground-up body of at least Valerie Bryer.

"Yes, I think it can," Pino said.

I turned to retrace my steps through the saplings and picked up the police blanket I'd shrugged off, wrapping it around the Muffster.

"Where you going?" Pete asked.

"I'm taking my hero and partner to the vet. I think his leg is broken."

"You can't take that blanket," Pino said. "That's police property."

"Bill me."

Epilogue

Ten days later . . .

OKAY, I'LL RAISE MY RIGHT hand and own up to it: I'm the world's worst procrastinator. Rather than saying, "Why put off until tomorrow what you can do today?" my motto lately seemed to be, "Why do today what could be put off until tomorrow?" Or, better, the day after that? Then, before you knew it, it was ten days later and I had just finished cleaning up the paperwork on the Laughton case from my uncle Spyros' office and was now seeing to other odd jobs that, truth be told, I'd have liked to put off until sometime next week.

I sat at my uncle's desk after closing time, doing one of those odd jobs: cleaning my gun.

While it was the one thing that I never left home without anymore, I hadn't really wanted to look too closely at it after forensics had returned it to me following that night at Sackett's. But now that things were settling down, beginning to resemble a workable routine (I couldn't say returned to normal, because normal had been forever changed somehow), I wanted to resume shooting practice at the firing range, and in order to do that, I had to take care of my gun.

I finished wiping down the exterior of the barrel and then popped the clip. It was light three bullets. I really didn't want to think about why just then. As with the office around me, I was trying to wipe away all signs of the Laughton case. The whiteboard sat clean, the corkboard empty, paperwork filed away. If only I could order my mind to do the same.

I took a deep breath and immediately regretted it when my senses filled with the scent of a dozen autumn roses. A gift from Hannah Greenberg's family. I'd tried to talk Rosie into taking them home with her, but considering the sad state of her love life, she wouldn't touch them. As for me, after the Nick Papadakis episode, I would just as soon not smell anything associated with flowers or fresheners or perfume or all things rotting for some time to come.

Hannah was doing well. As was Little Johnny. His attorney, Gene Shipley, had wasted no time appealing to the court, and in light of the new evidence, the case against Laughton had been dismissed.

I'd been there in the courtroom when the decision came down. Watched as John Warren Laughton was publicly given back his Little Johnny status. He had stood in shock as his sister hugged him. I'd followed them out onto the street, where I'd been the surprised one when Johnny was hugged by others he'd probably least expected to be hugged by: Valerie Bryer's family.

There had been follow-up media pieces done. Many on Floyd Sackett. But thankfully, they were pushed back to be-

neath the front-page fold on the day of Johnny's release or rele-
gated to the second news segment as Queens and the city at
large focused instead on Johnny's wrongful arrest . . . and the
embrace of the family of his murdered girlfriend.

I liked to think that Richard Bryer and his family would be
all right now that they understood what had happened to their
daughter. And that their bringing Johnny back into the fold
would provide the salve they needed to heal their family.

As for Floyd Sackett, it was beginning to appear that my
cousin Pete had been right in his serial killer assessment. Pino
had told me that the police suspected that ever since Sackett
had been released from the institution five years ago, he had
been kidnapping women every year on the day of his sister
Scarlett's birthday. The first had gotten away but had been unable to identify her attacker. The second, it had been determined through DNA tests of the mulch and scouring through
unsolved missing persons files, turned out to be a victim who
had looked eerily like his sister, although the day of her disappearance had been listed wrong. The third, well, the third was
Valerie Bryer. And it appeared that Sackett had been perfecting
that art of killing. Not merely the process, but the setting up of
a false suspect that would divert attention from himself.

I shuddered, hating to think that he might have gone on
killing had I not lucked out on the day I'd spotted him at the
Greenbergs'.

A sound vied for my attention. I looked over to see Muffy on
the oversize dog pillow I'd put in the office for him. He gnawed
madly on his third cast, his low growl bespeaking his dissatisfaction.

"Muffy, stop."

He snapped his head to look at me. Licked his chops. Then returned to work, redoubling his efforts.

A broken femur, the vet had said. He'd need to be kept immobile for at least six weeks.

I'd stared at her as if she were crazy. I couldn't get Muffy to sit still for longer than it took to do my hair. How was I going to get him to sit still for a whole month and a half?

It was recommended I get a dog crate. I'd considered it for all of two seconds until I'd figured out that "crate" was human-speak for "cage." After everything he'd been through recently, there was no way I was going to put my hero in a cage.

So instead I kept him with me at all times and tried to stop him from chewing off his latest cast (nothing worked, including a dog Elizabethan collar he either managed to get out of himself or got me to take off him by running around nonstop like a maniac, and some sort of god-awful spray the vet had given to me that had made him sick but hadn't hindered him). Exercised him moderately. And even took him for car rides, just him and me and an Eleftheria Arvanitaki CD as we drove down streets painted with color-draped trees that looked as if Renoir himself had set the scene.

As for Tee the cat . . . well, the day after Halloween, he'd just seemed to disappear. I'd woken up to find him sleeping next to me, he'd eaten breakfast, and then he was just . . . gone. And he hadn't come back in the past week.

I gave a little shiver, remembering Rosie's warning that cats possessed the ability to foretell someone's death. Now that the threat from my life was gone, had he moved on to the next possible victim? Or had he gone out for a walk and found his way back home?

Whatever the reason for his disappearing as quickly as he'd appeared, my window was open to him any time he wanted to return. Although Muffy's access was currently on suspension. I'd spent the past ten days carrying him downstairs and walking him short distances on a leash, careful not to let him put too much strain on his healing leg.

Funny how the instant the sun rose on November, thoughts of ghosts and ghouls and interest in the neighborhood vampire all but vanished. Thank God. I couldn't imagine living my life in constant fear of the shadows, especially when those shadows lengthened as the days grew shorter. Now, rather than dodging all things paranormal, I was looking forward to Thanksgiving and Christmas thereafter. My mother and I had already done a bit of holiday shopping, the outings bookended by coffee before and lunch out after.

Of course, my sister, Efi, might usually be a part of such outings, but we were still navigating a wide arc around each other. Probably she was upset that I hadn't reconciled with Dino. Probably I was still upset that she'd taken his side over mine. Either way, I knew that we'd be back on even footing again soon. Just not yet.

Then there was Jake. . . .

I sighed, staring at the empty whiteboard. He'd called the other night. He hadn't left a message, but I'd recognized his number. I hadn't called him back.

Over the past week and a half, I'd come to appreciate the fact that danger was overrated. And that predictability was way underrated. If I had my choice, I'd choose something in between the two. Unfortunately, life didn't work that way, did it? But I also knew that I didn't have to accept either extreme.

Besides, I figured it might do me a little good to coast for a while, alone.

What was it about relationships that for every high there had to be a low? And did the same philosophy extend to people? Was there for every good person a bad person? Was life about balances? After all, you couldn't have spring without winter, summer without spring, fall without winter.

I grimaced at the direction of my thoughts, which were a little too philosophical, and perhaps more than a tad nonsensical, even for this Greek girl just then.

I opened the box of ammunition and took out three rounds, feeding them into the clip one by one. I hadn't used my gun often in the course of my job. And while I understood there would be times when it would be necessary (thus the reason I carried it), I thought it important that I consider it with more than casual regard. I never wanted to reload the clip as a matter of course, a regular part of my day, like checking my messages and finding parking spaces. It was vital to me that every time I took the firearm out of my holster, I regarded it with serious contemplation, approached it with a sense of gravity that it deserved.

And I made sure I did so now.

Of course, I'd gotten more than my fair share of publicity since that night at Sackett's. Much to my chagrin. Which was strange because I'd always thought it would be cool to be in the papers for reasons other than drinking worm shakes or shooting my own client in the knee. But this . . . well, it was overwhelming to be held up as some kind of hero. I glanced at Muffy, thinking that if there were any heroes in all of this, the title belonged to him, hands—or paws—down. But I guess since he couldn't speak, I had to be the mouthpiece for us both.

I'd come to the conclusion that what I had done wasn't anything outside the norm of what now comprised my life and career. I'd been hired to find the real killer of Valerie Bryer. And I'd done that. Yes, I was satisfied with my success. But it was no different really from putting in a full, productive day at my grandfather's café or my father's steakhouse.

Simply, I'd just been doing my job. Nothing more, nothing less.

I was an average Josephine who found much to like and dislike about her job. But in the end, a working stiff just the same.

There was a knock at the front door. I leaned to my right to watch a woman standing with her hand against the glass, trying to see inside. She wore a long dark winter coat with a fur collar, her long dark hair blowing around her pale face. The agency had officially closed over an hour ago, as the hours posted to her left clearly indicated. She must have seen the light still on and figured she'd give it a shot.

I finished adding the fresh bullets into my magazine, loaded it into my Glock, and pulled the slide to load the first round. I tucked the firearm into the holster under my left arm even as I rose from the chair to continue doing my job. . . .

Τελωφ

Recipes

Dear Reader,

Since most have heard of Greek gyros, we thought you might like to become more intimately acquainted with Sofie's favorite Greek fast food, souvlaki. The word translates literally into "small skewer," and you'll see why below.

We're also delighted to include a delicious Jewish recipe from dear friend and editor Melissa Ann Singer, something that Sofie's neighbor Mrs. Nebitz would definitely make and feed to our hungry heroine.

Kali orexi and *Es gezunterheyt!*

Warmest wishes,
Lori & Tony Karayianni
aka Tori Carrington

TZATZIKI

1 large English, seedless cucumber, peeled
1 32-ounce container plain yogurt
8 cloves garlic, peeled and chopped (more or less garlic to taste; we use a whole bulb)
1/2–1 cup extra-virgin olive oil to taste
1 tablespoon salt (kosher salt preferable but not necessary)
1 teaspoon vinegar (cider vinegar preferable, but any type can be used)
Dash of pepper

In a medium-size bowl, grate the peeled cucumber and squeeze out the excess liquid by hand. Add the remainder of the ingredients and stir well and vigorously. Refrigerate an hour or so before using, if possible. Stir again before serving. *Opa!*

SOUVLAKI (MAKES 10)

1 4-pound cut of pork roast (or lamb or chicken or steak equivalent)
1 package of 10-inch bamboo skewers (soak in water for 1 hour before using)
Mix together: 1/2 cup of olive oil, juice of 1/2 lemon, 1 teaspoon Greek or regular oregano

Trim fat (or not <bg>), cut pork into 1-inch squares, and then put on skewers (say, 5–6 squares per skewer, tightly positioned). Grill on medium-high heat for approximately

20–25 minutes, until pork is thoroughly cooked, brushing with oil mixture and turning frequently.

1 medium-large red onion (white is okay)
1 bunch of fresh parsley
2 medium tomatoes
1 package regular-size pita bread (10)
Olive oil for brushing
Salt and pepper (optional)

Quarter red onion and slice thinly. Chop parsley greens. Add parsley to onion slices in a bowl and squeeze together until well mixed and the onions are separated and soft.

Halve the tomatoes and then cut into ¼-inch slices.

Lightly brush the pita on both sides with olive oil and warm slightly on grill.

Using paper towels (or foil) to protect your hands and for folding purposes, pick up a pita, put a skewer in the middle, and squeeze the pita closed so you can remove the skewer. Next, add a bit of the onion-parsley mixture, a few slices of tomato (I like to add a little salt and pepper at this point), and then *tzatziki*. Fold the pita over ingredients, wrapping the paper towel to hold it closed. Enjoy! (Add a bowl of *tzatziki* sauce to the table for those who would like to add more as they go.)

Greek fries: French fries sprinkled with sea salt and Greek oregano.

Kali orexi!

The basics of a Shabbat meal differ depending on where your family came from and what traditions they have established over the years. While many people think that all Shabbat dinners include roast chicken, the entrée can be (among other things) a different sort of chicken dish—say, chicken paprikash or a beef brisket or pot roast.

Most Jewish women I know learned to roast a chicken from their mothers. Unfortunately, my mother, though an excellent cook, cannot cook "Jewish food"—as she will be the first to tell you. So I never learned to roast a chicken. . . .

When my mother made a plain chicken, as opposed to her dozens of fancier chicken recipes, she "broiled" it on an electric grill. Though our New York City apartment was a decent size, it had a tiny kitchen with insufficient counter space. So the electric grill lived at one end of the dining room. If we turned on the TV in the living room while the chicken was cooking, we'd blow a fuse.

—Melissa Ann Singer

GRILLED CHICKEN

Whole chicken, 2½–3 pounds, or the equivalent in parts
Salt
Pepper or paprika
Oil
White bread

While grill is preheating, cut chicken into serving pieces. Season with salt and pepper or paprika. Brush with oil.

When grill is hot, place chicken parts on grill, skin side down, 2–3 inches above heat. If your grill is not adjustable, cook farther from the heat and cook longer, turning more than once.

Take a piece of aluminum foil. Double and fold up the edges so you have a small, square foil "bowl." Place giblets—liver, heart, kidney—on the foil to cook.

Cook 6–7 minutes on a side. Baste with oil when you turn the chicken.

After the second side is done, raise the grill and cook an additional 10 minutes or so until done. Baste again if necessary.

When chicken is done, remove from grill. Unplug grill. Take 2 slices of white bread and lay them in the chicken drippings at the bottom of the grill. Don't leave them there too long or they will become too sodden to eat.

Remove bread from drippings, turn over so the grease is on top, and eat—be careful, it's hot! Can you feel your arteries hardening? (In truth, we haven't eaten the drippings in decades, but sometimes I am so tempted. . . .)

Fight over giblets and other favorite chicken parts.

Serve with noodles or *kneydlach* (dumplings), green beans, and a nice salad.